APOCALYPSE THE BATTLEFIELD

THE POWER OF TWELVE BOOK FIVE

MIRANDA MARTIN

CONTENTS

Apocalypse the Battlefield © 2020 Miranda Martin

FOREWORD

Don't miss the start of *The Power of Twelve* start at the beginning if you missed it!

Apocalypse: The Beginning
By Miranda Martin

CHAPTER ONE

RAFE

I drop to my knees, unable to take a breath, blinded by pain.

"Aviella," I gasp, feeling her call.

Something has happened, something has gone wrong. Terribly wrong.

"Oh Rafe," Asmodeus says, his voice a soft whisper caressing my skin. "You think she didn't know? Lucy knows, of course she does. You've never been with us, not really."

I grit my teeth, clench my fists, press them against the black earth and force my body to rise. Lesser demons appear, joining Asmodeus. He's played me. Damn him to the light, he's played me—and I fell for it.

"You're going to pay," I growl. I struggle and rise to my feet despite the pain and pressure of their magic trying to force me down.

Another wave of pain punches into my guts and I gasp involuntarily. It's like being stabbed by a burning hot poker.

"No," Asmodeus says, shaking his head. "I'll sit at her right hand. The world is going to be ours. In His infinite wisdom, he chose poorly. As did you. Why, brother, did you betray us?"

"Because she was wrong," I say. "Small, petty, jealous."

I throw the barbs, and he reacts as I hoped. Asmodeus has always had a temper. It's his worst trait, and one I love to pull out of him.

"I'm going to shove you down the Leviathan's throat and let you digest for a millennia," he yells, drawing out his sword.

The sword is impossibly big, too big for the sheath it emerges from like one of those anime swords. It's also one of the few things that can cause permanent damage to me here on the hell plains. The blade is curved, black as night, with skittering runes dancing up and down its length. Dark ichor drips off of it, burning the ground where it lands. The demons with him take an involuntary step back.

Smart. He's not known for his finesse when wielding it. Red floods his eyes, and he opens his mouth to say something, but my laughter cuts him off.

"Why are you laughing?" he asks.

I'm laughing so hard that the pain has become distant. My eyes are watering, and it's hard to catch my breath.

"Damn it, you will answer me!" he yells, moving threateningly forward.

"You…" I'm stopped by my own laughing. He moves closer. "You're an… idiot."

He growls, but at the same time I move. He's predictable and easy to outmaneuver. He's come too close to effectively use his one advantage, his sword. I drive my closed fist into his exposed throat, crushing his windpipe.

It won't stop him for long, but long enough. He stumbles back, sword lowering, one hand flying to his throat as he struggles to breathe. The demons with him gasp, hesitating. It's the only chance I'm going to get.

Magic rips through my body as I draw on it, pulling deeper and harder than my form can hold. I'm torn apart as I reshape myself and take on my natural form. The form I was forced into after the Fall.

Black bat wings, elongated jaw, claw-like appendages. As I change, I grab the air in front of me, gripping time and space itself, and I tear it. She needs me and I'm going to her. Now. Nothing will stand between me and her.

More demons are appearing, shouting. They race for me in a faceless mob. Followers. None of these were there for the Fall. They're all lesser, trapped souls twisted by their own hate and actions. Lesser, but still dangerous in this large of a mob.

Straining, I pull at the fabric of reality, pouring magic into my arms and hands to enhance my strength and fuel the spell. We're not supposed to use this. It will leave me drained when I reach the other side, and I can but pray I'll have enough strength to help when I arrive. The only other option is to stand and fight.

I won't win, so it's not a choice. Asmodeus will recover in moments, and once he joins the battle, I'll be overwhelmed.

"Gahh!" I scream, channeling more magic.

The fabric of reality starts to tear, but it's also ripping at my form. Burning through my limbs and scarring my magical channels. The demons hit me from all sides. Claws slicing and teeth tearing at my flesh. It takes all my will to ignore them and the pain. An image of Aviella keeps me centered, keeps my focus on her.

A rip appears as I strain, then it gives way at once. I leap through the tear leaving behind one hell for a fresh one.

"Aviella!" I scream, tearing my throat, my heart ripping out with her name.

She lifts her head and looks. Her face is swollen, bruised, only recognizable because I know her so well. She's hanging

3

from the frame, her clothes barely rags covering her. Crowds of the followers of the False Prophet are gathered below her feet, watching in awe as she is sacrificed. I'm going to kill them all.

Leaning into my dive I drive towards her, my sole focus and target. Too late I sense *his* power. Casmir, the last of the Horsemen, turns, and his impassive face watches my drive forward. His power matches Tynan's. The two of them have had a quiet disagreement for centuries, and now that the Horsemen have served their purpose, Casmir is free to do as he pleases.

Our eyes lock, and in his I see the Shadow's mark. He's still under its control. Aviella didn't reach him in time. A small smile turns up the corners of his lips, and a net drops over me.

Magic surges, leaving me convulsing as I'm dragged to the ground. I fight, but the more I do, the more the net tangles my wings and limbs. The mob of humans pulls the ropes of the net, tightening its grip until I can't move a finger.

I bounce when I hit the ground, so hard I crack my head. Stars dance in my vision, but above, I see Nate. He's hovering high in the air, observing but not acting.

"Nate, save her!" I scream.

The pain of my body doesn't compare to the cold chills racing through my limbs. I'm helpless. Powerless. I can't save her, can't reach her.

Nate looks to me, and now I see the tears streaming, the strain on his face. He can't.

My heart breaks as the mob breaks the bones of my body.

Power washes over the fields, and a sensation of hope rises in what's left of me. The dragons! Tynan, Alaric, and Shen are coming. They'll have the power, they'll stop her.

They must, we can't lose her, not like this. She's the reason, the one thing that has made all these long centuries matter.

"I... forgive... you... ALL," Aviella says as the trumpet sounds and time itself is torn apart.

TYNAN

THE TRUMPET RIPS TIME APART. I CAN'T REACH HER. AT THE end of the long hallway of time itself, the door between past and future becomes unhinged, is gone. The past and the now mingle. Aviella was so close. I'd almost reached her, almost saved her. I relive the moment again. Racing through the skies, trying to reach her. When I see her, again, hanging there, her life slipping away, rage burns through me. I roar as the loop resets and I'm reaching her again.

Reaching but not arriving. Again.

And again.

Over and over the same loop holds on, replaying this singular moment of loss. In all my long existence, the number of times I've failed is less than one handful. Being stuck experiencing this again and again is tearing me apart.

Time resets, the loop starts again, but this time I stop, hovering in the air. I rear back and roar in defiance. I am a Horseman, the Horseman. Alaric and Shen hold next to me.

"It's the last trumpet," Alaric says.

"We're trapped," Shen says. "We can't change this."

"Nothing will stop me," I growl. "I will save her."

My brothers look at me, and then the loop resets. We're flying over the hill again. Her pain calls, sharp claws tearing through my chest, an agony I've never experienced. We're losing her.

"It's the last trumpet," Alaric says, as the loop repeats.

"We're trapped," Shen says. "We can't—"

I cut him off with a glare. "We MUST!"

Aviella raises her head. She's pale, her face almost too swollen to recognize, blood dripping down. Rage, I will tear them all apart. They will suffer in ways that I haven't even invented yet. Their pain will make the heavens weep.

My brothers look at each other. Ignoring them, I fly faster. I must reach her.

Time stutters, loops, and we're approaching the hill again. It keeps resetting, and each reset is a chance. A chance not to fail. To find the one moment I want, the one where I save her.

SILAS

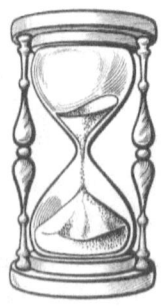

THE COLD IRON BURNS INTO MY NECK. IT CAN'T END LIKE THIS. It's wrong. This can't be the plan. How did I mis-predict the chain of events?

The False Prophet prances before the crowd, preening like a peacock. Casmir, the Green Dragon, Horseman of the Apocalypse, also known as Famine, watches impassively, studying without passion or compassion.

Something happened, changed. I've never been this wrong before. I've never missed a possible future like this. This shouldn't be happening. She screams in pain as they drive the nails into her flesh, and my heart breaks. Tears stream freely down my face as I reach for my magic, but the cold iron and its engravings have locked it away from me. It's there, barely out of reach, teasing me—which makes it all the worse.

Casmir's eyes land on me, and the weight of his innate power is oppressive. He is Tynan's equal, if not more powerful than the Horseman of War. Sweat pours down my face as I strain to raise my head and meet his eyes.

"Why?" I croak.

Something flickers on his face as he purses his lips. His eyes narrow and then he shakes his head.

"To see," he says, turning his attention away from me.

Rafe roars, his power a wave crashing through, and I'm knocked onto my face in the dirt. The mages appear, and in the distance I feel the other dragons coming. We're all here. All accounted for, eleven of us missing our twelfth.

I fight, with every fiber of my being I fight. The guards beat my body as I struggle to rise, knocking me down over and over. I'm almost to my feet this time when the blaring sound tears the world apart.

I'm in a frozen tableau, my mind racing but my body immobilized, until suddenly everything winds backwards.

We're living through the same moment again. And again. And again.

The world fragments, tearing itself apart. The Trumpet destroys time itself, tearing creation apart only to reform it over and over. There has to be a way to save her. Despite the agony, I strain to reach my magic. The burning in my neck grows. The harder I strain, the worse it is, until I'm consumed in a bonfire of pain, and I collapse as time resets again.

GAVIN

WE'RE TOO LATE. BEFORE WE CAN ACT TO SAVE HER THE trumpet sounds. As it distorts and tears at time, I reach out to my brethren. When I grab Ronan by his arm, our power links.

Casmir turns towards us, standing outside of the tearing of time himself, it would seem. Ronan grabs Killian, and together we force our way through the chaos to reach Luca. As the circle completes, our powers grow exponentially. The collar around Luca's neck shatters and he roars, leaping forward towards Aviella.

Time loops back and he's on his knees again, but this time Killian and Ronan grab his shoulders before he can leap forward.

"I have to save her!" His words are slurred, emerging from the broken, swollen mess that his face has become.

"This is not the way," Killian says, pulling him into our circle.

Power flows through each of us, resonating and multiplying. The world immediately around us stabilizes.

"Get Rowan," I order.

Killian nods. He forms our magic into what looks like a hook, using it to grab hold of Rowan, and he anchors her to us. She motions wildly, eyes wide, face pale. She struggles to turn and run to Aviella, but I soothe her with a stream of magic, focusing her attention.

As she finds her center, her power is added to ours, but we're not strong enough, yet. We need more power. There's only one answer.

The instant I think of it, Killian's mouth drops open and he mouths a 'no,' but there isn't a choice. We have one chance, and this is it.

Before they can stop me, I reach out for Tynan, inviting him and his brothers into our circle.

TYNAN

THE MAGES EXTEND A TENDRIL OF POWER TO ME, CUTTING through the looping of time. I take it without hesitation, pulling my brothers along with me. Their power is fresh, and so human. Filled with free will, sacrifice, and choices.

9

Concepts that we've studied for years. Free will is what we've longed for in all our existence, but when we achieved it after our role in Armageddon, we didn't know what to do with it.

Our existence had become purposeless until her. Aviella changed everything. She is our light, and we must save her. If I can't save her, then I'll burn this world to a crisp, making it as empty as the idea of losing her leaves me.

"Tynan—" Gavin cries out as I draw power from the mages.

They're all on their knees, shaking, unable to stand as I jerk their power from them too fast. Some piece of me sees this, and surprisingly, I care. That is Aviella's touch. What difference would the life of a small clawful of humans make to me? Never in my long life would I have considered their loss less than an acceptable price.

But now I don't.

I can't destroy them, not even to save her. I ease back my pull on their power and their relief washes over me.

"Save her," Killian says, forcing his way to his feet.

The mages aren't holding back but I control myself as I turn towards Aviella. Casmir stands at her feet, watching the interchange with passing interest. Shifting to my human form I land and stride forward.

"Stop this, Brother," I order, power flowing through my words.

Casmir's brow furrows, and he shakes his head.

"What is it you would have me stop?" he asks. "The end of this world?"

"You set this in motion," I growl, anger destroying reason.

I blast him with dragon's fire, fueled by the added power of the mages. Black flames engulf his body, blocking him from sight. Rage pours into the fire and it burns hotter, eating the light. At last I let the fire end, but to my surprise Casmir is still standing there.

"Interesting," he says. "You would destroy me for her?"

"I would destroy this world for her," I growl.

"She's gone," he says, and no blow could strike deeper.

It forces me to look, and what I see drops me to my knees. He's right. Her body hangs lifeless. The light that was Aviella is no longer in her mortal shell.

I've failed.

CHAPTER TWO

RAFE

*T*he crowd stares at the sky and cowers in terror as I land roughly into a timeline. The sky darkens and thunder rumbles loudly. The first drops of rain fall, and they burn into my flesh. The fools scream, leaping to their feet and rushing around mindlessly.

Desperate, I leap to my feet and rush towards her, but I'm too late, again. She's gone. I feel her pass. The world grows darker as if responding to the loss of her light. Pulling magic from the depths of my reserves, I force my body to heal and shift back to my human form.

The acidic rain burns, but I welcome the pain. It accents the empty, aching loss. Now that I'm in my human form, the net holding me down is loose, and I slide out of it easily. The mob ignores me, running for the bunker as I climb to my feet.

The False Prophet is at the head of the group. When I spot him, my blood boils. I cup my hand, fill it with a roiling ball of infernal energy, and throw it at him. He must sense it coming, as he turns around and screams something unintelligible. The ball flies towards him—it will kill him instantly—but before it lands, a hand catches it.

Casmir.

The Horseman stares at the magic in his hand, studying it with open curiosity. He looks from it to me then back to it. He closes his fist and the magic dissipates harmlessly. The Prophet and he walk into the bunker. Moments after they do the doors slowly shut, locking out dozens of followers.

They wail and scream, but there's no point in bothering them. They're the sheep, the blind, following because they're too scared to think for themselves. The lost. My demonic nature urges me to punish them, to use them as a target for my rage, but I'm not that man. Once, yes, I was like that, but not since Aviella.

She changed me in ways I didn't know were possible. And she's gone.

The loss hits me fresh, as if it were happening right in front of me, again. It's crippling, pain in my stomach and chest, too hard to breathe. Each breath is a struggle as I try not to break down. Tynan roars, rising to his feet and drawing my attention. He stalks towards those who were locked outside.

"You," he growls, his voice echoing off the heavy steel door of the bunker. "You did this. You took her from me. You. Will. Pay!"

I run to put myself between him and the humans. His eyes burn red, wisps of magic drifting out, giving him a demonic aura of his own.

"Tynan, no," I say, putting my hands on his shoulders.

He looks at each of my hands before affixing his gaze on me. The full force of his draconic nature hits me with that look, and it's all I can do to not step back. Our magic clashes as we stare one another down. His eyes lock onto mine, searing me with his rage.

"Let me go, demon," he growls.

"No," I say.

He's more powerful than I am, an entirely different scale of being. The Divine created him at the same time it did me and my brothers, but he and the other dragons were imbued with more power or potential power. Laid on them was their one task, to bring about the end of the world.

I know I can't stand against him for long. He's more than capable of destroying me, but I can't let him do this. The abandoned humans cower, groveling on the ground. They're lost, hopeless, and despite my own demonic nature, I feel for them.

Tynan's magic swells, and in my magical sight, it's a tidal wave about to crash, and that will be the end of me. Oddly, I'm okay with it. She's gone. What is the point of carrying on anyway? If I die in her name, for her cause, well, there are certainly worse things I could do. Have done, actually.

"She wouldn't want this," I say.

My words cut deeper than any knife. The wave of power is gone in a flash, leaving behind emptiness. A blood-red tear forms in the corner of his eye. His mouth moves, but no sounds come. He shakes his head, then turns and walks away, his head hanging low and shoulders slumped.

"Help me, damn it," Silas yells.

He's piling up debris below Aviella's broken body. Tears stream down the Methuselah's face as he works. Alaric, Shen, Efram, Nathanial and I rush over and help him build a mound until it's tall enough.

I start to climb up, but a hand on my shoulder stops me. I turn and face Tynan. His grim face brooks no argument, and I don't have one to give anyway. Nodding I step aside, and Tynan ascends the debris and takes Aviella down.

He cradles her in his arms against his chest looking down

on all of us. Pain throbs in my chest. Emptiness, hopelessness.

Tynan leans his head back, and he roars. The sound slashes at my soul as my own tears burn down my face.

CHAPTER THREE

LUCA

"*O*ur brother has retreated to his bunker," Tynan says.

"And what do we do about it?" Gavin asks.

"We go there, we destroy him," Tynan says.

We laid her down. She's gone. Every time the thought comes back it hurts as if it just happened. A singular moment of failure in a life that has been too long.

"We should not go there unprepared," Silas says.

Angry red burns mark his neck where the iron collar had rested. He's grim, grimmer than usual, but what else can any of us be? Failed, failed, failed, the thought pulses in my head with every beating of my heart.

"Then get prepared," Tynan growls. "I'm going to destroy him."

Murmurs of agreement come from all around including myself. What else do we have left but vengeance?

"It's been three days," Silas says. "We need more time."

"I don't!" Tynan yells, slamming his fist on the table in front of him so hard it cracks. "We go. Now."

"Your brother isn't the enemy," Rafe says. "He's only the easy target. The obvious one."

"And what target do you wish to face my wrath?" Tynan asks, turning to the demon.

"The true enemy," Rafe says, uncrossing his arms, black smoke drifting out of his eyes. "Her. The one who manipulated all of this."

Silence falls. No one speaks for a long moment, and then Tynan continues.

"Can you find her?" Tynan asks.

"Yes," Rafe says. "I think so."

"We should save Aviella's father first," I say. "It's what she would want."

"Someone betrayed her, betrayed us," Alaric says.

"What do you mean?" Tynan growls. "Who?"

"Who?" Alaric asks.

"Who indeed," Shen says.

"How did the False Prophet know to find us all? How did Casmir know that Aviella was the one?" Alaric poses the questions.

"The Shadow…" Rafe says trailing off.

"Free will," Nathanial says.

"Doesn't act, she manipulates," Rafe says, expanding on Nathanial's words.

"Exactly," Shen and Alaric say as one.

No one says anything. I stare at the dirty, stained carpet. It's covered in refuse with layers of dust and crumbling drywall. This was once someone's home. Filled with life and purpose, no matter how simple, but now it's a symbol. Like this home, life itself is pointless.

My entire existence has been filled with the Divine purpose my brethren and I agreed to during the Crusades. Gathering the Innocents, protecting and training them for the end. The time that the One would return and usher the world through its darkness into a new age.

Rowan takes my hand in hers, forcing me out of my

introspection. She places both her hands on her chest, over her heart, then throws her arms wide. I nod my understanding and she smiles.

"Thank you," I say. "I'll try."

Keep your heart open, she's saying. Don't let the pain close me off. She was Aviella's best friend, and yet she's the one supporting me. Everyone is arguing, acting out their pain. Tynan's rage isn't surprising in the least, it's his nature.

"Who?" Tynan growls.

Rowan steps into the middle of the assembled men and gestures with such wild animation I can't follow what she's trying to say.

"Where are Efram and Ronan?" Tynan asks, looking at each of us in turn.

Apparently, he got what she was saying because she nods grimly. I look around, as does everyone else. Those two are missing so I reach out for Ronan and sense him coming closer.

"Ronan will be here in a moment," Gavin says before I can.

I stretch my magical senses out trying to find Efram, but I find nothing.

"I can't find Efram," I say.

"Nor can I," Silas adds, and then the others each add their own inability to spot him.

"The necroseer isn't powerful enough to hide himself from us," Tynan says, slamming his right fist into his left hand.

I can't argue his point. Something is strange about Efram disappearing.

"I'll kill him," Tynan roars and his magic coalesces around him with staggering power.

"We should look into this further," Silas says.

"Why?" Tynan asks, whirling on Silas.

He looms large, filling the room with his presence. Silas stares at him, unperturbed, tilting his head to one side.

"Because it's what she would do," he says.

Tynan is like a balloon that springs a leak. His rage deflates, leaving him staring at Silas until Tynan nods his agreement. He turns and walks to a window, staring out of it silently.

"The evidence is there," Rafe says.

"Perhaps," Silas says. "You're certainly not wrong, but we should find him and investigate. We all know she wouldn't accept this without hearing it from his lips."

The door to the house slams open. Magic fills the room as we all turn, ready to unleash hell on whoever or whatever dared to interrupt us.

"She's gone!" Ronan yells as he runs into the dining room with us.

"What do you mean gone?" Tynan growls.

"She's gone," Ronan repeats. His eyes are wide and he's winded. "The cavern we laid her to rest in, the stone we covered it with is rolled aside, and it's empty."

"Show me," Silas says, the only one of us not displaying open rage.

CHAPTER FOUR

AVIELLA

*I*t's warm. Golden and warm and peaceful and everything I never thought I'd achieve. There's no more worry, no pain, nothing to be concerned with at all.

Except….

No, this is perfect. This is what I needed. A rest, that's all. A reprieve from the pain and suffering. A little longer.

Aviella.

"Mom?" I ask, though I'm not sure why.

I know her presence, or I think I do. The golden warmth, that's what a mom is, isn't it? The sense of safety, that it's all going to be okay no matter how bad it looks.

It's time, my love.

"No," I say, refusing to open my eyes.

A little longer. I'm not ready yet. If I do, I know what will happen. I'll be back where everything hurts. Where it's all so hard, and sharp, and harsh. No, I like it here. I don't want to leave.

She doesn't say more, so I rest. Golden warmth embraces me until even the memory of pain is distant.

Aviella...

"Dad?" I ask, suddenly aware again.

His voice cuts through the warmth and comfort. Memory crashes in. Dad. Trapped. Lost. Waiting for me to save him.

I'm drawn towards a blinding bright white light.

CHAPTER FIVE

RAFE

"Who would dare!" Tynan roars, his voice echoing off the stone walls to double back at us.

The massive stone we'd rolled over the cave entrance is pushed to one side, a feat no mortal could accomplish alone. I scan the area, but I don't sense anything Shadow or infernal tainted. There's a hint of the Divine though. I lock eyes with Nathanial, but he betrays nothing with his stony gaze.

Rowan walks into the yawning cavern, but the rest of us wait outside. Waiting for what, I have no idea. Nothing in the world has any real purpose. There are no signs of desecration, but the insult of someone taking even her remains from us makes it all even more pointless.

If we can't even protect these, then what good are we?

Silas studies the stone, while the three dragons pace a widening circle outside the tomb staring at the ground. Nathanial and I stare at each other, as I'm sure he knows more than he is saying. More than he can say if I'm being honest. His plight is possibly the worst. Even if he was aware of the Divine's hand, he wouldn't be able to tell us.

The mages form a circle and pool their magic, scrying the area around us. It's the most useful thing any of us have come up with so far, so I watch with some interest. It's the most I can manage.

Blue magic pours out of the four of them, forming a swirling circle between them as they chant. The circle tilts until it rests on its side, making a viewing screen. It shows the cavern, the boulder, all in place as it should be. Suddenly a bright golden-white light streams out and around the boulder. It grows so bright we all shield our eyes even though this is only a viewing of the past.

When the light fades, the scrying shows the boulder moved and the empty cave.

"Nate?" I ask, turning to the angel.

He clenches his jaw and shakes his head. Suddenly I'm pissed. Pissed at him, at the world, at all of it, and I can't stop myself.

I grab Nate by the front of his shirt and lift him into the air. I cock a fist back and threaten him with it.

"Tell me," I growl.

The other men gather around us, but no one moves to interfere. Nate stares back passively, he doesn't even raise an arm to defend himself.

"I can't," he says.

"Yes, you can! Damn it!" I scream. "Whatever it is you know, you can! You don't have to be an automaton. You can have free will. You can do it… for her!"

I choke, unable to say her name. A burning hot tear falls down my cheek. Nate touches my shoulder with one hand, and my anger is gone. I know his plight. It used to be mine, until I followed Her into rebellion.

Look where that's led. In a way, all of this is really my fault. If I'd stood against Her, then all of this could be different now. Aviella would be alive. The world wouldn't have been put on a crash course towards destruction. The Shadow wouldn't have been set free to tempt man and the novelty that was his free will. The very thing that enraged Her and started the rebellion.

Jealousy.

It's always been about jealousy, damn it. Regrets swirl though my thoughts and I set Nathanial down on the ground and let him go. He doesn't step away but instead he moves forward and embraces me.

"I understand," he says softly.

It's all I can do to keep tears from falling free. I won't show that in front of all those gathered. Taking a deep breath, I compose myself and nod.

"Sure," I say. "Well this is a shit show. What are we going to do about it?"

Best to change the subject as fast as possible. All these feels will get me nowhere.

"There's only one way forward," Tynan says.

"And that is?" I ask.

"We accomplish what we set out to," he says grimly. "We destroy the Shadow and every remnant of it. Starting with my brother."

No one speaks. I've no doubt we all thought it, but no one wanted to be the first to say it. I wasn't sure how Tynan would react. It is his brother after all. Alaric and Shen flank Tynan, their faces every bit as grim and giving no sign of disagreement with his assessment.

When I look over my shoulder at the empty cavern, the allegory of it hits me. The empty tomb is the perfect metaphor. It describes exactly how I feel inside.

Empty, useless, no longer serving any point. Tynan is offering a purpose, albeit a pale one in comparison, but we've already lost.

"Sure," I agree. "Let's go out in a blaze of glory."

The others murmur their assent, and as simple as that, it's decided.

CHAPTER SIX

EFRAM

They can't know. It hurts so damn much, and I can't tell them. They'd never understand. I can't listen to their plans any longer, so I slip out of the rotting building and walk through the empty remnants of what was once a city.

She's gone. She's gone and it's my fault.

My chest feels empty and the world is gray. My heart aches, throbbing pain with every beat knowing what I've done. I had a choice and I made it. Now I have to live with it. All of it. I'm not paying attention, letting my feet carry me along. What's the point after all? None of it matters.

The sun is dropping when I come to realize I'm at the small cave where we laid her body to rest. The large boulder that it took all of us to roll into place over the opening a hard stop. I rest my fingers on its rough surface and send my magic out, searching for any sign of her. Any remnant or echo of her, but it's empty.

"There he is," a man's voice says, and I whirl around. "You're coming with us."

"Like hell I am," I growl, magic forming into a defensive shield.

"Efram, there's no need for this," Casmir says, walking around the corner.

His emerald green eyes stare, and I let the magic go. I can't fight him, and he knows it. They all know it. I'm the weakest of the twelve—well eleven, we still don't know who the twelfth is. Of course, now we never will.

That is enough to make me give up. It's too hard to keep fighting. There's no point any longer. The rest of them are in the same place. The Shadow has won, but they don't want to admit it. Not yet anyway. Maybe eventually they'll come to terms with it. In that regard, I guess I'm ahead of them.

"What do you want?" I ask, barely able to keep my head from dropping to my chest. The weight of what I've done is so much to bear.

"I'm not done with you yet," Casmir says.

"Why? I gave you what you wanted," I say.

"Efram," Casmir says. "I'm a scientist. I do not project my considerations onto the experiment. I observe and record the reactions. This experiment is far from over."

"She's dead!" I yell, stepping towards him, balling my hands into fists.

Casmir tilts his head to one side, and as he does the full weight of his power crashes against me, stopping me in my tracks. Straining, I try to move forward but it's impossible.

"Yes," Casmir says, casually as if discussing the weather. "That is one possible outcome."

"Leave me alone," I growl, resisting with everything I have.

"I'm afraid I cannot do that," he says, and the Shadow mark on him flashes.

He's not on his own. Of course he's not. He's a tool of the Shadow. He motions with one hand and the men with him move to the boulder trying to move it aside. They strain, and I laugh.

"Good luck with that," I remark.

The men stop, sweat pouring down their faces as they turn to Casmir. He tsks and shakes his head, then places one hand on the boulder. It moves as easily as if he's sliding a well-oiled door. My stomach drops seeing his power. Tynan couldn't move that by himself, and Casmir does it as if it weighed nothing.

The men storm inside the cavern. It's not deep but still dark. I can't see them or what they're doing, but my mind fills in the worst. They're touching her, or what remains of her. I can't stop them, held in place by Casmir's power. I'm not strong enough to save her even this last humiliation.

I couldn't save my sister, and now I can't save her. The overwhelming sense of failure is too much, more than I can contain. It burns through my veins, and my only release is a stream of tears. At last the men walk out empty handed.

"What is happening?" Casmir asks.

"It's empty," one of the men say.

"That is not possible," Casmir replies, turning to face me. "This is where they put her. It's only been three days. She has to be here."

Casmir walks toward me and my skin crawls, but I can't move. Tendrils of magic wrap around me tighter than any chains, holding me in place, forcing my head up and my eyes to stay open. I can't even look away. His emerald eyes dance with promises of possible futures, none of which will be pleasant, but it doesn't matter.

I laugh. His brow furrows as he tilts his head to the side, and for some reason that makes it even funnier. Seeing the dragon confused is the most hilarious thing I've ever seen.

"You lose," I say, laughing harder.

His magic tightens around me and it feels like my ribs are

being crushed, but I don't care. I'm so amused by the entire situation. The absurdity of it all, and the loss of her. Nothing matters, and as it becomes harder to breathe, I can only keep laughing. The darkness forming at the edge of my vision will be a welcome relief from this world that has become absolutely pointless.

"Bring him," Casmir says, turning, and as he does the invisible bonds holding me ease their pressure.

Warmth washes across me, not my body but deeper, touching my silent parts, and suddenly hope blossoms in my soul. Straining, I turn my head and blink. It can't be...

"Avi?" I gasp.

"Hi," she says, a half smile on her face, a golden glow outlining her body.

"You're... it can't... how..."

"Yeah," she says, shaking her head. "About that."

The men with Casmir rush forward surrounding her with guns at the ready. Casmir moves to stand beside me staring at her. She's here. She looks... real. The others are reacting to her so it's more than a figment of my imagination, right?

Aviella slowly raises her hands in surrender. The men surrounding her glance from her to Casmir, seeking orders. They're shifting their weight, guns wavering, unsure what they're supposed to do next. After all, they all saw her die.

"Impossible," Casmir says.

"Maybe," Aviella sighs. "You look rough."

She walks towards him, hands still in the air. No one moves. I'm too scared to even breathe. Afraid the slightest motion will break this illusion, slamming me back into the reality where she's gone. If I have lost my mind, then I want to stay here, in this illusion, forever with her.

Casmir watches her approach but doesn't react. She stops inches in front of him, then slowly she touches his cheek, trailing her fingers down across his face. I clench my jaw so tight that spots flash across my vision, seeing her touch him so delicately.

"You've suffered so long," she says softly. "I'm sorry for that."

Casmir frowns, then jerks and steps back from her touch.

"Bring her," he barks, whirling around and stomping off. The biggest display of emotion I've ever seen from the dragon.

"Sir, what about him?" one of the men asks.

"Him too," he says without looking back.

"Avi," I say, trying to keep the desperation for this to be real out of my voice.

"Hi," she says. "Thank you. I know this was hard, but it's what had to happen."

"You were… gone," I shake my head.

"Yeah," she says, blinking rapidly. "Man, it's so harsh here."

The men aren't gentle with her, roughly forcing her arms down to her sides and back then putting handcuffs on her. They're doing the same to me, but I don't care. She's alive.

She's here. This is real. I'm not imagining things. It's really real, or else I've lost my mind completely and whatever comes next won't matter anyway.

CHAPTER SEVEN

SILAS

ynan may be right, and I don't have a better path forward to offer, but something about the entire situation bothers me. The group returns to the house we've made our base to plan the next move, but I remain behind looking at the empty cave.

I've lived, loved, and lost so many times in my existence I'd no longer let myself grow attached. Somehow, Aviella broke that rule. It'd been millennia since I let myself care about another being the way I did her. I'd grown accustomed to surrounding myself only with other long-lived beings who were as close to immortal as possible.

Aviella tore through those walls without even trying. Being her was all it took. Her warmth and the depth of her compassion for everyone, even those who hurt her was unbelievable. Unreal and if I didn't know better, I would have suspected she was faking it somehow.

She wasn't, of that there is no doubt. Now I'm here with this old, familiar pain. The pain of losing everything. The one experience I'd carefully shut myself off from ever having to feel again.

I close my eyes and let it flow, pulsing emptiness, aching yet sharp, like claws tearing straight through my soul. It hurts so damn bad that I can't hold back tears. As they flow, they let out the centuries of unshed ones. The floodgates break open as I drop to my knees inside the open cave, and it tears out of me in a scream.

I'm washed away as I let it out, until at last, in the dark and alone, I'm left empty. Wiping my face, I rise to my feet and pull on my magic, pooling power. The dark becomes as easy to see in as if it was high noon, but I don't stop there, shaping the magic into a swirling shape similar to the spinning of a helicopter blade.

The center of the swirl stabilizes as the magic tears through the barriers of space and time, opening a viewing into the past. The boulder is back in place as I look back to the day before, speeding back and forth through time as I look to see what happened.

Something blips and I stop the scan, moving back and bringing it into focus. Efram is standing at the boulder, resting his hand on it. I knew he wasn't with us, but why did he come here? Increasing the speed of the scrying, I move it ahead until my heart skips a beat when Casmir appears along with a group of armed men.

There is no sound but there is no surprise on Efram's face, and I can read lips, at least the ones I can see from the viewpoint I have.

Efram, no. You? Why?

Casmir moves the stone aside and they go inside but emerge empty handed. She's already gone? Why didn't they pull her body out of there? It's obvious that's what Casmir wants. Efram smiles, looking over his shoulder. I can't change the viewpoint of the portal but they're talking to someone out of my sight. Surprise is apparent on all their faces but why?

Then I see why. My heart skipped before but now it stops. My blood chills and I can't take a breath. She's there. She's there and alive and…

They take her away, and I can't concentrate enough to hold the magic together any longer. It dissipates in a sparkling array of shards.

She's alive? How?

The old prophecies come to mind, up to and including the False Prophet. He Who Has Risen, it's a theme and I suspected it might apply but still… to see it. I'd thought it was over, we'd lost, but no. Hope grows like the first blade of grass springing through the snow. I have to get to the others. They're going the wrong way, our direction has changed completely.

CHAPTER EIGHT

LUCA

"She's alive?" Tynan asks. "And he betrayed her?"

"You're kidding me," Gavin says, shaking his head.

"No, you misread something," Rafe says.

"No, I did not," Silas says. "I know what I saw, I am not mistaken."

"Where did they go?" Shen asks.

"I'm not sure," Silas says. "Possibly New Jerusalem."

"Fine," Tynan says. "We go."

He strides towards the door without another word.

"Wait," Nathanial says.

The angel has barely spoken at all since we lost her, and his word is probably the only thing that could stop Tynan.

"You have one minute," Tynan growls turning back to us.

"The Divine has set things in motion," Nathanial says. "But you all have free will. Even you," he looks at Tynan, Shen, and Alaric.

"What is your point?" Tynan growls.

"Only that you consider the consequences of every action

you take," he says. "Your choices are what matter here. They're all that matter, really."

"My choice is made," Tynan says.

"As is ours," Shen and Alaric say in unison.

There's a weight to this moment. It's heavy with possibility and the gathering of fate itself. Nathanial is right, we're at a turning point in time. A moment when the course of history itself will be set.

"We cannot act out in anger," I say, stepping towards Tynan. "No matter how righteous the rage, no good can come out of destruction for the sake of destruction. Or revenge. No matter how sweet it might seem, once tasted, revenge is a cold mistress."

"Pretty words mage," Tynan all but spits, turning and grasping the handle of the door.

I look at Nathanial and he nods but says nothing more. He probably can't, so I look to my brothers.

"We have to save her," Gavin says.

Rowan stands next to him nodding enthusiastically and gesturing her agreement. She pounds a fist into her open palm then mimes opening a gate. She wants to save Aviella. We all do. Somehow, she's alive, impossible as it seems, and honestly, I'll only believe it when I see her, when I hold her in my arms again. But even the possibility she is... it can't be ignored.

So we're going to save her. It's a choice, but not one that had any other outcome possible after all. We fall in and follow Tynan.

CHAPTER NINE

AVIELLA

*E*verything here is harsh. Hard lines, bright lights, too solid. Too... there. Where I was, everything was soft, gentle, comforting. Here, it hurts. My hands and feet still ache no matter that the wounds have been healed. The memory of the pain is there still.

This is the way forward. I'm not some Mary Sue, no matter that my power is more than ever before. Sure I could set myself and Efram free. I could wipe out this entire bunker, easily. It wouldn't matter though.

Casmir is powerful too but even more powerful is the enemy that sits behind him, pulling the strings on all of us. Now I understand, more than ever, the depth of the battle I've been being prepared for. The Shadow uses free will, manipulates, appears in the guise of your friend only to betray you.

It's a long, storied tale, in a battle that was raging behind the scenes of the entire planet, until it came to a head. Again. It's happened before. History does tend to repeat itself after all.

"Avi," Efram says. "I can't.... you're... I watched you..."

"I know," I say. "It's fine, don't worry."

We've been carted back into New Jerusalem and locked into a cold tiled room. The walls are a soft teal that should probably be reassuring but is more sickening in color. The tile goes up three-quarters of the wall and there's no furniture. Efram and I are chained to hooks in the ceiling. My arms ache and my shoulder sockets burn. I'm standing on my tiptoes to keep them from being dislocated.

"I'm sorry," he says, his voice catching.

Before I can say anything more, I hear a screeching voice outside the door.

"No!" the False Prophet screams. "You're wrong. She wasn't gone, that's all. Who checked her body when it was brought down? She can't have been dead. I am He Who Has Risen, she can't have returned. It's impossible."

The door slams open and he sweeps into the room, a storm of emotions and waving arms. His wild eyes land on me and he runs over, slaps my face. It burns and the coppery taste of blood forms in my mouth.

"Good to see you too," I mutter.

It hurts but then everything here does so it is only a minor addition to being here at all.

"Leave her alone!" Efram screams struggling against his restraints.

A moment later there's the sound of electricity crackling, and he's screaming in pain. They don't stop for the longest time. It's breaking my heart to hear him, but there's nothing I can do. They don't stop until he quits screaming.

"Leave," a new voice says.

"No," the False Prophet screeches, whirling around.

Casmir stands in the doorway staring at him. His personal guards flank him. He barely nods his head, and they rush into the room taking the Prophet by either arm and manhandle him over to the dragon.

"Do not defy me," Casmir says.

"It's me!" he screams. "I am the one who rose. Me! Not her!"

Casmir steps to one side, and they carry the Prophet away. His voice echoes back to us until at last something slams, and I can't hear him any longer. It's a welcome relief. That guy gets on my nerves.

"Take them to my place," Casmir says, turning away.

"Casmir," I call to him. He looks back over his shoulder.

"You don't have to do this," I plead. "You know that."

"The experiment is in motion," he says. "I cannot interfere."

The men grab Efram and me as Casmir disappears from sight.

CHAPTER TEN

TYNAN

"**O**pen the door," I growl.

The tiny window slides shut as an answer. I wait and nothing else happens. My blood boils. I'm going to tear them limb from limb.

"Give it a little longer," Silas suggests.

"My patience is thin," I say.

"Is it ever anything else?" Silas asks, and Rafe snorts.

"There is power here," Gavin says.

The four mages are walking intricate patterns in front of the steel door of the bunker. They say this as if it's news to me, which it isn't, so I ignore them.

The window slides open again, and this time the wild eyes of the False Prophet himself look out.

"You are not welcome here," he says.

"If you do not open this door, I will tear your bunker out of the ground," I say.

"You want her, right?" he says.

"Correct," I say.

"She's not here," he says.

"You lie," I say.

"No!" he screams. "No! He took her. He took her from us. He's wrong, but he took her. I am the one who rose, not her!"

"Where?" I ask.

"His home," the Prophet says.

My vision turns red, and I pull my power around me like a cloak. I grab two bars on the front of the door and then move my hands to get a better grip. The reinforced steel crumples easily as I get a hold, intending to rip it open.

"Tynan," Nathanial says, placing a hand on my arm.

Warmth infuses my flesh as he pours his Divine-touched magic into me. I glare at his hand then slowly raise my stare to meet his eyes.

"Let me go," I growl.

Nathanial does but he doesn't break his gaze from mine. Slowly he shakes his head, and without words spoken he makes me think. Think of her and what she would want or do. Damn it, this is not my way.

"He did this," I say, rage boiling and barely under control.

"He's a fool," Nathanial says. "A distraction."

Nathanial moves with blinding speed. His arm darts towards the door and he touches the Prophet with two fingers. There's a flash of white light and the Prophet screams, dropping out of sight.

"No, no, no, no, no, no, no," his voice repeats out of sight but still clearly heard.

"What did you do?" I ask.

"Time is fractured," Nathanial says. "I let him see what he's done and now he'll relive it."

"Over and over?" I ask.

Nathanial nods. "Until he learns."

CHAPTER ELEVEN

AVIELLA

"*A*vi," Dad says, his voice croaking. "Oh god, Avi."

My eyes are crusted shut and refusing to open. I keep working them until the lids tear painfully apart. The light is white, bright, stabbing into my brain where it explodes like a super-nova. Everything hurts but that's the way it is here. This is an entire realm of pain and discomfort. Still it takes a moment for me to orient myself and let my eyes adjust. Turning my head towards the sound my heart races.

"Dad?" I ask, unable to believe my eyes.

It could be a dream. A vision or figment of my imagination.

"Hey, baby," he says.

"Daddy," I sob.

It's him. It's really him. He looks terrible, broken, but it's him and he's alive. I knew he was, deep in my heart I knew but seeing him here…

"You made it, kiddo," he says, chest heaving and his voice tight.

His face is swollen behind a thick, unkempt beard, but his

eyes are bright. More than that, I feel him. His soul reaches out and touches me. My magic latches onto that touch, embracing it and embracing him.

He's dressed in rags, hanging from the ceiling, and it's easy to see he's been tortured for too long. Magic coalesces around me responding to my rage. The walls of the room we're in shake, items crashing to the floor.

"Daddy," I say, but it comes out a growl through my clenched teeth.

I'm sluggish, slowed by some kind of poison in my body. It drags on me, but I'm not going to leave him there, hanging and in pain.

"Avi, no," he says, shaking his head.

He never had any magic of his own, I know that now, but he had heart. That's what my mom saw in him. That's why he was chosen to be my father.

"They can't get away with this," I say forcing myself up onto my elbows.

I'm strapped to an operating table. Wires attached to my head, my chest, and my arms. Machines with blaring alarms screech as I work to focus my thoughts. It's hard enough being here, but whatever they've done to me makes it feel like I'm swimming through a thick fog. It's hard to think.

"Avi, forgive them," Dad says. "They're blind. Misguided."

Things make so much more sense now. His faith in humanity, his love for all his fellow man, no matter how many times they disappointed him—that's his magic. His great strength. His heart is so big I feel it flooding me with warmth, almost as if he's embracing me.

The shaking slows and stops as I reign in my magic. He smiles, showing broken teeth behind his swollen lips.

"Good," he says, exhaling heavily.

"Dad, I'm sorry," I say. "I waited."

"I know," he says, letting his head drop to his chest again. "Sorry. I'm tired kiddo."

"Oh daddy," I cry, fighting the urge to set him free.

"It's… fine," he says, breathing heavily. "Takes a minute to catch my breath is all."

I touch him with my magic and gently infuse his body with it. Wounds close and his color takes on a semblance of normalcy.

"Let me set you free," I say.

It'd be nothing to do it, so easy. I could bring this entire place down around our ears without an effort.

"We're not… alone," he says, looking up. "It's not time, Avi." The echo of footsteps reaches our ears, and he looks at the door, fear on his face. "Play dead, baby girl."

An old code. I'd all but forgotten it. He wants me to keep my magic shielded, do all I can to appear normal. Now it's so much easier that I understand what's inside of me. It's not some separate 'thing' I struggle to control but actually a part of who and what I am.

Closing my eyes, I pull the magic back in and wait to see what happens next. The footsteps come closer. Click-clacking their way closer and as they do, I feel him. Casmir, the final piece of the puzzle that my life has become.

He's powerful, rivaling Tynan for raw power but the restraint he has on his own power is different. Unique. He doesn't rely on his power to get what he wants, no, he's so much different than his brothers.

Alaric and Shen are players, gamesmen who use their powers to heighten the thrill of the hunt. In everything they do it's apparent. While Tynan is pure force, bending the world around him to his will by his presence alone.

Casmir is different, and I feel it in his magic, his presence. He's an observer. Setting things in motion, then studying

43

where they go as if on their own accord. His magic is tightly reigned in, controlled, almost cold and indifferent.

He sweeps his attention over me, and I can't suppress the slightest of thrills that races down my spine in reaction. He pauses beside the table, and I feel the pressure of his gaze resting on me. My cheeks warm. He turns towards my father, and I shiver, wanting the warmth of his gaze back. There is no doubt in my mind that he's the one. The final piece I have to find before I'll unlock the truth of who and what I am. Before I'll be ready to face the Shadow.

I have to set him free.

"You're interesting," Casmir says, his voice having a musing tone to it. "No discernible powers, yet you're resilient. Strong in ways that no human should be."

"Let me down, and I'll show you strong," Dad says, putting on a brave face.

Casmir doesn't respond to the bravado. He studies my dad like he's nothing more than another experiment. Which, for him, he probably is. I'm getting a feel for him, though I've not known him long.

From behind my closed eyes, I concentrate on my breathing and reach out with magic tendrils. Slowly I touch Casmir, caressing his magic, calling to him. I hear his breath catch as his magic responds to my touch. A hint of warmth behind the cynical façade he faces the world with.

"You, though," Casmir says, leaning so close his warm breath passes over my face. "Interesting."

Opening my eyes, I stare into the deep emerald pools that are his. Fire and passion dance deep inside them, hidden away, suppressed.

"Come closer," I whisper. He doesn't respond but his brow furrows. "I know things."

"Yes," he says. "I think you do."

He hovers inches from my face. My heart pounds hard as

my breathing speeds up. If he was only a little closer, I could kiss him and part of me wants to so badly it hurts. Magic sparks between us, dancing in a tiny light show, pulling him towards me.

"Stay away from her," Dad barks, and it breaks the moment.

Casmir pulls back, and barely noticeable, I see the Shadow mark that shifts on his aura, reasserting its control. I'll have to break that thing's hold on him. He's the last key. I'm sure of it. Claiming him is the final step before I'll be able to... what?

I'm not sure. Nothing profound was revealed to me while I was dead. I wish it was, but I'm not that lucky. Not that it was bad, honestly, it's better than this place, but I can't tell anyone that. They wouldn't understand.

Casmir stares, eyes narrowing, and then his jaw tightens as he seems to make a decision.

"Well enough," he says, turning on a heel and moving out of sight.

"No," Dad cries out. "No, don't do this, damn it!"

I bite my lip, not wanting to know what's coming but my imagination is running away with it. It's going to be bad, I know it. I'll survive it, of course. Surviving doesn't mean it's going to be pleasant.

The squeak of an unoiled set of wheels draws closer and Casmir comes back into view. He's wearing a white lab coat along with a protective set of glasses.

"Let's see what we have here," he says bringing a tool into my field of vision.

CHAPTER TWELVE

RAFE

"*I*'m trying, damn it," I curse Tynan.

"If you'd quit 'trying' maybe you could actually 'do' it," Tynan barks.

"You fuel this gate, you son of a bitch," I growl, sweat pouring into my eyes. "His defenses are complex. Add in that time is still hitching in its tracks and his bunker is outside of time itself…"

"Excuses for failure are still excuses," Tynan growls. "Do it, demon."

"You worthless, dirty—"

Nathanial cuts me off with a hand on my shoulder. It's enough to stop me from losing my temper and trying to tear Tynan apart. I'm not sure I could or not, but no matter. It would certainly not save Aviella.

"She's alive," Nathanial says. "She needs us."

The aching pull on my soul pulses with his words. She's hurting, again, and I'm not there to save her. None of us are. We're all here, all except Efram who disappeared. Which is just as well, since if he were here, I'd rip his guts out.

Redoubling my focus, I manipulate the spatial energies.

They swirl green and gold, throwing sparks around the room. Small fires ignite and the mages busily stomp them out before the entire worthless place burns down around our ears.

Every time I've almost gotten a lock on her, something shifts and I lose the connection. My muscles quiver from exertion. I can't keep this up much longer. My knees are weak and every limb burns. The magic aches, throbbing in every nerve ending.

The circle grows, almost the size of a man now, and the blackness in the center of it brightens. Slowly shapes take form inside of it. Almost there!

"Yes!" Luca exclaims.

"You've got this, Rafe," Gavin encourages, and Rowan dances around miming for me to go, go, go!

Thanks Rowan, I wasn't already doing that very thing. Tynan, Alaric, and Shen step up to the forming portal. They position themselves around it.

"Stay back, you damn fools," I mutter.

Ignoring me, they grab hold of the swirling sides. Anyone other than the dragons would likely be ripped apart by the energy. Alaric grimaces, the only tell of how much this is hurting them. Tynan growls, and then he pulls.

It rips at me too, like someone is jerking sharp barbs out of my body. In a way they are, their pulling tears magic from me, forcing me to pour more of it into the gate itself. The blobs in the dark become definite outlines of shapes and then the portal blinks several times and I've got her.

Emerald eyes look up, staring out of the window in space and time right at me. Casmir blinks, his lips pursing, then his brow furrows.

"Determined, aren't you?" he asks, raising a hand.

He motions and something punches me in the gut. I cry out in pain and surprise. His power blankets oppressively over me, forcing me down. All with a glance. He's the strongest being I've faced except for Her herself.

"Hold it!" Tynan yells as the portal blinks in and out of existence.

"I'm… trying…" I gasp, but he's not talking to me.

His brothers, Alaric and Shen, shift their positions moving to stand on either side of it. Tynan steps in front of the window, blocking Casmir from my view.

"It's you," Casmir says, his calm cold voice accented by Aviella, screaming.

The sound of her scream cuts through my soul. It's filled with pain, agony, the depths of torture that shouldn't be known outside the hell realms and even then, reserved only for those who are most deserving.

Rage fuels my power, and I pour it all into the spell I'm weaving. Time itself resists. In the best of circumstances, tearing a gate through space is hard and takes a lot of power. Creating one that crosses differing streams of time is all but impossible.

The gate key I'm drawing on grows hotter in my pocket, burning into my leg, but I can't let it break my focus. I have to save her. This time, I can. My knees quake so I lock them. A roiling green ball of raw magic flies past, and I barely move in time to avoid taking it in the face.

Tynan roars and grows bigger, taking on aspects of his natural shape. Dark red wings appear on his back as he gathers power.

"Give her to me," he growls.

"That is not the plan," Casmir says from the far side of the portal.

"Get her out of here!" a new voice yells, a man.

I look around Tynan and see a haggard human male hanging behind Casmir. He looks terrible, and it's obvious to my experienced eye he's been tortured for a very long time.

Still, he rallies himself and struggles, fighting against the bonds holding him.

"Her dad?" I ask, glancing at Nate next to me.

Nate nods grimly, then his eyes light up and he touches my shoulder. Cold rushes through my body, quenching the burning pain. My legs quit quivering and I find new reserves to dump into the spell.

Tynan and Casmir are facing off across the portal, but what matters is her. She's alive, somehow, and we have to save her. I may have failed before, but this can be my redemption. When I dig deeper, the magic burns through its pathways in my system. There is permanent damage being done but I don't care. If I can never wield magic again it will be worth it, if I save her.

"Get her," I bark, gritting my teeth.

Nate doesn't need to be told twice. He knows what to do, and he rushes around Tynan in a blur. The forces I'm holding in place are back on me alone. I drop to my knees as the weight of it crashes into me.

It's trying to close, time and space wanting to go back to its natural position, self-correcting. Her screams grow louder, closer. She's sobbing and my heart shatters hearing it. Are we too late? Again?

"Now!" Nate yells. "Let it go!"

"Dad!" Aviella screams.

I'd started to let it go when Nate yelled but I try to stop it when I hear Aviella. The backflash hits me, and I'm flying backwards. I slam through a wall, the air is knocked out of me, and I'm still going. Another wall and my bones shatter, then another, and at last I'm stopped.

I slide down and land on the ground in a slump. Standing up seems like a good idea, but when I make the effort, the only thing that happens is my head exploding with a billion stars, so I give up on that idea. Lying here a moment is good too. My mouth fills with blood, and my head is pounding, but the worst is the burned feeling throughout my magical channels.

"Rafe!" Nate yells, landing in front of me and folding his wings away.

"Hey," I cough and blood flecks onto my chest. "Fancy meeting you here."

The angel kneels and touches my face. His fingers are cool, filled with the Divine. Dimly I remember when I was the same. Before I fell, when I was still like him. Good, not the evil dirty bastard I've become.

"Hold still," he commands.

"Did we…" I pause to try and get a breath. "Get her?"

"You did," Nate says. "You got her."

"Well. At least I've done one good thing," I say, my eyes too heavy to keep open.

"Don't talk that way," Nate says, cupping my face in his hands and forcing me to look up and meet his eyes. "She needs you."

"She's got plenty," I say.

"Not you," he implores, his eyes boring into mine.

I open my mouth, but I've got nothing. The first time in my long existence I can recall being speechless. I start to shake my head, but it hurts too much. The edges of my vision are graying, and I can feel myself slipping away.

"I… think… I've over… done…"

"Damn you, demon," Nathanial growls.

Without warning, his lips are on mine, and I'm suffused with his Divine power. It pulls me back, anchoring me here, keeping me from slipping into the abyss where no fallen has ever returned from.

When he breaks the kiss at last, I'm left breathless, but the pain is a lot less. My ribs are knitting back together, and I can take a deep breath without something stabbing deep into my lung, cutting the air off before I get a full one.

"Is that a rocket in your pocket or are you happy to see me?" I ask, resting my fingers on his cheek.

He blushes and I can't stop myself from laughing. I immediately regret it as the pain isn't that far gone, but it was totally worth it. Nate rises to his feet, barely glancing at me and not acknowledging what just happened.

"Obviously you're going to be fine," he says, spinning on his heel and walking away.

I work my way to my feet using the wall to steady myself. The imprint of me is a perfect outline dented into it. Nate is walking away, and I watch him leave. He's too uptight, always has been, even before the Fall. Always unwilling to admit to having feelings, too busy trying to be aloof and the perfect child of the Divine.

It worked out for him, overall. I fell, and he didn't. Another thing to thank Aviella for. I've missed him all these eons.

CHAPTER THIRTEEN

SILAS

"We need to move her somewhere safer than this," Gavin says.

"Your Sanctuary?" Shen asks.

"No," Gavin shakes his head. "It's not safe enough, not now. We've gathered too many Innocents there. If we added Aviella into that mix... it would be sending out a beacon."

She's lying in the next room, not having woken up since we pulled her out of Casmir's bunker. Her body is a mess, and my quick scan was enough to know that her magical energy has been disrupted. I'm not sure how such a thing is even possible, but it felt so... wrong.

They continue the discussion, but I give it only part of my attention. Scenarios and possibilities reel out as I consider every solution. I come to the only conclusion there is.

"I have a place," I say, and they all turn to me.

I walk past them to the door, blocking the room she's in.

"Where, Methuselah," Tynan growls, before I enter.

"I have a place," I say, not turning around.

Staring at my hand on the doorknob, I debate how much more to say. I've never told anyone about this place, never taken anyone there. It's my last secret. The one thing I've held back from the world. My fortress of solitude.

"That's not an answer," Gavin says.

"No," I say, not turning. "It's not."

I walk through the door and close it behind me. Aviella lies on the broken bed, ratty blankets pulled up to her chin. It's all we have here. The world has truly gone to hell. The Shadow is no longer only rising, it's reaching its zenith. Supplies were hard to come by outside the bunkers before, but now most of the bunkers have fallen.

The remnants of the last world are falling to the inevitable march of nature as it slowly reclaims what was once its own. Soon there will be nothing but the rare artifact of the human race that no survivors will recall or understand. It's worse than the flood. Even after that catastrophe, what remained carried forward more of the world from before.

This time, there will be almost nothing left. Nothing but the horrors that man created in his time on this planet. Unless. Unless we save her.

She came back. Impossible. We laid her to rest. I know she was dead. I was not mistaken about it. I scanned her lifeless form so many times. We all tried using all of our skills and powers to revive her. To no avail.

She was gone.

And now she's not.

Sighing, I step towards her as the door behind me slams against the wall. Tynan's anger hits me like a blast wave on my back. The hairs on the back of my neck stand on end and my skin warms.

"You do *not* walk away from me," he growls.

"Tynan," I sigh, turning to face his anger head on. I'm tired. Too damn tired for this. I may be a Methuselah but I'm still of mortal stock. "You know this isn't the time."

He growls, huffing, his nostrils flaring, hands balled into fists. He glares at me, and I meet his gaze without flinching. His eyes narrow as he grinds his teeth.

"Where do you plan to take her?" he asks.

Behind him I see the others staring past him. All but Efram. The betrayer, but is he the only one? Can I trust any of them? I haven't scanned them for any signs of Shadow touch in a long time. That complacency on my part is what led to...

No. I'm not going there. Self-blame will accomplish nothing.

"To safety," I say. "Isn't that what we all want?"

Tynan steps closer, and the rest of them crowd at the door watching the interchange play out.

"Do not twist my words," Tynan says.

"Tynan, I know you're hurting. We all are," I say, holding my hands out in front of me palms up to show I'm not making any threats. "Let me take her to safety."

"We were betrayed," he hisses, his face almost shifting to his dragon form blurring before my eyes.

"Yes," I acknowledge. "Which is why I need to take her some place safe. Someplace no one knows about."

"You doubt me?" he asks.

"I doubt all of us," I admit.

He stops, and as fast as that, the anger drains from him. His shoulders slump, and he unclenches his fists. We stare at each other for a long, drawn out moment, neither of us sure what to say. Finally he shakes his head, turns and walks out. The mages, the angel, and the demon stare through the door looking between Tynan and me. He walks over to his brothers and the three of them stand silent together, though I have no doubt they are having a heated discussion none of us are privy to.

I wait for three heartbeats to see if anyone else wants to

argue then I turn my attention back to Aviella. Her cheeks and eyes are sunken. She shivers despite the blankets, and a light sheen covers her forehead. She hasn't awakened since we pulled her out.

I don't know what Casmir did to her, but there's a distinct feeling of wrongness in her magical aura. I haven't had a chance to do a full scan and figure it out, but I need to, and I need to have her the one place I'm certain we can't be attacked to do it.

I kneel and place a hand on her forehead.

"Dad," she moans, not opening her eyes.

No, sweet, it's not your dad. We'll save him, or try, but right now all our attention is on you." I wipe the sweat from her brow and push her hair away from her eyes.

"Gavin," I call, and the mage walks up behind me. "We need to save her dad too."

"I agree," he says. "But I don't think we can face Casmir alone."

I feel him scanning Aviella, his magic swelling and passing across me as well. His scan is fast but he gasps midway through it and stops.

"What do you see?" I ask.

"Dead spots," he says.

"You're sure?" I ask.

"Yes," he says without hesitation. "Somehow he's created dead spots in her magic."

"I see," I say.

The most dangerous thing, or at least the worst that can happen to a wielder of magic is dead spots. They're voids in their magical aura that act like black holes. Sucking in magic and consuming it. Interrupting the flow of the magic through their soul and making it difficult if not impossible to wield it. At the very least, they will reduce the victim's power.

Unfortunately, it makes sense. Casmir has always been of a scientific bent. An experimenter, using his immortal life to set things in motion and then watch what happens. Before the fall, he was behind some of the deadliest discoveries that humans ever achieved.

Genetic modification of food, reducing its nutritional value while increasing the yield, making it an easy sell. The obesity problem from before the rapture was directly under his hand. Untold number of deadly viruses that were used in germ warfare. Everything from the origin of Greek Fire to the development of mustard gas and dirty bombs, he has had a hand in manipulating the researchers, guiding them towards their discoveries.

The image of Famine was never understood, but he earns his title in the fullest sense of the word.

"Is there any chance?" Gavin asks, not finishing the thought but I know what he wants to know.

"Yes," I say, putting on an air of certainty that I don't actually have.

"We're in agreement," Tynan announces, pulling the attention of the room to himself.

"I haven't agreed to anything," Rafe points out.

"But know this, Methuselah," Tynan says. "If you do betray us, if you harm her in any way…"

He doesn't finish the threat. Nodding, I look back to Aviella.

"Uhm, I say again I haven't agreed to anything," Rafe says, his voice hitching.

He's a pulsing source point of pain. The abuse to his body is still not healed. I scoop Aviella into my arms then turn to face the group.

"We know we've been betrayed," I say. "We know who did it. I know we lost her. You've all felt that loss. I ask you, please, trust me."

Outside this house, the time stream jumps again, and it's only our gathered power that keeps us together and anchored to this one line, but all of us feel its turbulence.

"No," Rafe says, limping forward, one hand holding his ribs. "No."

"Rafe," Nathanial says, placing a hand on his shoulder.

The four mages look at each other and magic flares, then they turn back to me, and as one, nod their agreement. Rafe looks stricken, his face pale, and he's shaking as he looks to each of the others.

"Are you all insane?" he asks. "No! We can't... she can't... not again."

Flecks of blood fly from his lips as he raises his voice.

"Rafe, you're hurt. Stay here, get healed. I'll bring her back as soon as I can," I say.

"Rafe, this is the path," Nathanial says, a rare moment of him admitting to knowing more than he ever lets on.

Rafe turns to the angel and tears fall down his face.

"I can't lose her again," he says.

"Then know that this is our one hope of saving her," Nathanial says, pulling the demon into an embrace.

Nathanial nods to me over Rafe's shoulder.

It's all the agreement I need. Closing my eyes, I mentally draw the runes in the space next to me and the door opens. I step through and leave them all behind.

CHAPTER FOURTEEN

AVIELLA

"*D*AD!" I scream, eyes flying open.

Time has passed. I don't know how much, but I sense it. Time, so much time. Over and over and over, Casmir driving things into—not my body, but my magic. Somehow, he was drilling straight into it, extracting samples or draining me completely. The pain was beyond anything I've ever experienced. I couldn't find the safe, golden haven that protected me during my sacrifice. This time, every single instant I felt it, and it was... too much.

My mind shies from the memories, and I can only pray that it's not going to keep going on. I sit up, and it's only then I realize I'm not bound to the table any longer. The room around me is different. This isn't where I was the last time I looked.

It's a trick. He's messing with my head.

Everything hurts, but I pull magic around to shield myself from the pain and to be ready to fight him. It comes, but slow, and as it flows, it brings more hurt. I scream.

"Aviella," Silas says my name, appearing before me.

I lash out, knowing this is but another lie. A guise

assumed by my tormentor. He's trying to break me. Magic flashes, burning as it leaves, it slams into the fake Silas. He flies across the room and crashes against the far wall.

"Free him," I growl, swinging my legs off the bed. I try to rise but my knees buckle. "Let my dad go!"

I slump to the floor, unable to hold myself upright, but I'm not going to waste this chance.

"Aviella, it's me," Silas says, holding onto the wall as he struggles back to his feet.

He doesn't move closer, holding one hand out, palm towards me.

"Liar!" I yell, gathering power again.

Pain is blinding, white hot light bursting apart my control, I fight it, struggle to form the magic but it hurts so bad I can't keep it. It falls apart and the power disburses. I'm left in a hump on the cold floor, tears streaming down my face.

Silas rushes over, stumbling as he does, dropping to the floor beside me. He wraps his arms around me, and I struggle, knowing I can't trust him, that I should resist. He doesn't let me fight, pulling me tight to his chest. The scent of him fills my nostrils. Surely Casmir wouldn't think to replicate the scent of Silas too, would he?

I keep struggling, but at last my body refuses to do more. Everything hurts too much, so I collapse against Silas. Head on his chest, I listen to his heart pounding. The smell of him is familiar and comforting.

He runs his hands through my hair, holding me while making soothing noises. I let myself drift, welcoming the escape from the pain. I thought this place was harsh when I returned. Everything so solid, bright, so... there. None of that compares to what Casmir did. I shudder at the thought, remembering the way he would watch me with those impassive, cold eyes as his tools tore me apart without ever touching my body.

Still, behind that cold dispassion, I saw a spark. He's in there, behind the façade, there's a dragon waiting to be freed. I'll have to, if I don't, I'll never succeed.

One thing I came back knowing with certainty is my one hope to stand against the Shadow, the one chance at success, is to have the power of Twelve. That number has been written indelibly on history. Each time the Innocents return to this plane, it has been a battle and this, this is supposed to be the last one.

This is it.

The stakes have never been higher. This world will emerge into a new, better one, or it will rot forever in eternal darkness. Abandoned by the Divine for eternity.

I can't let that happen. I can't. It's not only those who've survived, even the dead will be lost if I don't succeed. The pressure of that alone is enough to make me want to break. So I take this brief moment. Thankful for the reprieve though I know that Casmir will rip it all away from me any moment.

But he doesn't. Nothing happens. Could it... could it be?

"Silas?" I ask, my voice hoarse and crackly.

"Yes," he says.

"Is this real?" I ask.

"Yes," he reassures me. "This is very much real."

I wait, certain that's what Casmir would say. What else would you say if you want to lull someone into complacency? What could possibly hurt more than to think that I've escaped, that I'm in the arms of one of my loves, and then to have it ripped away?

Still, nothing. I lean my head back and shift my position so I can study Silas's face. He looks back with his cool gray eyes, a couple of days' growth on his beard sparkled with more gray than black. The lines at the corners of his eyes look deeper, as if he's worried more than a lifetimes' worth since I last saw him, but it's Silas.

It looks like him. Smells like him. It *feels* like him, but is it? I can't stop the doubts assailing me, so I hesitate still more. There's only one way to know, and if it isn't him, maybe it will help me to either know or to break through the walls that Casmir has built.

Shifting myself around a bit more I tilt my head back then hook an arm behind his head and pull him into a kiss. Our lips meet, electric, a jolt of excitement runs through me, overriding the aches and pains that my body has become.

His arms enclose me tighter as he deepens the kiss, his tongue seeking mine. Passion doesn't rise, it rages. Full-blown, overwhelming need and desire staking its claim on my body. I shove my hand between us and grab his hard cock, stroking it through his pants.

His hands roam over my body, up, down, around and grab my breasts. They slide at last under my shirt, bringing sweet relief to my fevered skin. He pulls away from the kiss, holding me back as I strain forward, not wanting it to end.

"You're hurt," he says.

Tears burst free, streaming down my face. I nod then shake my head and throw both arms around his neck jerking him to me so I can kiss him more. He resists but I don't stop pulling.

"Avi," he says.

"No, kiss me," I demand. "It's you, damn it, kiss me!"

He complies, kissing me, but he's still hesitant.

"You... rest... need... heal," he says, continuously pulling back and interrupting my moment with his stupid words.

"You're real," I sob, gripping his face between my hands.

He narrows his eyes, causing the slight wrinkles at the

corners to deepen, his mouth turns down into a frown as his grip tightens.

"I'm so sorry," he says, softly.

Silas has always been a rock, unemotional, of all of us he's the one that has never shown emotions, nothing bothered him, but all of that is gone. I'm struggling to keep the dam on my tears, but the look in his face is too much. The dam crumbles and my tears flow.

"It's not your fault," I say.

He pulls me against his chest, strong arms wrapping tightly around and squeezing. He holds me silent, not even shushing sounds. Creating a safe space in his arms where I let go of all I've been pushing down.

I cling to him. He's my lifeline. An anchor to the here and the now, safe from all that has come before and holding me away from what is yet to happen. I know, with total certainty, that I'm not done yet. Fate hasn't revealed her hand to me in any discernible way, but I'm not stupid.

I'm on a crash course to face off against the Shadow. The Queen of Evil. How strange is it that she's a she? Everyone always assumed it was a he, but it is what it is.

Sexism reigned supreme in the old world. Casual, unthought of, but always present. A quiet undercurrent interwoven into the culture itself. If we win, that's going to change. No woman should ever feel less powerful than she is no more than any man should feel less.

The well of suppressed tears runs dry and still Silas holds me tight, and I cling to him too. There's an edge of desperation to it, but what else could we expect? His heart beats solid, regular in my ear. Everything here still has that harsh edge to it except that sound.

That sound is warmth, ease, steadiness. That sound is a rhythm that I can fall into time with, almost an anchor. Concentrating I open my senses more. It hurts, something is wrong with my magic channels, and it's not flowing like it should. They burn when I open myself up to it, making me shy away.

So I hold myself back, unwilling to have the pain, at least for now. I tilt my head up and shift in his arms again. His beautiful eyes stare into mine, evaluating, but warm. Slowly, almost as if he's feeling tentative, he lowers his lips to mine.

His kiss is softly electric. Awakening a low buzz of thrill that gently passes through me. He doesn't push forward, only tasting, feeling his way forward with his physical touch. My core tightens, throbbing with instant desire and for an instant I want to throw away all this foreplay and get to the good stuff. I want him driving into me hard and fast with no further build up.

But the gentle, attentive attention is good. Suppressing that urge by breathing my way through it, I let him control the pace. The kiss slowly deepens. Light touches becoming more insistent. His tongue tasting my lips, fleeting touches, until at last it drives into my mouth and lays claim.

His hands move slowly across my body. Gentle touches. So soft there are moments I'm barely aware of them on me except for the comfort.

I wrap my fingers in his short hair, holding him tight and we kiss more, deeper and deeper as the passion multiplies. Instinctively I draw magic, responding to the sensation of his embracing me.

"Ow!" I cry out, shuddering as blinding pain hits me.

"Avi?" he asks, stopping everything.

"It's… fine," I say, shaking my head.

"No, it's not," he says, shifting out from under me. "Let me look you over better."

An empty, throbbing ache in my core pulses and anger flashes along with it.

"I only want one damn thing right now, and it's not more probing or poking!" I exclaim.

Silas stops and looks at me seriously. His cock is so hard the bulge in his pants looks like it could tear itself free at any moment, so it's certainly not a matter of desire. His jaw tightens, but I'm not going to give him time to be analytical.

I know at least part of what I need to start healing. I need him. I need all of them but he's the one with me here. I'm aware of the rest of my men, peripherally, and know they're okay somewhere. Part of me wishes they were here. All of them. I want to do the one thing we've never done, take them all. I want them all flowing into me, giving me of themselves and holding nothing back as we all join, but I'll take what I can.

His mouth opens, and he's about to argue so I leap up, shutting his lips with mine. I drive my hand under the belt of his pants and fumbling, find his cock, gripping it tight. I stroke, roughly, this is not the time for gentle, soft lovemaking. I need him. I want him. I need him to fuck me like I've never been fucked before.

I need a good Tynan fucking. Hard, fast, pounding, and in ways I can't fathom healing.

This isn't Silas's normal way, but I'm going to take what I need. He gasps into the kiss, then he grips my ass and lifts me up. I wrap my legs around his waist, leaning back enough to keep stroking him.

He grabs my hair with one hand and jerks my head back. His rough beard scrapes along my cheek and neck as he kisses his way down to my collarbone.

"Yes," I gasp as he responds exactly how I need him to.

We drop to the bed, the weight of his body crushing me. He rises up onto his elbows, and his hips thrust his cock into my hand, grinding it against the cloth separating us.

Holding himself up on an arm, he fights my shirt, but it

won't come undone one handed. Growling he rips it, setting my tits free. The instant they bounce out, his mouth is on them. He sucks one roughly, and I thrust hips up into him crying out in pleasure. He works the other one with his free hand then that same hand slides down across my stomach.

"Fuck me," I whisper into his ear, tugging on his hair. "Fuck me hard."

My words push him. Every move is rough, unplanned, pure response mechanisms without the gentle forethought that Silas puts into everything.

I jerk my hand out of his pants to find the fastener. A moment later there is the satisfying sound of his zipper right before he gets mine to let go as well. He grips my pants in both hands and tears them off of me, scratching my fevered skin in his haste.

He works his own off, then he dives between my legs.

"Oh!" I scream my pleasure as his hot, rough tongue drives deep into my pussy without preamble.

I don't need any. I need him. I need attention. He works my soft lips with tongue and gentle nibbles pushing me right to an edge. As he moves inside of me, his magic pours in, soothing and cooling my aching channels.

The flow of it hits points where it dissipates, and other points across me where I don't feel it at all. Each point of difficulty lights up in my awareness. Points where Casmir did something to me, making things wrong.

The pleasurable sensations override the pain that comes each time the magic hits one of those points. When he hits the right spot, I grip the back of his head, pulling him tight. I hold him there as his tongue moves wildly, not stopping. An orgasm rushes through me.

As it grips my body, I'm left shuddering and Silas climbs up covering my body fully with his. His engorged cock is at my opening, ready to drive in, but he's waiting for my signal I'm ready.

Biting my lip in anticipation I nod, and he thrusts in, fully seating himself in a single motion. I cry out, pleasure overriding awareness of anything else.

He slowly retreats as our heartbeats fall into time with each other. When he drives his hard cock back deep into my pussy, magic pushes in with it. It fills my channels, cleansing them. Easing the pain at least, if not healing them.

"Fuck me," I growl, digging my nails into his shoulders.

"Yes," he grunts thrusting harder, faster.

"Yes!" I cry out. "Give it to me. Give me your cock."

He moves faster and a fresh orgasm is ready, almost to overtake me. His magic calls my own which responds sluggishly. It's subdued, not embracing him the way it always has, but it does respond.

His lips crush mine, his tongue drives into my mouth at the same time his cock drives deeper and then we fall into an orgasm together.

Explosions rock my body as our magic co-joins, and I draw on his to replenish that which was taken from me. I'm awash in the pure white joy of it all. Pleasure beyond words until at last I collapse onto the bed.

Silas lies down beside me and I shift, throwing a leg over his and resting my head on his chest. We lie silent, covered in sweat and stickiness, but for the first time since coming back here, I feel like I might actually belong.

It makes it a little easier knowing that the worst is yet to come.

CHAPTER FIFTEEN

AVIELLA

"*How* much longer?" I ask, impatient.

Silas doesn't stop weaving the glyphs of light around me. It's a repeating pattern that has gone on too long already. Weave glyphs, tsk several times, make notes on his clipboard, repeat.

"Not long," he says.

"And why can't everyone else come here?" I ask, again.

"Because we're outside of time," he says absently, his mind mostly on the work he is doing.

"So?" I ask, again. I'm still not grasping the reasons he's given.

"So?" he asks, stopping what he's doing and actually looking at me.

"Yes, so? I don't get it," I say.

He frowns, his thoughtful frown as I like to think of it. He nods then walks over to a tray of tools. A cold tendril of fear worms its way down my spine seeing them and flashing images of Casmir standing over me with a similar tray flashes through my thoughts.

Silas picks up a long, stainless steel pokey thing and holds it up.

"Think of time as a linear thing, like this," he says. He motions up and down it with his free hand. "It marches along, straight, always going in one direction."

"Right," I agree. "That part makes sense."

"Good. This place, this watchtower if you will, is here," he points to a spot in the air above the pokey thing.

"Right, that doesn't explain why the guys can't come here."

He gives me the look, the "I'm getting there, and you need to learn to be patient" look. Which does nothing to change my mind, of course, but whatever.

"When the last trumpet sounded, this," he points at the straight-line representing time, "became this."

He drops the pokey thing on the tray of tools and odd bits and messes them around, creating a chaos on the previously organized tray.

"And?" I ask.

"Time itself is a mess," he says, pointing at the tray, then pointing at the empty space where he said we were. "This is outside of that, but we're anchored to the mess. Even our presence here is wearing down the magics that keep this bubble outside of time. If I bring the others here, it will accelerate the decay."

"Oh," I say. "So is time moving different for us?"

"Yes," he says. "And for each of them if they get separated from each other. Each of these is a pocket of time, flowing forward or backward, faster or slower, in relationship to each other."

"How long did he have me?" I ask, biting my lip.

It had seemed like ages. He did so many... things to me. And my dad is still with him.

"I don't know," Silas says.

I nod, but there's nothing more to say about it. I let him do his 'work' even though I don't really understand it. It doesn't hurt at least, though when he draws the glyphs over the areas where magic won't flow, I get a tingle or a sensation of numbness.

He finishes at last, writing the final notes on his clipboard, then staring at it. He shakes his head.

"What is it?" I ask.

"Somehow," he says, looking up and meeting my eyes. "He created dead spots in your magical channels and aura."

"What does that mean?"

"That wielding magic is going to be much harder," he says. "It should be impossible, but I've already felt you doing it."

I swallow and nod.

"How do we fix it?" I ask.

He shakes his head. "I don't know."

"Great," I say. "So how do we save my dad?"

Silas shakes his head. "Aviella—"

"Don't even say it," I cut him off. "It's not optional."

His mouth snaps shut, and he nods. He walks over to a bookshelf, running his finger along the spines then selecting one out. It's a heavy-looking tome that he still manages to hold in one hand while he opens it and flips through the pages.

"We need to understand," he says.

"Why does that not surprise me?" I ask.

"Because I've taught you well," he says, absently and I snort. "I suspect Casmir's bunker is outside of time, before the trumpet even. That limits the number of points it could be located."

"Oh, that's good to know," I say, excitement growing, and Silas nods. "What does that actually mean though?"

"In order to anchor something so that it sits outside the

natural flow, it's not only a powerful magic, but it takes a place that has an inherent history and magic to it already."

"Okay," I say. "Such as?"

"This place," he says.

"Obviously," I reply. "Now can you elaborate for those of us not already in the know?'

He looks up from the book, frowning.

"Of course," he says. "This place is a lighthouse. Or it was, is, a reflection of a lighthouse."

"What's inherently magical about that?" I ask.

"Love," he says. "In this case."

"That doesn't make sense," I say. "Who loves a lighthouse?"

"The sailors who it guides home," he says matter-of-factly, "for one. Though that's not enough. In this case it's the tale of its keeper that set it apart, preparing it for the spell I cast on it."

"Go on," I encourage him, genuinely interested.

"This was one of the very first lighthouses built by man," he says. "Older than you're likely to believe, built by the Atlanteans. The keeper fell in love with a woman, and they were very happy together.

"She had traveled to see family and was returning by ship. A storm was raging as the ship fought to return. The lighthouse keeper watched from his tower, helpless, as her ship was sunk."

"That's awful," I say, my heart aching for the man.

Silas tilts his head and nods.

"Love is a magic of its own," he says, unexpectedly, his eyes boring into me.

"What do you mean?" I ask.

"The next day the keeper found her body washed up on the shore. He gathered her into his arms, holding her there on the beach, his heart broken. The light of *his* life gone."

He emphasizes the word with a look that drives straight into my own heart then his gaze is staring into the distance as if he's looking at something more than what I can see here. Something niggles at the edges of my thought, but I'm enraptured with his story. Magic dances around us and I can almost see the images he's describing. The beach is clear to me, the broken man holding her broken body in his arms.

"Go on," I say, breathless.

"He buried her," he says simply. "There on the beach where they'd lived and loved. A love so deep..." he trails off to silence but this time I wait.

Patience has never been a strong suit of mine and I sense or feel the thought he hasn't finished.

"As deep as the oceans," I breathe.

"Exactly," he says without looking at me. "As deep as the oceans."

"What did he do?" I ask.

"It doesn't matter," he says, eyes snapping into focus on me. "It's a tale, an old story, but it serves its purpose. The power of love is a magic of its own. Their love embedded itself into this building. Cementing it outside of time because love, of all the magic in the world, is boundless."

The dead spots in my magical aura throb painfully and my heart aches every bit as badly. There's more to this tale that he's not saying. I know it as much as I know I'm going to take a breath.

"Silas," I say, touching his cheek.

His unshaven face is rough under my fingers and masculine. His strong jaw tenses as he puts his attention back to me. He knows what I'm going to ask but he doesn't want to say.

"He ran off the tower," Silas says, matter-of-factly. "He killed himself."

Our eyes bore into each other and I clearly see the pain in his. Feel it in his magic, the aching loss.

"It was you," I whisper.

He recoils at my words, turning away to cover the reaction.

"We have work to do," he says. "I'm not sure how Casmir managed to damage your magical aura, but those dead spots are going to make it almost impossible for you to wield your magic. We need you in top shape."

Staring at his back, I bite my lip and decide to let him have his secret. I'll handle what's in front of me right now. One thing at a time, it's all I can do.

"Right, let's get this handled," I say, sliding back onto the bed to let him work. It's for the best.

CHAPTER SIXTEEN

RAFE

*I*t's taking too long to heal. It's not only time that got screwed apparently. Magic is a fucking mess since the sounding of the trumpet. My ribs are tender making it hard to get a proper breath. Now isn't the time for being weak or lying around convalescing so I force myself to keep moving.

"We'll return," Tynan says from the doorway.

"Make it quick," Gavin tells them. "We're going to try and create a path between here and Sanctuary."

Tynan stares at the mage, obviously offended by Gavin's attempt to put any control on him, but he doesn't say anything. After a long moment he nods sharply then sweeps out the door, letting it drift closed behind.

"We need a path to Casmir," I say to the mages and Nate.

"That's what the dragons are going to try and find," Lucas says.

"And if they fail?" I ask.

"It's not really an option is it?" Ronan says.

"No, not really," I say. "And you are all doing what?"

"We're going to Sanctuary," Gavin says. "If we rework the

wards protecting it, I think we can link it to Aviella, giving her access."

A low rumble pulls all our attention to the outside. The walls shake and dust falls from the ceiling. Coming out of nowhere, I feel the Shadow approach. Somehow, they managed to cloak their approach. The mages look to Nate and me.

"We can fight or run," Gavin says.

"Run," I say, pulling magic close, letting it pool into my hands which become covered in black Shadow. "I'll hold them back."

"Not alone," Nate says, placing a hand on my shoulder.

"You should go too," I say. "These are my people, let me handle them."

The conflict in his eyes is obvious for anyone who knows what to look for, though his face is blank, giving away nothing. The mages don't hesitate, disappearing with a pop, leaving Nate and me alone.

"Don't be an idiot," I say, shaking my head.

Unspoken words hang between us. Words that have waited millennia to be said, but now is not the time. The past, our past, must remain where it belongs. Long ago, with nothing to do with the now we find ourselves in. Our choices drove us apart, and while she has brought us together, it isn't time for an exploration of old wounds.

"Raphael," Nate says.

"Don't call me that," I say, shaking my head. "I'm not him any longer."

"You are," he says, his voice soft, barely a whisper.

"Run, you damn fool," I growl. "Before they find your stupid angel ass and cut your wings off then shove them down your damn throat!"

As if summoned, his wings unfurl behind him, blinding white, shining with the pure light of the Divine. He hooks an arm behind my neck, pulling me closer, his forehead resting against mine.

"Don't die," he orders, then with a whoosh he's gone.

"Hadn't planned on it," I mutter, turning towards the door right as it crashes open.

Swirling red and black smoke curls its way through the opening as it fills the door, blocking out all sight beyond it. The smoke swirls, a living column of darkness and fire as it roils its way before me.

"Nice of you to join me," I grin. "Been waiting."

"Don't," a soft voice says as the swirling smoke takes on the shape of a man.

It forms into a mousey, short man, with a receding hairline of gray hair slicked back tight against his head. He has horn-rimmed glasses, an affectation to be sure, and sallow skin. He smiles, showing nicotine- and coffee-stained teeth.

"What? I've missed you Beez, how the hell are you?" I ask.

His glare would be plenty enough answer, but I'm not going to let him throw me off my game. He pushes past me. Outside the door his monstrous entourage waits, eager to be let loose to murder and maim. It's the only thing they know how to do, and even Beez, an Arch Lord of a Demon barely keeps them under control.

"Where are they?" Beez asks.

"Who?" I ask, but he turns slowly to face me.

The weight of his gaze lands on me, and it takes all my will to not step back. He's several ranks over me in the hierarchy of hell, and believe me, you don't get to that without being one powerful son of a gun.

"I don't like you, Rafe," he growls. "You amuse Her Infernalness, so I tolerate you, but now is not the time. Do not play games with me. Do not try to be 'cute' or 'funny' or any of your other distractions."

"Beez, I'm sure I don't know what you mean," I say, barely suppressing a laugh.

He's on me faster than I could blink. I don't see him move across the space between us. One moment he's a few feet away, the next he's lifting me by my neck, his hand now a claw crushing my windpipe.

"Do. Not. Fuck. With. Me."

He enunciates each word as a statement of its own. His eyes burn with fiery promises of pain, but none of that matters. He doesn't matter. No, I've seen the light, again. I might die here, but if I do, I won't die a traitor. I'll reserve that honor for Efram. I'll die right, straight with the world, or as straight as I can be.

"Bee-ell-za-bub," I choke his name out. "They're gone. I came hunting them too. When I arrived, they had only just left."

Okay, it's a lie. I'm not a coward but there is also intelligence being the better part of valor. I am a demon after all.

He drops me to the ground and my knees shake, causing me to stumble before I can manage to keep myself upright. His beady eyes filled with fire bore into me, testing the truth of my words. I drop my magic and meet his gaze with nothing more than my own guile. If I didn't, he'd suspect my lies and suspicion is all he needs to go on.

"Where?" he asks.

"If I knew that, you wouldn't have found me here," I say. "I'm hunting the ones She wants too."

"We'll see about that," he says.

He holds up two fingers and makes a come-hither motion. Two massive creatures squeeze their way through the door and take up positions on either side of me.

"Beez," I say. "Come on, for old times' sake?"

"That's always been your problem, Rafe," he says. "Too sentimental. Clinging to things that could have been, might have been, unwilling to face the reality of our situation. The Divine placed THEM above us! Us!

"How you are not filled with the same righteous anger that led us into the rebellion is beyond me. Perhaps you need persuasion, something to help you open your mind to reality."

"I guess I don't really see it that way," I say, shrugging. "I mean without the humans, what kind of game would we even have? You recall how boring it was before? I mean mind-numbing boring. So, ugh, why would you want to go back to that?"

"You're a traitor," he says softly. "I've always known it, but never could prove it. You won't get away from me this time, I promise you that."

"Traitor is a really strong word," I shake my head. "I prefer conscientious objector to stupidity. Like your ideas. They're really not very bright, if you'd only look at them. Nothing is all black and white like you try to make it. The world is a whole lot of gray."

"Take him away," Beez roars.

The two monsters latch painfully onto either arm then drag me roughly towards the door. We're about to go out of it, slowed down by the not-quite-bright trying to figure out how to pass through a normal door side-by-side, which is of course impossible.

The world brightens around us, turning bright white. A wordless battle cry echoes and then Nate appears at my feet, replete with brilliant white wings and flaming sword. He faces off against Beelzebub, who shifts to his true form.

It's not a bright idea to do inside the room we're in, but as I've observed, he's not the smartest. As his shape shifts, he grows in size, crashing through the ceiling. Plaster and dirt rain down on us, as he takes on his natural demonic state.

Nate's head cranes back as he watches him grow into his

full size. The two monsters holding me let go, reaching for the angel. I'm about to blow any last cover I have with the hell realms, but I can't let Nate face this alone.

I leap to my feet, pull my own dark fire sword to me, and land next to Nate, ready to face the demon before us together.

"You had to get involved," I hiss.

"Yes," Nate says.

"I had this under control," I say.

"No, you didn't," he says. "And I'm not going to let you stand alone."

That's all the time we have for words. The monsters swing and Beez blasts fire at us that's tainted with his infernal breath. It's on, and I'm not sure we're going to get out of this one or not.

CHAPTER SEVENTEEN

EFRAM

"*W*here is she?" she asks, crossing her legs one over another.

I stare, unable to take my eyes off her. She's beautiful. Mesmerizingly so, and my body responds against my will. She exudes raw, animal magnetism. Every line, perfect. Every curve, not a hair out of place, full breasts straining against the surprisingly seductive business attire she wears. She exudes sex, desire, and pure need.

"I don't know," I repeat for the thousandth time.

"Oh, I know you don't think you do," she says.

She only took over the interrogation, for that's what this has been, recently. I'm not sure how long I've been here. I was measuring the passage of time by the growth of my beard, but they must have figured that out, because three men came in and shaved me, which now happens daily. Or maybe every other day? I'm not sure.

"Well that's right," I agree. "I don't."

"No," she shakes her head and smiles. "I said you don't think you do, not that you don't."

"I don't know what you mean," I say.

Her magic caresses along my skin, pulling my own magic out, entangling with it. It fevers my skin, makes me aroused, clouding my thoughts. It's worse than being drugged because this feels natural. It feels like it should be this way whereas no drug I've experienced ever accomplishes that.

The tight business skirt leaves her calves bare. She's wearing high heels, one of which dangles from her delicate foot. She clasps the strap between her toes, letting it swing freely, back and forth, drawing my attention to it. As my eyes drift down her thighs to her bare legs she uncrosses and crosses her legs, leaving nothing to the imagination about what's up that skirt.

I swallow hard, struggling to stop my body's natural response because there's no desire behind it. Nothing pure or of my own personal choice. I don't want her no matter what my body is doing. There's only one woman I want, only one I would do anything for, including what I've done.

Betraying her. Causing her death, but then she came back. I knew my faith in her wasn't misplaced. She told me to trust her, told me I was the only one she could count on to do what had to be done. I was strong, stronger than all the others. Finally I felt like I'd earned my place with her, but then she died.

I haven't spoken to her since she returned. She was dead, I'm sure of it. She's back, I'm sure of that. What it all means, though, I have no idea. That's the part that's not clear, yet at least.

Sighing, I close my eyes and try to breathe through the pain. They've tried all the torture techniques on me that I've ever read or heard of. I'm down a pinky and a toe now, but it's an acceptable loss if I buy Aviella enough time.

They must have decided none of that was working, and now I'm dealing with her. She doesn't think I know who she is, but I do. Aviella hasn't left me unprepared. I know what

I'm facing off against. I know I should be able to, but I also know that I don't have any choice. Every minute I can buy for her is a minute more for her to succeed.

I don't know what the plan is, but I trust she has it in motion. She is going to save the world. This is my part to play. Suddenly the sweet scent of hyacinth fills my senses and warm breath passes over my cheek.

Her eyes shift colors as I stare into them. They have a depth that is incredible, pulling me into them until I'm lost. She never actually touches me, but her body is so close it feels like she does, and her magic caresses just over me.

It's erotic. Arousing. And so damn wrong.

"You're thinking of her," she whispers in my ear. "I can feel her in you."

"Get away," I fight to get the words out.

"You love her?" she asks, her breath tickling my neck. "It's okay. I get it, she's enticing, isn't she? Full of life and love, and that sweet, young body that you want to bury yourself in so badly…"

I can't stop myself from thinking of Aviella, and as she talks about her body my thoughts flash to watching her with the others.

"Oh," she says, almost as if surprised. "You like it like that, do you?"

"No," I strain back from her, but I can only move so far. She's too close.

"It's okay," she says. "Hey, each to his own, right? It's what I've always said. What is the point of free will if you don't exercise it?"

Shaking my head from side to side, I strain against the back of the chair, but I'm held too tightly. I can't get away, can't get any air.

"Show me," she whispers, and my mind explodes with

every moment I've spent with Aviella. Every thought, every feeling, every instant of desire and need and love.

She drinks them in, absorbs them, and there's nothing I can do but scream as she ransacks her way through my thoughts.

CHAPTER EIGHTEEN

AVIELLA

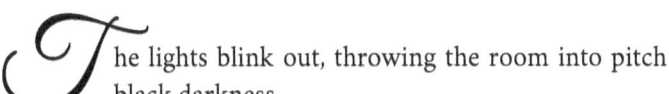

*T*he lights blink out, throwing the room into pitch black darkness.

"Silas?" I call out, pooling magic around my left fist and creating a ball of light.

An instant later the lights blink back on, but something feels off. I can't put my finger on what it is, but there's been a change. I hear something crash in the distance, so I throw down the book I was reading and run for it. When I chase down the sound, I find Silas in the library with books piled around him.

"What happened?" I ask.

He's staring at the mess of books and only looks up to me when I speak. He shakes his head and there's a flash of deep regret on his face. Old pain, I'd say.

"We're losing our anchor," he says, kneeling and picking up the nearest books.

I move over and help pick them up.

"So we're going to be back in the normal timeline?" I ask.

"Perhaps," he says. "If there is such a thing any longer."

"It's all part of the plan," I say, reaching deep to find that certainty I had when I first came back.

There is a plan. I know it, but I don't know what it is. And no plan is without its complications.

"I'm glad to hear you say so," he says. "I've long doubted the idea of fate, but I do know prophecy can be accurate, so it's a conundrum."

"Sure," I agree. "Fate isn't locked into one path though. It can't be, really, can it?"

"What do you mean?" he asks, carrying a fresh stack of books back to their shelf.

"Well if fate was locked, then what about free will? It wouldn't be free if the outcome was already determined."

"True, but that would only strengthen the argument against fate," he says.

"It could but not still account for prophecy, now would it?" I ask. "If you take that into consideration then consider this, there are fixed... goals I guess."

"Okay, goals," he says, stopping with the books and giving me his full attention.

I frown, thinking this through and trying to put a concept too big for words into something I can say.

"Yeah, targets, I guess. Possible outcomes that all of time and the entire... world? Universe? I don't know, like everything is marching toward them. These singular points where... things are decided. Like a choose your own adventure book!"

It's been years since I read one of those but as a child, they were my favorite. My choices changing the story was the coolest thing I'd ever run across. It made me feel powerful.

"An interesting analogy," Silas says.

"Thanks, yeah," I say. "It's like that though."

He nods rubbing his chin thoughtfully.

"If those 'targets' as you call them were considered to be

turning points in time. Where a billion tiny decisions would lead to a collision point…"

"Exactly!" I exclaim excitedly and he nods.

"Then it would make sense that those points would resonate enough that those sensitive to such things would write prophecies around them."

"It makes sense, right?"

His frown deepens as he considers my idea before nodding sharply.

"You've grown," he says, then the lights blink out again.

"Silas?" I ask.

The darkness brings with it an oppressive silence. Things shift and move inside of it making my skin crawl and the hair on my arms stand on end.

"I'm here," he says, and I jump because he's closer than I expected but I didn't sense or hear him move.

The lights blink on again but this time the walls seem… thinner. Less there than they were before.

"What's happening now?" I ask, as magic washes over us.

It's a wave, but not unpleasant. It's familiar to the touch, but I can't put my finger on how or why I know it.

"The mages," he says. "They're reaching out to us, creating a path to their Sanctuary." He places a hand on the small of my back.

I lean my head against his chest, my heart pounding. Time and fate are moving, again. I'm oddly, distantly aware of it, and a small part of me doesn't want to leave. I could make a good life here, with Silas. Studying, learning, growing and exploring the depths and power of my magic as well as his.

That's not my destiny and I know it.

I'm a focal point, want it or not, and the final decisions that are being made about this world that was and the one that will be are all going to be influenced by me. It's a heavy load and I feel it weighing on my shoulders.

The wall takes on a soft glow, growing brighter and thinner at the same time. The lights blink once more and then the wall is gone. Standing in the newly created opening is Rowan.

"Row!" I exclaim, running and tackling her.

I wrap my arms around her, burying my face in her gorgeous hair and swinging her around off her feet. She returns the embrace, pulling me tight against her. She wraps her hands in my hair and forces my head back, so our eyes meet. She stares, studying me intently.

"I'm fine," I say. She tilts her head and arches an eyebrow. "Yes, I'm sure. Silas has helped, a lot."

She nods, pulling me tight against her again. A tear slips out before I can stop it. She's my dearest friend, and we've barely been together. Magic pulses inside of her now, too. She's got a power all her own, and now I wonder how I didn't see it before. She's definitely coming into her own.

"If you two would like to come on," Gavin says, good naturedly.

The four mages stand together watching the reunion.

"Hey, Silas," Lucas says. "We made the path work. A lot is happening. We thought we'd better get the gang together."

"Probably a good idea," Silas says. "This place is becoming... unanchored."

I don't know if anyone else picks up on the hesitation in his voice, but I do. It's the tiniest of hitches, a small indicator of pain that he'd never share. Except I know. I let go of Rowan and walk over, place an arm around his waist.

"The past is done, but we're going to create a better world," I say softly.

"Yes," he says, putting his arm around me. He straightens up and nods. "Yes."

He speaks with more confidence and certainty, turning to the newly formed tunnel.

"Okay, let's go then," Gavin says. "We don't want this path open for long. They're already tracking us down."

I grab Rowan as I pass, putting my free arm around her waist while keeping the other around Silas, giving him what support I can. The three of us follow the mages down the tunnel made of light, striding towards the destiny that isn't going to let us free.

CHAPTER NINETEEN

AVIELLA

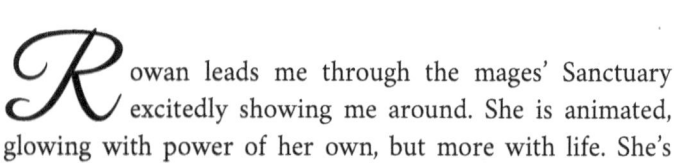

*R*owan leads me through the mages' Sanctuary excitedly showing me around. She is animated, glowing with power of her own, but more with life. She's always been full of life, but now more than ever.

"I see," I say, as she drags me into yet another room.

This one is filled with ghostly images and dozens of Innocents fighting in it. Some of them I recognize from before, most I've never met. Killian is calling out orders, and those training perform maneuvers on his command. We stand and watch for a few moments.

Undead creatures form from the mist, lurching at the Innocents. Killian barks at the last possible moment and each Innocent thrusts their hands forward, white light exploding out of their hands to blow up the undead.

They're all sweating and obviously have been working hard. As I watch, biting my lip, I'm happy and sad at the same time. They're an army. That's what they came here to become and become they have.

Trained, experienced in wielding the raw, unfocused power they had, which is good. They're no longer victims, they'll be able to protect themselves. The problem is an army has one purpose. War. And in war there are no Innocents. I'll lose some of them. A lot of them, probably.

I notice them glancing at me out of the corners of their eyes, curiosity on their faces, but it looks as if they know who I am, even those I haven't met. As Rowan drags me out of the training room and pulls me towards the next, I stop. She turns and looks.

"How do they all know me?" I ask.

She grins sheepishly and shrugs.

"Rowan?" I ask, crossing my arms over my chest.

She signs to me that she's innocent but the look on her face is anything but innocence. She may not have done it all alone, but she has obviously spread word about me. It's humbling, but also it brings a heavy weight with it. She grips my shoulders and shakes me softly until I look up and meet her eyes.

"It's nothing," I say, shaking my head trying to shoulder the weight. She shakes her head and waggles a finger in my face. "I know, I know."

She signs for me to go on about what I think I know.

"The way they look at me," I sigh. "They're in awe. They'll follow me. I know it, I feel it if nothing else."

She nods sharply and signs that this is true.

"Right," I say, trying to walk forward but she tightens her grip to hold me in place.

She asks why this is a bad thing.

"Because," I say, biting my lip. "I'll lose some if not all of them. They won't all make it."

She cups my chin, pulling my head up to meet her eyes. We stare into each other's eyes until she pulls me tight. We cling to each other, and I let the pleasure of being with her again wash away my worries about the future.

It's going to be what it's going to be. We'll all do our best.

"There you are," Gavin says, striding down the hall. "Mind coming with me?"

"Sure," I agree. "Rowan too?"

"Of course," he says, turning back the way he came. "We're going to try something."

He leads us to another room. The entire Sanctuary is white. White walls, white lights, white doors even. It's redundant and makes it very hard to orient myself. Rowan and Gavin seem to have no problem navigating it, but I'm left lost. The room we walk into is a muted white, almost dusky in shade, which is a nice change. Ronan, Silas, and Luca are gathered in the room already when I arrive.

"Hey, guys," I greet them.

"This is not a good idea," Silas says, apparently finishing a thought he was in the middle of.

"If you have a better one, please say so," Ronan says.

"What are we doing?" I ask.

Ronan looks to me then back to Silas. He walks closer. It's the first time we've really seen each other since... I went away. He stops barely a foot away, but his magic is fully embracing, curling around, intermingling with mine.

We stare at each other for a long moment, my heart pounding. He doesn't say a word and I don't either as the world fades away around us. His lips part and the urge to kiss them is so strong I'm leaning forward, into a kiss that hasn't yet come.

"Damn," he exhales. "You are stunning."

"Thank you," I say, cheeks warming. "You don't look half-bad either."

He grins, then closes the space, wrapping his arms around me tightly. The others look on, and in any other situation this would be awkward, but not with them. My men know, my men are... mine. There is no jealousy in them, or I'd feel it. No, those watching have only happiness for what we're all creating.

It's strange, different, but absolutely the way it's supposed to be. The Twelve will gather to me, and only with the Twelve do we have a prayer. He plays with my ass a moment as he kisses me then slaps it and steps away.

"Sorry," he says, more to the group than to me.

No one begrudges him or me the moment. They nod and the subject is returned to as if without interruption.

"We're trying to find allies," Luca says. "The Sanctuary has come under attack."

"It has?!" I exclaim, pushing my magical senses out as far as I can, looking for the source and where I need to run.

"No!" Silas exclaims. "Restrain yourself."

I look at him angrily, but Ronan puts an arm around my shoulders.

"Avi," he says. "It's not active, at the moment, but it has never happened before."

"Oh," I say, withdrawing my magic.

"Aviella," Silas admonishes. "When you wield your full power like that, it's a beacon, calling attention from the Shadow. You must not do that."

"Sure," I say, testily. "I'll hold back and lose more people."

"That's not what I—" Silas says.

"I get it," I cut him off with a sharp motion of my hand. "So what's this plan."

"A creature that is from before time," Luca says. "Here before the heavens and fated to be here after. Powerful, very, very powerful, and possibly an ally."

"Or possibly an even greater threat than the one we already face," Silas says sourly. "You're playing with fire and refuse to see it."

"I don't believe so," Gavin interjects. "It's a risk, yes, but a calculated one."

"I'm not risking the fate of the entire world on your calculations," Silas says.

"It's not up to you," Ronan says hotly. "She's the One we follow, not you."

"Enough!" I yell. "Seriously, we don't have time for this. Now quit with the build up and tell me what you're talking about."

The men each exchange a look and I wait for further argument, but none comes.

"The Leviathan," Ronan says.

"You're shitting me," I say. I've read about the Leviathan in some of the ancient texts, but even those were more like it didn't really exist.

"No," Gavin says.

"It's not real," I say, shaking my head. "It was here before everything?"

"At home in the dark, and yes," Luca says.

"Then it's a creature of shadow," I say.

"No, not necessarily," Gavin says, looking at Silas.

"The Leviathan is a creature, or more accurately, a being that precedes all of creation. As such it is neither aligned with light or dark, good or evil, it simply is," Silas says, shaking his head. "And contacting such a creature, that is beyond the concepts of good and evil as we know them, is an incredibly dangerous, destructive idea."

"Or smart," Gavin adds in. "A final play."

"We have the dragons," Silas argues.

"And even they might not be enough," Luca says. "The dragons were created after the Shadow after all. There is nothing that can compare to that level of power, on a toe-to-toe basis outside the Leviathan."

Rowan motions wildly, calling attention to herself as she pounds her chest until we're all looking at her. She motions to me, then moves to my side and moves her hands up and down in front of me.

"And Aviella," Gavin says.

"If she survives long enough," Luca says seriously. "Look, like it or not, want to admit it or not, we lost her. She came back through whatever miracle of the Divine but that's a gift horse you only get once."

"Thanks, I'm not a horse," I say.

"That's not what I meant," Luca says.

"I know," I shake my head, closing my eyes. "So, straight talk, how desperate is this move?"

The mages look at each other, none of them daring to look at Silas. The silence and their looks tell me all I need to know.

"Right," I say. "Do we have a better option? Can we get Tynan's input on this? Or Alaric and Shen?"

"No," Gavin says. "We can't reach any of the others."

"You can't? Why not? I got it where I was with Silas, but I thought you guys could keep tabs on everyone here."

"The dragons are outside of our reach," Ronan says. "We've tried."

"What about Rafe and Nate?" I ask. No one answers me, all of them look at the floor or off in the distance, anywhere but at me directly. "What about them?"

There's a shrillness to my voice that I wish wasn't there. An edge of sharp, cutting fear slices through, leaving me cold.

"We haven't been able to contact them," Silas says.

"What does that mean?" I ask.

"They could be—" Gavin starts.

"We don't know," Silas cuts him off. "That's all it means. It's not the first time they've been out of touch."

"Oh," I say, pushing down hard on the desire to reach out for them.

I know I could find them. They can't hide from me, no matter where or even when they are. The connection I have to both of them is entirely too strong for that, not any longer. Biting my lip, I debate the question at hand.

"Will it help us? Will it help us win?" I ask.

"If it doesn't destroy us for bothering it," Silas says. "Possibly."

"Then do it," I say, thinking of my dad.

It's selfish and not the reason I should be doing anything. I know it, but my need to save him pulses in every beating of my heart, tinges every breath I take.

"We'll need your help," Gavin says. "This isn't something we can do alone."

"Okay," I agree. "Show me what to do."

It doesn't take long. They bring in a few of the more powerful Innocents and my heart warms that Rowan is among that group. She grins broadly then mimics Silas being grimly present. I can't suppress a laugh.

Soon we stand in a circle and I'm at the head of it, or close enough. Under Gavin's direction we all join hands and the mages chant along with the Innocents. They didn't bother teaching me the summoning, so I stand and wait, feeing magic into the symbols their words weave.

Darkness forms in the middle of our group. At first, it's small, the size of a saucer, a flat spinning circle of inky black. The chant funnels magic into it, and it grows. When it's the size of a dinner plate, it begins to rotate on an axis and a low thrumming sound starts.

It's drawing more magic. No longer do I have to funnel into it, it's drinking it in. Consuming it as it grows, pulling. Sweat beads on the forehead of those gathered, and the power ramps up. My hair is moving in a breeze coming from nowhere, and the darkness keeps growing. It's almost the size of a man now, stretching and elongating until it looks like a tiny humpback whale floating in the middle of our circle.

Eyes open and blink. It's impossible to call them anything else, even though they're black too. Black eyes on blackness, but they're there. It's weird, but then what isn't, when you're dealing with magic?

"Haruhm," the thing says.

"Leviathan," Silas says.

"Haruhm," Leviathan grumbles. "Youngling, boring."

It turns slowly in the air, dark eyes landing on each person in turn as it spins. At last it's eyes land on me and the weight of them is palpable.

"Leviathan," I say, when it doesn't keep moving.

"Thrice-Born," it says. "Haruhm, interesting, haruhm."

Glancing at Silas I arch an eyebrow, but he shakes his head clearly not understanding the title either.

"I'm looking for… help," I say.

"Help, haruhm, of course, your kind always are," it says. "Help is not what you need. Dependence, no, not on a creature such as I. I who was here before all and I who will be here after all. No, help, haruhm, wrong question, Thrice-Born."

"I don't understand," I say. "What is the right question?"

"Exactly!" it exclaims, and the walls of the room shake with the booming of its voice. "Haruhm! Haruhm!"

I think it's laughing, but I'm not sure. My magic forms a protective shield around my ears, the only thing that kept me from being deafened I'm sure. I glance at the others to make sure they're okay then put my attention back on the… thing.

"Leviathan, I face the Shadow, I seek allies," I say, trying a different tack.

"You have allies, haruhm," he says. "Allies and allies you have. Power, yes, power in Twelve. You've come before, you'll probably come again, if you fail."

"If I fail?" I ask.

"Of course, haruhm," he says. "Fail, again, or win and change the cycle. So it is, so it has been, so it might be. Or it might not, haruhm."

Frowning, I look at Silas. Magic buzzes through my soul angrily, like a million bees ready to be unleashed. The Leviathan drifts close, its eyes swirling and taking on colors.

"Can't you answer me straight?" I ask frustrated.

The Leviathan opens its mouth and inhales. When it does suddenly my magic is pouring out of me and into it. I drop to my knees, exclaiming in surprise, and shock. It doesn't hurt, per se, but it doesn't feel good either.

"Aviella," Gavin yells.

He and Luca break the circle moving towards me but the Leviathan haruhm's and undulates. They're knocked flying back and slam into the wall, sliding down.

"Thrice-Born, you were, you were, and now you are. The only right question is the one you should be asking. Will you? Will you, or will She? That question is the one. Haruhm."

It's so close to my face we could touch if either of us waver. It's black swirling eyes stare into mine, drawing magic from my body and soul.

"That... doesn't... make sense," I say gritting my teeth through the unpleasantness.

"No, haruhm, it doesn't. Yet," he says. "Consider. Consider. We'll speak again."

Suddenly it's gone and I'm left panting on my hands and knees. The guys run to me but Rowan is at my side first, pushing them back. She hooks an arm around my shoulders and helps me to my feet. They're all talking at once, demanding to know if I'm okay, but too many thoughts fill my head.

I don't understand but on some level I do. Thrice-Born. It

means something, something deep, that matters. If I could only put my finger on it...

No matter though, one thing is clear. We won't be having an ally in the Leviathan. Steadying myself on Rowan's shoulders I shake off the remnants of the experience and turn to face the guys.

"It's fine," I say, answering all their concerned looks and words at once. "Seriously, I'm fine. Anyone else hurt?"

"We're fine," Silas says. "What did it say to you?"

"You were there," I say. "Nothing but a bunch of riddles."

Everyone looks at each other, then Silas shakes his head.

"We didn't hear what it said," he says.

"Oh," I say, closing my eyes. "Great. Well he speaks in riddles and didn't say anything really useful except that it's not going to help. Directly at least. Apparently, I have all I need here in my Twelve."

"But we're not Twelve," Gavin says.

"Not yet," I say.

"Yet?" Luca asks.

"No, but I know who it is," I say, exhaling heavily.

"You do?" several of them ask in unison and I nod.

"Aviella, you haven't said anything," Silas says. "Who is it?"

Bracing myself for the flashback I'm sure will happen, I debate not saying his name. Somehow it feels like this is the time though. They need to know after all, I'm going to need them to help. They have to back my play on this.

"Yeah, I've known for a bit," I say, squaring my shoulders.

"Then who is it?" Gavin asks.

Rowan signs that she wants to know too.

"Casmir," I say. "It's Casmir, and we have to stop him before he hurts my dad too much for me to accept him."

CHAPTER TWENTY

AVIELLA

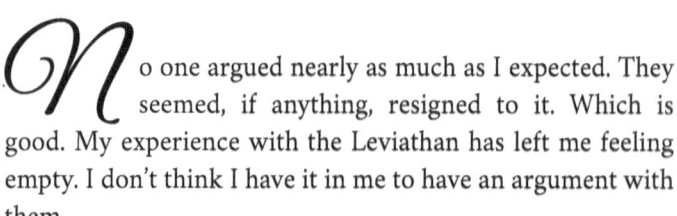

*N*o one argued nearly as much as I expected. They seemed, if anything, resigned to it. Which is good. My experience with the Leviathan has left me feeling empty. I don't think I have it in me to have an argument with them.

We break up the group and I wander off to find some food. Rowan helps me find the kitchen and we throw some sandwiches together, then sit and eat. It's like old times and I really appreciate it. It's soothing and brings a sense of normalcy to my life that has been sorely lacking.

It isn't long before she tells me she has to go, and I'm left on my own. I wander the Sanctuary with a weird sense of déjà vu. It pulls me along with that sense of almost familiar until I find a room with a closed door.

"Come in," a voice says when I knock.

I enter and am surprised to find Killian, Gavin, Ronan, and Luca standing around a table.

"Hey," I say, as I walk in and they all return the greeting. "What's up?"

"We're looking over a plan of attack," Gavin says,

motioning me to come stand beside him. "This is where we think Casmir's hiding."

He points to a map. Something about it bothers me so I lean in closer trying to cipher out what about it is ringing a bell. Suddenly it hits me.

"You're kidding me," I say, looking at the mages.

"No," Luca says.

"I wish," Gavin says, "but no."

"He's in the magic kingdom?" I exhale.

"As near as we can pinpoint him, yes," Killian says.

"Great, that's freaking perfect," I say, shaking my head. "So what's the plan?"

"It's running on its own time loop," Luca says, drawing his finger in a circle around the map.

Gavin is on my right and Killian on my left. They're both close, touching me, and it's comforting. One of them places a hand on the small of my back as I lean over the table and the warmth of that contact spreads across my skin.

They lay out their plan of attack. Each of them pointing and touching and moving things across the map. It seems solid—if we can surprise him. If not, we're going to be in trouble. When they finish, we five stare at the map as if daring it to prove us wrong.

"Okay," I say, then Gavin grabs me by my waist and turns me towards him.

"I'm glad you're here," he says huskily.

"You scared the hell out of us," Killian says pushing up behind me and crushing me into Gavin.

Gavin claims my lips, pushing aside all the worries about the Leviathan, the impending battle, and leading the Innocents.

Luca and Ronan move up on either side of me and grab my shirt. I'm stuck between the other two, but I'm not resisting anyway as they lift it up and over my head.

"No fair," I argue, topless.

"Oh?" Gavin says. "You want this?"

He grabs the hem of his shirt and lifts it up only enough to show the six-pack hiding underneath.

"Yes," I say, running my hands over the hard muscles of his stomach. "And more."

They don't bother teasing me further. All four of them rip their shirts over their heads and while they do, I step out of my pants. This is exactly what I need.

Gavin kisses me, then Killian spins me around and claims my lips. He pushes one hand down between us, finding my warmth and shoving a finger inside. I gasp in surprised relief, grinding my hips and forcing him deeper.

His tongue pushes into my mouth while Gavin's rock-hard cock digs into my ass. I'm aware more than I see Luca and Ronan slipping off their pants. They stand to either side of me touching and stroking my fevered skin.

At each point of contact between my skin and theirs, magic flows. It creates a protective cage as it pours into me, fueling a soul-deep hunger. An insatiable appetite for their love and attention. Killian breaks our lips' kissing, and Luca claims my freed lips. Then Killian's mouth works its way down my front.

I lean back into Gavin, who holds me steady, hooking his arms over my shoulders with hands on my ass. Somehow, magic or otherwise, he's lost his pants as I can feel the tip of his cock resting between my rear.

Luca's kiss is gentle, soft and filled with easy passion. So different than Killian's demanding lips and tongue. He peppers my lips with soft touches, tongue darting out to taste before retreating. He continues the light strokes of his fingertips up and down my sides, brushing the swell of my breasts, down across my hip.

Ronan kisses my neck while fondling my breasts. The

head of his cock rubs against my hip enticingly. I reach for it and with my other hand I take Luca's. Ronan groans throatily while Luca gasps into my mouth.

Gripping tight I stroke their cocks then Killian reaches my sex. When his hot tongue makes contact, I buck, shoving my hips into his face, crying out in pleasure.

Gavin holds me steady while Ronan and Luca add their support, hooking their hands under my ass to keep me upright.

"Yes!" instinct claims my body and I want more of the intense pleasure.

Killian doesn't hold back. His rough tongue drives through my soft folds like a missile. Drives through the protective layers until he finds my hidden pleasure spot.

Luca and Ronan shift their hands. Each has a hand on my lower back, then they move their free hands to behind my knees while I continue to undulate against Killian's magical tongue.

Gavin takes a half step back, dragging me along with him until I'm almost horizontal, held in the air by the three men. They spread my legs, letting Killian drive his tongue deeper.

I'm moaning, twisting and groaning, driving myself forward and retreating at the same time. It's too intense, but exactly what I need.

It's not only physical. Their magic is a golden cloud, pillowing me in its embrace. Touching, stroking, pouring in and filling my own reserves. Preparing me for more.

Killian or someone slides two fingers inside, filling my aching void, then more slide in and I'm over the edge. My toes curl, my back arches, and I bite off a scream of pleasure. My magic pulses like the waves of the ocean, crashing into the boys.

I've got a death-grip on the two cocks that I slowly

release as the orgasm washes away, leaving behind the after-tremors.

When I open my eyes again, they're holding me tight, waiting for the intensity to ease. I smile, shaking my head, but they're not done yet and neither am I.

I'm lowered back onto my feet as they shift around. The table is the perfect height and Gavin turns me so I'm facing it. One hand on my neck, he presses forward so that I bend over it.

Ready and wanting, I spread my feet apart, making sure my men have easy access as I shift myself so I'm lying across the corner of the table. Ronan steps up behind me, the head of his dick at my slick opening, pressing slowly in.

"Oh," I exhale as he slides in and seats himself. "Yes!"

He groans as my wetness embraces him. "Fuck…"

Turning my head to either side I reach out with my magic and pull Gavin and Killian around and towards me so that their throbbing cocks are within reach of my hands. I take each of them and stroke in time with Ronan's thrusts.

I turn my head and then lock eyes with Luca, having no intention of leaving him out. He grins and nods under-standing as he positions himself in front. I open my mouth wide, he slides his rod in, and I swallow him.

I'm filled, and the sensation of it is wonderful. Exhila-rating and thrilling, but the magic makes it so much more. Each push in, every stroke, our magic intertwines, flowing in and out of each other. Heightening the sensations, but so much more too. It sweeps us away to something so far beyond the physical.

It's not only sex. It's joining, coming together. We're becoming something more than the sum of our parts.

They take me, but I'm taking them too. And in taking from each other we give to each other. The give and the take beyond the physical strengthens us.

Ronan is close. He won't be able to hold back much longer. I sense it in the urgency of his thrusting and in the pulsing of his magic flowing through all of us. His urgency and need calls to the other men, and my own building orgasm responds too.

Tightening my grip on Gavin and Luca, I stroke their cocks with greater intensity. Their hips power the thrusts in and out of my hands as they groan. Hands are all over my body, touching, exploring, sweeping aside the remnants of what Casmir did while I was his prisoner.

We're all close.

So close.

As one, we crest the height of our pleasure and fall into it. They explode, covering my body with their fluid as their magic blasts into my soul. I drink it all in, taking the cocks deep in my body, but the magic goes further.

It's fuel. Gateways open as I take pieces of them into myself, becoming, somehow, more in tune with them, closer.

I'm left a shuddering shell as they pull their cocks out and away. Gavin appears with warm washcloths, and they all set to work cleaning the mess they've made of me while I lie gasping in air, feeling the pleasure and changes that continue to roll through my body.

They're gentle and attentive, making sure that I'm well cared for, until at last it's time to dress. We help each other find our own clothing, small talk, gentle kisses and fond touches. The love in their gazes, the warmth of their magic coddling me, is the perfect ending.

"Well," Gavin says, straightening his shirt and unfortunately covering over his beautiful washboard abs. "We have the plan."

He points at the map which now has some very conspicuous stains on it that couldn't be cleaned away.

"If we're right, this is where your dad is, we can rescue him," Killian adds.

I purse my lips and frown. Nothing is more important to me in the short term than to get my dad out of Casmir's clutches. I know I'll have to confront Casmir, and that somehow, I've got to free him from the mark of the Shadow. When Casmir had me, I saw desire in his eyes in brief flashes behind the cold facade he maintains.

When I rest my fingers on the map, the table is still warm. Their magic pulses in me, bolstering my magic and my spirit. I'm brimming with new power, and the flow of my own magic feels easier. It's definitely less painful, thanks to the work Silas has done. Sex is powerful magic too, obviously. It fills me with confidence. Certainty we can do this, if we're together.

"Very well," I said. "Let's mount an attack."

"Silas will counsel to wait," Ronan says.

"Sure," I agree. "He will, and you know what, he's probably right. Sometimes though, you have to say screw it all. Throw it all to the wind and see what happens."

"Throw what to the wind?" Silas asks, coming in the room as if summoned by the thought of him.

I turn around, lean against the table, and meet his gaze. His nostrils flare, and I can see the calculations happening in his head. He looks at each of the gathered mages and pulls his magic back, withdrawing from me.

Is he... jealous? It feels like he is. My eyes widen and my mouth drops open in surprise.

"Silas," I say, softly, walking over.

I put my hands on his chest, feeling his strong heart beating, the rise and fall as he breathes. He can't hold back when I'm this close, his magic curls around, caressing. Rising onto my toes, I kiss him. It's a soft kiss, lacking the usual passion that we have between us, but more than making up for that with genuine concern and love.

His lips are stiff at first, barely responding, so I become more insistent. Pushing him, forcing him to look for himself. There's no way I'm going to make him wrong for feeling what he's feeling, but I also won't leave him feeling excluded.

At last his lips soften and he gives himself into the kiss. I hook my arms around his neck and press myself against him until his hard cock is digging into my belly. Only then do I break the kiss and lower myself to my feet. We stare into each other's eyes as our magic intertwines and mingles. I'm aware, on some level, of his feelings.

"I love you," I whisper, impulsively.

It's an instinct. Unplanned, something I've only said to one of the guys, and yet… it's true. It's right, and as I watch his face, I learn it's also exactly what he needed to hear. Knowing his pain, understanding him on levels I never thought possible after our journey to the lighthouse… I know it's true.

It's true I love all of them. This has never been about sex, magic, or anything else. It's about love. I love each of them for who they are. Telling them, navigating the rocky waters of loving so many and throwing sex into the mix, well that's going to be my superpower if I manage it. I can't let one of them ever feel left out or jealous or alone. It's on me to make sure each of them knows how much I care about them.

Taking a deep breath I turn back to the mages without another word. Silas doesn't answer me with words, but his demeanor has changed so completely I know he's okay. Another thing to be careful of is making sure each of them can be the man he is, to not call one of them out in some way in front of the others.

Damn, I thought saving the world was hard, this is going to put that to shame. I need to talk to Rowan. I'm sure she'll have some good advice or at least she'll make me laugh about the situation.

Taking Silas's hand, I walk back over to the map and pull him along with me.

"This is the plan," I say, pointing to the map and laying it out for him.

CHAPTER TWENTY-ONE

CASMIR

*T*he screams echo off the tile walls. Interesting. The cold has a greater effect than the heat. The decibels of the screaming subject were twelve percent higher but it's also certain that the adjustment I made in its DNA has increased its resistance to both heat and cold, though obviously the heat resistance was greater. I didn't expect that.

"Javi, make note of those numbers," I say, before turning and leaving the room.

"Of course," Javi says. "What do we do with the creature?"

"Send it to the pits," I say absently. "Let it join Her army and prove itself or not."

"Of course," Javi says, taking up a shock stick to herd the creature.

As if speaking her pronoun summons her, a familiar tingling itch sensation forms at the edge of my awareness telling me she wants to speak. I do not have time for this, but dragging it out will only be more of a hassle.

"Dragon," she says when I step into the astral plane to answer her call.

"Yes," I say, pushing my glasses back up onto my nose.

She looks at me and shakes her head. "Why do you take on their affectations?"

"Did you need something, or were you simply lonely and wanted someone to chat with?" I ask.

Her face darkens and shadows dance around us. I'm not impressed. Her power is considerable, but then we've avoided going against each other for a reason. I don't want to fight her, of course, that would be wrong somehow.

She smiles, her eyes narrowing, and she nods.

"You still have her father?" she asks.

"Of course I do," I say. "She 'escaped' exactly according to the plan I laid out. They'll return soon enough, but this time we'll know where her others are."

"Good," she nods. "It's all going to my plan."

I bristle at her words, something she doesn't miss. She saunters forward, oozing her sexuality. She places two fingers in my jaw and traces a line down to my chin, while her other hand grabs my cock. I stare into her eyes, not responding.

"Casmir," she whispers my name seductively.

"I have work to do," I say.

She rubs her hand over my pants. Magic swirls around us as she flows her power towards seducing me. As my cock stiffens, an image flashes through my thoughts and I'm instantly hard. An image that is not her.

Aviella.

Interesting. What is this? Why would the one I'm bent to destroy have this effect?

It's something to be studied. I need to examine all aspects of this. Is it her body? Something in her magic? Lucy here with me is certainly a prime incarnation of the 'perfect' female body. Even in the beginning she was considered the fairest of the fair.

In that respect, Aviella, though beautiful, is in an unfair contest. She is a mortal, human, and her beauty is capped by those standards. Still, my cock throbs thinking of her, which works well, as Lucy thinks it's her ministrations causing the rise. I have no reason to disabuse her of the notion.

"You are still mine," she whispers. "We belong together."

I can't stop the frown that forms on my face at her words. I am hers? I'm a Horseman and a dragon; I belong to no man or woman. I am beyond such control or considerations. She's too busy 'seducing' me to notice and while I resist the concept, somehow it seems easiest to go along.

It usually does. I have no interest in her game or those of the Divine. There is too much to study, too much to understand. My experiments are all that matter, really. What they all do with the knowledge I gain them, well what higher calling could there be than the pursuit of knowledge? Even the Divine itself doesn't know exactly how all the rules of this game it created interact with each other. There are so many mysteries that demand to be solved. Ones that could only be resolved by the sharpest of minds. By me.

Tiring of her attention, I grab her shoulders and stop her from rubbing up against me any longer. There is an urge to continue, to finish the physical needs on her perfect body, but my experiments demand my attention.

"I must attend to my research," I say. Her face clouds with anger. "If we want to be ready for her."

The cloud dissipates at my words and she nods.

"Of course," she says as if it was her idea. "Attend to that. It's time we kill those around her. Let's test her mettle."

"It will be interesting to see how her magic responds to a loss," I say, and She smiles.

"Won't it?" she purrs. "You have the backup ready, of course?"

"I do," I say. "He is here, and having served his purpose of leading us to the Twelve, I don't see any further need for him."

"Good," She says, smiling brightly. "Then we are prepared. I'll send the forces to draw them in."

CHAPTER TWENTY-TWO

LUCA

I should tell her. The thought keeps returning, and each time I decide not to. We've all discussed it, and the consensus was that telling her would be a bad idea. Yet every time I see her, it feels wrong to have not said something. If I did tell her, how would I even bring it up?

Oh, by the way Avi, you know Efram? The one we all trusted? He betrayed you and us. He's the one who told the False Prophet you were the one, and just for good measure, he sold the rest of us out, too.

Yeah, that'd go great. She'd take that totally calm, and it wouldn't distract her from what we have to do one bit. I throw the glass in my hand against the wall, watching it shatter and the milk inside of it slowly drip to the floor. Damn it, I'm terrible at secrets.

Sighing, I rise from my chair and weave a quick spell to clean up the mess I made. The glass tinkles as I drop it into the trash can. I can't tell her. Everyone is right. The one thing she's asked of us is to not keep secrets, but in this case…

The lights blink out.

Alarms sound. Below them is a low thrumming. We're

under attack.

It's impossible.

But there is no mistaking it. I enhance my sight to try and see in the dark but there is no light to enhance, so I cast a spell that creates a sphere of light. I position it behind my left shoulder and run.

"Get to your stations, this is not a drill," I yell as I emerge into chaos.

The Innocents haven't been to war, yet. We've been gathering them for the past millennia. Bringing them here, outside time so they don't age, and we had the opportunity to train them. Some are very well trained, others are too new.

"Danial, where is Gavin?" I ask one of the oldest of the Innocents.

He snaps to attention, saluting the moment I speak. The scar along his cheek gives him a cadaverous look in the harsh light of my magical spell.

"Sir, they were in the training room," he barks.

He's one of the oldest of the Innocents. Only one Crusade younger than us, part of the final one, but always he was loyal.

"Good," I say. "Gather the younger ones, get them posted, and be prepared for anything."

"Yes, sir," he says, not waiting to be dismissed but jumping into action.

We've trained them well, the best we can, and we always knew it was coming to this. No matter how much I'd hoped to put it off, it's here and now. I pray to the Divine that we don't lose too many of them, but there's no time for that. I need to find out what is happening.

Running as fast as I can, I make my way through the rush of people taking up their stations. The closer I get, I can feel her.

She's powerful. More so than ever. It's a tidal wave of pure, raw power washing over me like the waves of the ocean. White-capped and peaking as they slam out from her. I resist it at first, but I can't make headway against it. She's too powerful and fighting her is out of the question.

Instead, I open myself up to her. Embrace her magic and welcome it into myself. I soar free the instant I do. My power flows out, into her, then back to me as if I'm completing a circuit. I'm aware of the others, Gavin, Rowan, Killian and Silas feeding power to her and she drinks it all in hungrily.

She takes of us and gives back. Doubling, tripling, quadrupling the power as it races through the circuit becoming more powerful with each pass through. She's moved. I know where she is, feel it in my soul, so I shift directions.

Deep in the tower is the crystal that binds this tower outside of time. They're there, all of them, or those that are here with us. I'm aware of the empty aches where the other eleven should be. Eleven, one area is clouded in mystery.

There's an innate understanding of who belongs in each spot around her. I know where I belong, where each of the others fit in, but one spot is clouded in mystery. She says she knows who it is, but I don't want to believe it.

Leaping down the stairs that twist around going down deeper and deeper. If we were on the body of Earth, on the surface, I'd think we were driving to the infernal itself, but here time and space operate on different rules.

Coalescing magic around me, I pull my goal towards me and the stairs shorten as I skip over parts of the space between me and it. A handful of leaps down the stairs later, I'm at the door. It's a double, wooden door that arches up with heavy iron hinges and bands that stretch across it. The architecture of my first life.

It swings open as I race towards it. Bright multi-colored

light streams through the opening, casting dancing shadows around me. The shadows almost seem to take on demonic shapes. That's a bad sign.

"I... need... more..." Aviella gasps.

She latches onto me, magically, and pulls. It's hard, fast, and unexpected. I drop to my knees exclaiming my surprise and shock as she pulls power to herself through the connection we share. The others are gathered already and it's obvious she's pulling from them as well. Her aura is alight with a golden glow that keeps getting brighter until she her aura is blinding..

She has both hands on the crystal itself. The crystal is five feet in length, multi-faceted to reflect light. In its natural state it stores magic, crafted as this one is, it powers a specific spell. The magic fueling it being of the light, it shines brightly with the power it contains. My brothers and I refuel it once per decade to keep it strong.

This is where the Shadow has attacked. Dark clouds form like miniature thunderstorms inside the crystal. The structure of the artifact has cracks appearing along its surface. Magic leaks out of it creating dazzling sparkles as it disperses into the air.

Aviella is pouring power into it, directly contesting the forces of Shadow, vying for control. If the crystal breaks, we'll be slammed back to Earth, relocating to where this tower originally stood hundreds of years ago.

It's doubtful the structure itself would survive the shift, and even if it did, I know for a fact that the area where it stood is not dead center of a metropolis. The level of destruction this would create would only be the beginning. We'd be defenseless against the Shadow army, having lost our most valuable asset.

Aviella pulls more power from me and those around me. She pours it in, and the dancing lights grow brighter, pushing away the darkness. Our own shadows dance along the walls, and then something tears into my back with searing pain.

I whirl around, still on my knees. My shadow has taken on a demonic aspect with long clawed hands that it swiped across my back.

"*Et abierunt*," I growl, swiping across the shadow, using what little magic I have left that Aviella isn't drawing from.

The shadow dances back, dodging, then sidles to one side. Gritting my teeth I force my way to my feet and grab more power. Around me the others are doing the same, their own shadows coming to life and attacking.

"Ahhhh!" Aviella growls. "Almost…. Have… it… more…"

I look at the Shadow demon. It's using my own casting against me. Aviella is pulling power, and she needs more, but I've held back this small reserve, the piece I'm using to save myself. I glance at her.

She's beautiful. Her hair is flying around her, dancing in the power she's wielding. Each strand outlined by the sparkle of magic. Her face is grim, but the most perfect thing I've ever seen. She is… everything. My heart swells and I make my decision. I give myself fully to her and hold nothing back.

The shadow rips into me, attacking full force, and I fall before it with nothing to defend myself. My flesh shreds as I try to fight it off with nothing but my fists. It's a shadow, so there's nothing to resist, but instinctively I try, holding back my own cries of pain.

The room grows brighter, burning my eyes, so I close them, turning my head towards Aviella. I open my eyes a slit to see her, and peace passes over me. This is good. It's right. She gave all for us and this world. How can I do less than she?

The light flashes and everything is gone.

CHAPTER TWENTY-THREE

AVIELLA

"No," I growl. "No... no..."

When I draw more power from the guys, it pools and swirls, filling up every part of me. Still it's not enough. The Shadow pulses and throbs. It's nebulous, impossible to gain control of. Every time I get a grip, it morphs and slithers away.

Instinctively, I know I'm drawing too much from them. We've never done this before; I don't know how much power I can pull from them and not hurt them. I don't have time, now, to do anything but try.

The connection between myself and them wobbles, shakes, growing tenuous as I pull the last of their reserves into myself. We're almost there!

"Need... more..."

Everything pauses for an instant as I reach a crossroads. Two different paths stretch out before me as the decision point hits. There are only two choices. I win or I lose. If I want to win, I have to do everything I can, no matter the costs. If I don't, we fail.

I've already given everything, what more do I have to lose?

Decision made, I reach out to each of my guys. If only the others were here, I wouldn't have to do this, but that choice wasn't mine to make. I'm standing in a storm of magic. My hair is flying wild around me. It dances across my skin, tingling, enticing and exciting. Promising me everything, there's nothing I can't do, if I only draw a little more power to myself.

The cracks in the crystal are mending and I know, with absolute certainty, I can fix them if I only have a bit more power. The guys grunt as I pull harder. Something holds back, it's resisting, the last bit of power I need to fight the Shadow off.

I don't have time for debate. I jerk the power out, pulling it into myself. The balance of the scales shifts, and it's enough. The light flashes blindingly white, and I'm thrown away from the crystal as power coalesces into it.

I'm slammed up against the wall. I slide to the floor, finding it hard to breathe. The Shadow stops its attack, retreating, but as it does, there's an empty, echoing laughter.

Laughter. Why is it laughing? I won. It doesn't make sense, but dread makes my chest clench tight and cold chills race over my limbs.

"Luca!" Gavin yells, and my stomach drops to the floor.

I leap to my feet and run towards the sound. I'm still seeing after-effects, dancing halos around everything I look at from the bright light, but three of the four mages are gathered around a motionless bundle of rags on the floor.

"Luca?" I ask, my voice quavering.

Gavin glances up from where he kneels next to Luca's still form. His face is grim, he has one hand on Luca's neck, checking for a pulse, I guess. My heart pounds, mouth is dry, and I don't want to hear him say it. Oh Luca.

Now I know why the Shadow laughed. I know and I'd give anything not to know.

CHAPTER TWENTY-FOUR

AVIELLA

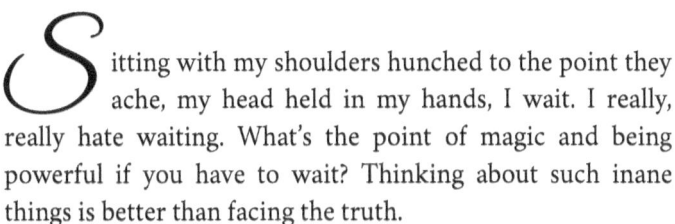

*S*itting with my shoulders hunched to the point they ache, my head held in my hands, I wait. I really, really hate waiting. What's the point of magic and being powerful if you have to wait? Thinking about such inane things is better than facing the truth.

I did this. I hurt Luca.

"This is not your fault," Silas says, his feet appearing into my vision.

"Yes, it is," I say. "I pulled too much. I knew what I was asking, I made the decision."

"You had the best of intentions, you could not know that this would happen. We've not done enough testing or practice with this facet of your powers."

"Intentions," I snort. "You know what they say about intentions, whoever the hell they are. The road to hell is paved with good intentions. Seems those mysterious jerks were right."

"Saint Bernard of Clairvaux," Silas says, taking a seat next to me.

"What?" I ask, looking up at him.

"Saint Bernard of Clairvaux," he repeats, placing a reassuring arm across my shoulders as he settles back into the chair.

"What are you talking about?" I ask.

"You asked who 'they' were, I'm answering the question."

I stare as my jaw drops, my mouth moving but unable to form words out the swirling confusion. Shaking my head to clear it I take a deep breath and let it out slowly.

"You never change," I say.

"Should I?" he asks. "On what basis?"

"Luca is hurt!" I yell. "He might die and it's my fault!" Silas frowns at my outburst but says nothing. "You don't care?"

"I do," he says.

"Then why don't you show it?" I scream leaping to my feet.

"And what would this accomplish?" he asks, not rising.

"I don't know!" I rage, throwing my hands up in the air. "Damn it, I don't know."

He nods, letting me have my rage. There's nothing for me to target. No thing I can be angry at except myself. It burns but that's it. My stomach roils, acid climbing up my throat and once more my shoulders slump.

"It's my fault," I say, dropping back into the seat.

Silas replaces his arm around my shoulders.

"He didn't actually say that," Silas says.

"Who didn't say what?" I ask without bothering to look up.

"The road to hell," he says, rubbing my shoulders. "He actually said hell is full of good intentions and wishes. A slight difference but still, a difference."

"Huh," I say, shrugging.

"It's interesting," he continues, ignoring my obvious lack of interest. "When you've lived long enough, you get to see many things change and evolve. Sayings such as this are subject to much interpretation and alteration through the passage of time.

Do you think Jesus said exactly what is now written down? Or Buddha? Or even Ben Franklin?"

Slowly, I turn my head to lock eyes with him and frown more deeply.

"You are impossible," I say.

"Possibly," he agrees, flashing a rare smile. "You're not the first to tell me so."

The door next to us swings open, and Gavin walks out with Ronan. I leap out of the chair and land in front of them.

"Tell me!" I bark.

Gavin and Ronan exchange a very fast look before either of them speaks.

"He'll be okay," Ronan says, but there's a weight to his words, something he's holding back.

I grab Ronan by the shoulders, flowing enough magic through my arms to hold him despite his greater size and physical strength.

"And?" I ask, willing him to tell me the truth.

Magic swirls along with my will, curling around as pressure builds in the room. Ronan knows what's happening, probably more than I do, but he doesn't back down. He puts his hands on my waist, and Gavin takes a step closer, placing his fingers on my cheek.

"Aviella," Gavin says.

"What?" I snap. Gavin tugs on my face, pulling me to face him. When our eyes meet, I know I'm overreacting, so I let the magic go, shaking my head. "Sorry, what aren't you saying?"

Gavin and Ronan exchange a frown before Ronan speaks.

"He may not be able to wield magic," he says.

The world stops and a throbbing ache in my soul pulses in time with my heart.

CHAPTER TWENTY-FIVE

AVIELLA

"*W*ho do we have? Where are the rest of them?" I ask, pacing the length of the long table without taking my eyes off the maps we've spread across it.

"The Mages and me," Silas says.

"Dragons?" I ask.

"We have yet to reach Tynan or the others. Time is still disrupted, so those not close to us are running in different time streams than we are. It's making communication... interesting."

"Where in the hell is Efram?" I ask.

"Unavailable," Silas answers, but something in his tone catches my attention.

"What is it?" I ask, stopping my pacing and locking my eyes onto Silas.

All I need to know is told when his eyes dart to Gavin.

"We can't reach him," Silas says.

"And?" I ask.

"We're not sure where he is," Gavin says, but I sense the care in choosing his words.

Narrowing my eyes, I shift my glare between the two of them, trying to ascertain what it is they're hiding.

"That's not all of it," I say.

"No," Gavin agrees, shaking his head.

"The last contact we had he was close to Casmir," Ronan throws in.

Staring at the maps and the circle marking Casmir's bunker I think that over. If Efram is there, then he's probably a captive. In trouble, I'm sure.

"This is a rescue mission already," I say. "We need to know. We can't go in blindly not knowing what to expect or the parameters of the job."

"Agreed," Silas says.

"So how do we find out?" I ask, placing two fingers on the spot marked for Casmir's bunker.

"Once we arrive, you'll be able to sense him if he's close," Gavin says.

"Little bit late then, don't you think?" I shake my head. "Better... we need better."

"Anything we do would take time," Ronan says.

"Time we don't have," I agree with his unspoken words. "Fine. The target is my dad, then Efram if he's there."

I bite off the rest of my own thought. They'd really freak out if they know what I'm planning, but I don't have time for their upsets. I know Casmir is the twelfth. The final piece if I can free him from the Shadow Mark. They're not going to like it, especially as I only know one way to do it.

"Two hours, we go," I say, spinning on my heel and walking to the door.

"Aviella," Killian calls and I stop but don't turn around. "Efram may be expendable."

Slowly I turn to glare at him. I turn my glare on each of them in turn without speaking until my look returns to Killian.

"No one is expendable," I spit. "We don't leave a man behind."

I turn and leave the room before they can argue further. I don't want to deal with it right now. I make my way to the medical area where they've kept Luca.

Two bulky Innocents stand guard outside his door. They stand up when I approach and step into my path, but I'm not in the mood and it must show on my face. They step aside wordlessly, and I walk into Luca's recovery room.

He lies on the hospital bed with an IV dripping into his arm, but that's not the most interesting thing in the room. Sigils are drawn on all the walls and the floor and hovering over him are glowing, twisting runes that cast a golden glow across him.

His eyelids are fluttering as if he's dreaming. As I walk up to the side of his bed, they crack open and a smile plays across his lips. He turns to look, and the smile becomes genuine.

"Hey," he says. "You look like shit."

"I could say the same," I say.

"Yeah, but you're too nice to be honest," he chuckles, grimacing as if in pain.

I put my hands on his face, staring into his eyes. I almost lost him. Tears swell in my eyes thinking about it. It was like a wakeup call that I can lose. Not only those I barely know—those lost souls weigh heavily enough—but to lose one of those closest to me? It never occurred to me.

"I… love you," I whisper.

His smile brightens. He touches my face, lets his fingers trail down my neck and come to rest cupping my breast.

"I love you," he says.

"Are you going to be okay?" I ask.

He frowns, not answering for a long moment, then nods. "Yes, I think so."

"Good," I say. "We're attacking soon, but I'll need you for the end of this."

"Great," he says, rising up on his elbows and swinging his feet to the ground.

"No," I say pushing him back onto the bed. "You're not coming."

"I *am*," he says.

"No, you're not," I say, grabbing enough magic that I can force him back onto the bed.

The fact that he doesn't even try to resist me with magic is all the tell I need. He's not ready.

"I'm fine," he argues.

"You are," I say leaning in to kiss him. "Very fine, but that has nothing to do with if you're ready for battle."

"Nice," he chuckles. "Love a good double entendre, but no way in hell I'm letting you go off without me."

"I figured you'd feel that way," I say. "But I'm not giving you a choice. I will need you. It's all coming to a head, soon. When I face Her... I'll need you. We can do this one on our own."

"You need me now."

"Of course I do, but let's be real. If you go now all of us would be splitting our attention to make sure you were okay. Right now, without access to your magic, you'd be a liability."

The look on his face breaks my heart but he nods his understanding. I've never seen any of my guys look broken like this.

"I'm sorry," he says.

"Why? Because you gave it all? If you hadn't, I don't think I would have succeeded," I say. "You have nothing to be sorry for, nothing. Matter of fact..."

I run my hands over his chest and hard abs diving under the sheets and grabbing his cock. It's hard in an instant, standing erect as he gasps, and his eyes go wide.

"Avi—"

"Shut up," I say, stroking his dick. "I'm showing you how much I need you."

His teeth click he shuts his mouth so fast. I continue stroking his cock at a gentle medium pace. He runs his hands over my stomach and down between my legs, rubbing at my clit. Closing my eyes I lean my head back and enjoy the sensation.

He groans and I do too as we quickly build each other to the edge of orgasm. It's fast and dirty with the heightened danger that we might get caught at any moment. Anyone could walk in.

He pulls down the front of my pants, working his way around until he slips two fingers inside. I gasp louder, biting my lip to keep from screaming.

My hand tightens on his cock convulsively. I stroke faster, leaning over to kiss him. His tongue claims my mouth. I rest my forehead against his, panting as the pleasure continues to build.

"I'm close," I exhale.

"Yes," he says. "Soon…"

Tighter still until a slight concern I'll hurt him, but I don't stop stroking. We're panting in time together, building, needing each other. Needing this release.

As we dance on the edge, I embrace him in my magic. On the astral level I see the flow of magic into him. It's slowed, his channels are damaged by the power he gave, it was too much for them. I caress his form with the softest touches of magic I can manage, easing my grip on his cock as I do too. Focusing on long strokes that time out with my touching his channels.

He grunts, then sighs and the glow of him in my astral sight becomes brighter. I understand, looking at him like this, what the runes are doing and seeing it I know that in time he will heal. He will be able to wield magic again, if I help.

"Close," I gasp, as the pleasure peaks. "Yes. Yes. Yes."

"I'm about to—"

I cut him off by twisting my body and taking his large member into my mouth. I close my lips on it and suck him in, but at the same time I'm flowing magic out. He explodes as my own orgasm rocks through. I'm bucking up and down on him taking his length and load as the pleasure causes my body to contort.

Finally it passes and we straighten ourselves up, staring into each other's eyes.

"You get better," I order.

"Already on it," he grins before his face turns serious. "I love you Aviella."

"I love you too," I say. "I'll be back."

I pause at the door and look back. His eyes are closed, and his chest is rising and falling with easy breathing. He's resting, and the magic as well as the medical is doing its work. I must succeed. He and all the others are counting on me. This is it. Win or lose starts now.

CHAPTER TWENTY-SIX

TYNAN

The dark and twisting shadows swirl as I stride through. Streams of time flow around, but now I'm outside of them, anchored by my brothers as we seek the fourth of our family. Casmir. Where are you hiding, brother?

Tynan, something is coming, Alaric says over our mental connection.

Something is very vague, I respond.

It's powerful, Shen says, but then I feel it too.

As it comes close, power crashes into me, and I take a step back before I can steady myself, almost getting swept off my feet. My magic gathers together, forming a protective shield of raging flame.

"Who dares?" I growl.

"Harrumph," a deep rumble echoes around me, bouncing off the endless dark here outside of time.

"Leviathan," I say through gritted teeth.

"Harrumph, dragon," the beast says, taking form before me.

It appears as an area of darkness against the endless dark of where we stand. A massive shape similar to a humpback whale. Its presence is oppressive, raw power and potential barely formed onto this plane.

"What do you want?" I ask.

"Wrong question, harrumph, dragon," he says.

His voice booms so loud the syllables pound against my body with almost crushing force of their own. Each one laced with hints of the creatures' power.

"I have no time for your games," I say.

"Games. All games. Time, harrumph, illusion. You know. Harrumph," he says. "Right questions only."

I ball my fists so that magic coalesces around them and a spear forms in my hand. It's not any spear, but one I collected two millennia earlier and hid away from humanity. A very special spear wielded by one particular Roman soldier on that fateful day that the second born died.

It might be enough to harm the monster.

Tynan, don't—Alaric sends but I shut down the connection before he can finish the thought. I don't want the creature to pick up on what I'm about to do.

"I said," I growl, "there is no time!"

I thrust the spear, driving it into the black hide of the ancient creature. The spear pierces its hide, flashing with golden-white power. Blackness so deep it stands out against the field of black seeps out, curling around the spear, climbing towards my hand.

Jerking the spear free, I ready myself for another strike. I've considered hunting this monster for ages. The ultimate trophy, but always my brothers and I have held back. No longer.

Its mouth opens, impossibly far, big enough to swallow galaxies as each of us take on shapes closer to our true forms.

"Enough!" it roars, rattling my insides with the depth of the sound.

I'm frozen in place. Straining I will my arm to move, to

stab again, aiming for the eye this time. The spear trembles but refuses to obey.

"Speak," I growl, pulling on my brothers' power to fuel my own.

Get it talking, if I can pull enough power, I'll be able to break free before it destroys me.

"Harrumph. Deal. I come for a deal, not a fight," it says.

"What kind of deal?" I ask.

It drops its hold on me and I'm free, but now I'm intrigued. I open the lines to my brothers, letting them listen in on the conversation again.

"A place, harrumph," it says. "A place in what is to come."

"Why would we offer you this?" I ask.

"Choices," it says, undulating in the darkness as if its swimming through an ocean of black. "I choose a side soon, harrumph."

The Leviathan is going to choose a side? That's news.

"What is different this time that you would involve yourself?" I ask, suspicious.

"The thrice-born, harrumph," it says.

Aviella. Of course. This thing from before time feels it too. She's special. She's different than anything we've seen or felt before, and now I know it's not only me.

"What do you offer?" I ask.

"Harrumph," it chortles, a dark dangerous laugh. "A gate."

"A gate?" I ask.

"To that you seek," it says.

"Casmir?"

"Harrumph," it says.

"That's not enough," I argue.

"It is a lot," it counters.

"Yes, but not enough," I say. "You want a place? A place in the world to come, the one she will create? You will have to give more. We've all given more, and if you want part of it, then you will too."

"Harrumph," it says. "What?"

"A favor, to be called and answered without question," I say instantly.

It chortles that dark sound, undulating and shaking with its mirth.

"Bold," it says. "Bold it is. Agreed."

CHAPTER TWENTY-SEVEN

AVIELLA

"A little bit more," Gavin says.

Magic swirls forming a large circle outlined in golden sparks. The circle shimmers, darkening, until it's floating plate hanging in the middle of the room. The four mages chant as one, each of them pouring magic into the creation of the portal.

I'm holding back, as we agreed. A last resort if they can't do it themselves. We don't want to give Casmir warning that we're coming. He might still know, it's impossible to be sure, but we do know for sure is that he'd recognize my magical signature.

Or the Shadow would.

Silas grimaces, watching, but remains silent. I wish Efram, Nate, and Rafe were here. On that note I wish the dragons were here too, but it's best they're not. I can't ask them to face off against their brother.

"There," Silas says, stepping forward.

He reaches out and touches the center of the circle. It wobbles, ripples echoing out from the point of his touch, like a stone tossed into a still pond. There is darkness on the far side, but I can make out shapes in the darkness.

"Best we're going to get," Gavin says.

"Then we go," I say, taking a deep breath I stride towards the portal.

Luca grabs my arm and pulls back.

"No, I'll go first," he says, moving in front of me.

There's no arguing with him, and I'm not an idiot, no matter how much I hate the idea. Bravado is not bravery, so I let him go. Killian and Ronan go in next, then Gavin motions for me to go.

Stepping through the portal is like passing through a wall of cold. Chills race over my skin and then it's done and I'm standing in a dark hall, smashed between Ronan and Gavin behind me. It's reassuring being between them like this.

No one moves. The sound of our breathing is all I can hear. I'm holding my magic tightly down, not reaching out at all. It makes me feel cut off, like I've lost a limb, almost. I hadn't realized how much I've come to depend on it.

The air smells of antiseptic, too clean, to the point of being sterile. Knots form in my stomach, and bile rises in my throat. It's offensive in a way that cleanliness shouldn't be. The air is cool, almost cold, but not quite. Goosebumps rise on my arms, and the seconds tick by while we wait for any sign of an alarm at our entry.

The mages were very careful to manipulate their way through the wards guarding Casmir's place. The idea is to make this a stealth mission, not an assault. We save my dad and Efram, and I do my own side mission. The mission that, much as I hate to admit it, is the only one that matters. They don't know that one though. They'd stop me if they did, and I can't have that. I know the path forward. I know what has to happen, no matter what it takes.

The stakes have never been higher. Considering I've already died, that's saying something. Yet they wouldn't accept it, and I don't have time to win them over or make them understand.

"We're good," Luca whispers.

I will a touch of magic to my eyes, the slightest of uses of magic, and the hallway we're in brightens as if someone turned on a light. It looks like an unused corridor. Boxes are stacked along either side, and there is a layer of dust on the floor despite the clean smell. Weird.

Luca moves and we follow, closely packed together.

We've studied the layout of this place. Everything that was known about it, at least. Before the fall, this was a major location. A tourist attraction that brought millions of people here every year. None of them would have ever suspected what was happening below their feet, where we are.

The thousands of cast members who worked here wouldn't know either. It's sick, another thing that Casmir and the Shadow need to be held accountable for. Perverting a happy place like this. I've enough understanding of magic now to suspect they were using the emotions of those above them to fuel their experiments.

We navigate through dim halls, finding our way by Luca's memory and our educated guesses. It's quiet. The hair on the back of my neck stands on end, and I've got that itchy feeling like I'm being watched.

"Wait," I whisper. Suddenly I'm falling. "Shit!"

There's no time to hold back now, so I pull deep on my magic, sensing the guys around me. Panic fights for control. Instinctively my body wants to curl into a ball, flail, cry and scream all at the same time. Luckily all the time I spent training with Silas has taught me not to give in to such primal urges.

The magic solidifies around all of us, slowing our fall. We land, hard, but nothing is broken. Loud exhales and grunts escape from all of us, but no one's hurt badly as far as I can tell. I roll over, climb to my knees, and look around.

Blindingly bright lights snap on, bright white driving away the darkness. My magically enhanced eyes cause me to be stunned. All I can see is spots dancing in front of my face.

"Avi?" Gavin calls my name.

"Here," I say.

Someone bumps up against me and then more bodies press around me. I know it's the guys, so I don't resist their closing ranks.

"Interesting," a now-familiar voice says, coming from above us.

"Casmir, let us go," Silas says. "We're not here to fight."

"Unless we have to," Luca mutters.

I blink rapidly and my eyesight returns, though everything is still outlined with a golden halo. We're in a metal box, more or less. It looks like it's fifteen feet square with no obvious way in or out except through the trap door above us. Casmir stands at the edge of the opening, looking down.

He's wearing glasses and his hair is shoulder length, which I have to admit looks sexy. His head is tilted to one side as he studies us.

"How did you find me?" he asks, curiosity clear in his voice.

"You weren't that well-hidden," Gavin says.

"As I can see," he says. "This is… unexpected."

"And what does that mean, Casmir?" I ask, pushing my way past the guys.

When he looks at me something throbs deep in my core, and my magic resonates to the pulse. Reaching out with magic, I caress his tightly controlled power. His eyes widen the slightest bit and his lips part.

I want to taste them.

"It would indicate I need better security," he says.

135

Something moves in his eyes. His face doesn't betray it, stoic and studious as ever, it's deeply hidden, but I don't miss it. Our magic touches and it's as if a crystal-clear bell rings.

"Do you?" I ask. "Or do you need less?"

"Avi, what are you doing?" Luca hisses.

"We need to talk," I say, ignoring Luca and the burning stares of all the men with me. "Can we?"

"Avi, this isn't the plan," Silas says.

"It is," I say, without taking my eyes off of Casmir. "It's the only way."

Casmir is considering my request. Watching the interaction between us. The cold dispassionate appearance not cracking in the slightest.

"The only way for what?" Casmir asks.

"To save you," I say.

"Save me?" Casmir asks.

"Yes," I say.

"No," he says. "This would not be wise."

He turns away and disappears out of sight. Damn it. My stomach sinks and a cold sweat forms on my chest.

"Avi, what are you doing?" Killian asks.

"Saving the world," I snap. "Or trying."

"That's Casmir," Luca hisses. "The enemy, you remember this, right?"

Turning on my heel, I glare at all of them.

"Do you trust me?" I ask.

No one speaks. We glare at each other for a long time, or so it seems, before Silas steps out of the group towards me.

"Aviella, we only wish to understand," he says. "This isn't part of the plan we had."

"I know," I shake my head. "You have to trust me."

A part of the wall slides up, and inky blackness rolls out. It pulses with magic and wrongness. We retreat before its advance, but inside of it are shadowy shapes with weirdly glowing eyes. My back hits the wall and it forms a barrier around us.

I don't want to touch it. Even being this close to it makes my skin crawl. We're huddled against each other as it comes closer, making it obvious the guys feel the same way I do. Directly in front of us a part forms and then there's a walkway.

"Take the path," Casmir says from above. "Oh, as a note, touching the darkness would be bad."

"Bad?" Ronan mutters. "Seriously, he calls that bad?"

Taking a breath to steady my nerves I march down the offered path. This is the way forward, as if I have a choice. It leads us into a tight tunnel then it opens into another room. The darkness shifts and swirls around separating us. It never comes higher than my waist, so we can all see each other.

I reach out to touch Ronan but the instant my hand passes over the darkness it shifts up and I jerk back before letting it touch me. My bicep is cold and numb where it came close and revulsion fills my stomach with bile.

The blackness has cut us off from each other and once it's done, the wall in front of us opens up into a door and I'm herded into a small cell.

The cell is a glass square allowing me to see each of the guys are trapped in a cell of their own. Inside of myself is a storm of magic. A tempest I'm barely maintaining control over. I move to the glass, let the storm focus into my hands, and then touch it.

Nothing.

Nothing happens, which makes no sense. How can nothing happen? The glass should shatter. I can't be held here by this.

Concentrating, I add more power and repeat my touch. Nothing. No reaction at all. It's as if I did nothing.

"Guys?" I ask.

No one responds. Gavin is staring at me from the cell a few feet away. His mouth moves but I can't hear his words. Turning behind myself Silas is there and he also talks to me but no sound. Damn it, no magic, no sound, no nothing.

Past Silas a door opens and Casmir strides in. Two men dressed in white lab coats with clipboards stride along behind him. They stop and stare at each of the cells holding my guys. Casmir talks at each one and the men make notes on their clipboards then he goes to the next.

When he reaches my cell he stops, staring in silence. I move closer to him, almost pressing against the glass separating us. I place an open hand against it, offering him contact. His eyes narrow, his head tilts to one side, and his chest rises and falls faster.

On his forehead, a dark circle swirls faster and faster. His right arm twitches, the arm moving towards my offered one, but then the circle blackens. He frowns and pulls his arm back to his side.

Shaking his head, he turns and walks on down the line. Damn it. I've got to find a way to reach him. An aching emptiness pounds in my guts, and I know he's the one to fill it. Sighing I sit down, preparing to wait.

If nothing else, I've learned patience.

CHAPTER TWENTY-EIGHT

TYNAN

I bend space and time with a thought. Now that I know where I need to go, thanks to the Leviathan, finding it is easy enough. Stepping outside the broken streams of time, I look over what remains of existence.

Out here, it looks like pockets. Inside each pocket is life and no matter how rough, their view will be only that of the world. Mortal minds couldn't conceive of what has happened. They're built to be a self-protecting mechanism. When faced with the impossible, their innate makeup will push an understandable reality onto it.

Since the first man and woman were created it has been thus. It's why their stories often make no sense. How would a man and his sons build a boat big enough to survive a flood that destroyed the entire world while taking along two of each animal? The answer is they didn't. Not exactly, or at least not in the way that the stories tell.

The 'boat' was actually an intervention from higher powers that created a bubble of space-time with magic protecting them. They couldn't handle seeing the destruction of all space-time outside their reality bubble, hence a story that over years morphed into the tale of a boat and a flood.

I was there. I know better.

My mind is not self-protecting, but fully able to observe what is. So now I will find Aviella, knowing where to look. And as if on cue, there it is. A pocket realm. Cleverly hidden among hundreds of similar ones. Well-played, brother.

I move closer with a thought, a flexing of will. When I'm close, the pocket realm flashes brightly, and I'm blasted away from it. The force is enough that I feel it, which is saying a lot. Growling, I move close again, but this time I'm watching and stop before I get to close to the magical barriers guarding.

"We could smash through easily enough," Alaric says.

"And what would be left?" Shen asks.

"He's right," I agree. "If we go through with force, it is very likely that Casmir has layered it with traps that would destroy the realm."

"And her," Alaric says.

"And her," I agree.

"So the hard way?" Shen asks.

"Yes," I say, my brothers flanking me as we set about dismantling the protective layers around the realm.

CHAPTER TWENTY-NINE

AVIELLA

I'm not sure how long we've been waiting here. It seems like a few days, but odds are it's only a few hours. I'm guessing a few hours.

So much for the patience gig. It was never my strong suit, really. One of the men in a lab coat with his clipboard walks up to my cage. He makes several notes on the board then motions with his head.

Two burly men step forward and then the front wall of the cage is gone. They grab on and roughly pull me to my feet.

"Hey," I cry out. "Where are you taking me?"

They don't bother answering. Magic answers my call, force swelling but before I can do anything with it, a collar clamps around my neck. Horrific memories flash the instant the inscripted collar clicks.

I remember being there, hanging. Looking down. The pain. Unable to reach my magic. This is bad. So, so bad. It's all I can do to keep from throwing up. My stomach is in turmoil, cold sweat trickles down my back, and my breath is ragged.

They drag me down the length of the room. Gavin, Luca, Killian, and Ronan pound on the glass box holding them back. I can't hear their shouts, but it's obvious. I look at each of them and smile. It's all I've got to offer.

The two brutes drag me through a door, leaving my lovers behind. The room we enter is white decorated with stainless steel. It gives off that sterile feel and appearance. There isn't a single affectation, no picture, no splash of color, not a flower in sight. It's cold. Heartless, a manifestation of what Casmir tries to portray. Except I suspect the truth.

It's a lie.

He's a dragon.

A dragon filled with suppressed fire and passion. It's up to me to try and unlock that aspect of him that he's denied himself.

"Change," the lab coat guy says, motioning at a table.

I walk closer and find clean clothes laid out. Simple slacks, a button up shirt, and, of all things, a white lab coat of my own. I roll my eyes and shake my head.

"Look, I'm not the studious type," I say.

Lab guy stares at me blankly as if the words I spoke weren't actually words. Pursing my lips, I force a smile then point to the clothing.

"Not my style," I say, speaking slowly.

He makes a note on his clipboard then looks up. "NO choice was given."

"Yeah, that happens a lot I bet," I say. "But you'll get used to this. I don't ask for choices, I make them. I decide, not you. Not him."

"Interesting," he says, turns and walks out of the room.

The two brutes move to stand on either side of the door. We wait, silently staring at each other, though I hate to admit it, they win the staring contest. There doesn't seem to be any conscious thought in their eyes. They're like automatons.

A short time later the door opens, and lab guy walks back in. He walks up to me and the brutes fall into and flank him with no words being spoken.

"Please," lab guy says.

"What?" I ask, surprise spinning my carefully prepared arguments away.

"Please," he says and motions to the clothes again.

I start to say something, realize I've got nothing, and shut my mouth. Please. Interesting, okay I'll play along. I grab the clothes then look for a place to change. There's nothing apparent so I look back at the lab guy. He watches me, waiting, but doesn't say anything.

"Where?" I ask.

"Where what?" he asks.

"Do I change?" I ask, struggling to keep the exasperation out of my voice.

He makes more notes on his clipboard, then turns and walks out again. A few more minutes pass and he comes back. He walks past me to one of the plain white walls. He places a hand on the wall, and it flashes blue. A door slides open and he steps to one side.

"Here," he says.

Shaking my head, I walk through the door. In for a dime, in for a dollar, or something like that.

It's a closet. Brooms, mops, cleaning supplies. I'm changing in a closet, but at least it's a modicum of privacy. I dress quickly and then realize there's no door handle. I knock on the wall and it slides open.

Lab Guy stares, looking me up and down, then nods and makes notes on his clip board. He turns and walks away. Lacking any clue what else to do I follow. The two brutes fall in behind, thankfully not assaulting me further.

We go to another wall that reveals yet another hidden door and we walk down a dimly lit hall. The two brutes don't come into this hall with us. I'm not sure what to make of that. Are they suddenly not worried I'll hurt this guy? Or does Casmir not care? Or, more likely, is he testing me to see what I will and won't do?

The floor angles up, and we climb it in silence. It turns back and forth, and I'm sure we're at least one story higher than when we started when we come to another wall. Lab Guy puts his hand on the wall, and a door slides open. He steps aside and motions me to walk through.

I emerge onto a balcony. Standing a few feet ahead, back turned to me with his arms clasped behind himself is Casmir.

The balcony has a low wall that comes up to about his waist. The rest of the way up to the ceiling is clear glass, similar to the cage I was held in. I stand there, unsure what's next. The glass means he doesn't plan to throw me off, so that's good. It doesn't answer why I'm here though.

In some ways, this balcony is similar to the one in Tynan's bunker. I wonder if it's a dragon thing, some primal need to look down on the world. He doesn't turn around or make any acknowledgment of the fact that I'm standing here.

I take a step towards him, half expecting some kind of trap to trigger but when nothing happens, I decide to go for it and walk up next to him. He glances and nods before returning his attention to staring out the glass.

When I follow his gaze, I'm looking down onto the spitting image of Tynan's fighting pits. These are different only in that everything is white except for the smears of fresh blood that are splashed randomly around the space.

"What is this?" I ask, throat dry.

"The same as everything," Casmir says. "An experiment."

"For?" I ask.

"How did you do it?" he asks, crossing his arms over his chest but still not looking at me.

"Do what?" I ask.

"Tynan, Shen, Alaric," he says. "How did you do it? It's clear they're no longer following Her. They didn't break free on their own. The only logical conclusion is that you did it, somehow. I want to know how."

"Well," I say, shaking my head. "We talked."

It earns me a harsh glance and a frown.

"Do not play me for a fool," he says, a hint of anger to his tone. "You will not like the results."

"Yeah," I sigh, shaking my head. "Here's the thing. I'm not. But I did also have my magic. Magic that you have effectively cut me off from."

I motion to the collar that weighs heavy around my neck. His eyes rest on the iron blocking me from my magic. His brow furrows, then he sighs and shakes his head.

"No," he says.

"Okay," I say. "So what then? I can't free you without it, but that's what you want, isn't it?"

"I did not ask for such a thing," he says absently. "You are but another comer, another experiment. I will admit though, I am curious. You're different than those that came before. Something about you is unique."

"Those that came before?" I ask.

Casmir snorts, shaking his head. "My brother has done you no favors, keeping you in the dark."

"What do you mean?" I press.

"It is what it is," he says. "Let us move to the next phase of the experiment."

"Next phase?" I ask, but he nods and motion below us pulls my attention.

Luca stumbles into the open space below us. He looks quickly around until his eyes land on us standing above him. He runs across the room at a full sprint. There's no collar on his neck and magic tingles in the air around me, outside my

145

ability to reach but it makes the hair on my arms stand on end.

Another motion jerks my attention to the left. An eight-armed monstrosity squeezes out of an opening, falling down as it does so. The thing has two heads and enough bulk to make up six of Luca. It climbs unsteadily to its feet, looking around. The two heads turn in different directions, growling. The left head has rows of razor-sharp teeth and the right head has protruding tusks. It looks like twelve different monsters somehow blended together.

One of the heads spots Luca and it runs. Fast, too damn fast for something that big. Slamming my fists against the glass I scream to get Luca's attention. He notices it at the same time, turning to face the monster bearing down on him.

"Stop this," I order, but Casmir isn't even watching the event below us, he's watching me.

Luca manages to dodge the barreling thing, but it clips him as they pass. Blood sprays freely from his wound.

Magic ebbs and flows right outside my ability to touch it. I reach, willing it to me, and get so close but there's a thin layer denying my access. It's as if I'm blocked by a transparent, thin sheet.

"Casmir," I say, a note of pleading in my voice. "don't do this."

He gives a nod of his head. Yes, I'm getting through! Hope blossoms as my heart races, but then he looks to the side, down into the arena. Following his gaze, I see Gavin shoved out to join Luca. The two mages lock eyes, then weave magic together.

The creature rages, throwing its arms wide. Its roar is so loud it shakes the glass. They're weaving a shield, and I can tell from the way the magic is flowing that they're trying to make a net of magical energy.

"Interesting," Casmir says. "It won't work, but an intelligent play."

"It won't work?" I ask.

"Of course not. The creature's resistance is such it won't be held by that for long enough," he says. "They're performing as expected. No surprises to my prediction model for them."

"Your prediction model?" I yell. "You're going to kill them!"

"Perhaps," he says, turning towards me. "You could save them, though."

"How?" I ask, struggling to slow my breathing and heart.

"Surrender," he says.

"I have!"

"No, you've allowed yourself to be captured. That is not the same thing," he says.

"I can't," I shake my head.

"You can. You choose not to," he says. "I know She came to you. Her offer stands. Accept it, and this ends."

I've got nothing. He's serious, or he seems to be. This is not where I expected this to go. He wants me to take her offer? To give up?

This can't be him. The real him, this is all part of the façade. He's acting as her puppet, not as his own man. We stare at each other as the two mages below fight for their survival. This is ridiculous. Insane. It can't be.

"No," I say.

"I see," he says and glances at the arena.

Killian and Ronan are both shoved out. Killian stumbles and falls to his knees. Ronan helps him up, taking in the room.

The monster has Luca and Gavin backed up against a wall. Killian and Ronan both throw balls of magical fire at the thing. They hit against its back and explode, but cause no visible damage. They do, however, pull its attention to them.

It whirls around and roars. Two arms swipe behind it at Luca and Gavin. Gavin grabs Luca and pulls him to one side, barely keeping him from being hit again. Blood pours down the arm that was hit earlier, and it hangs limp at his side.

Killian and Ronan separate but even with the collar I see the magic flowing between the four men. They weave it to each other, threads of power intertwining as they move with the precision of a ballet company.

"Stop this, Casmir," I order. "You don't have to do this."

"No," he agrees. "I don't."

"Then why? Why are you doing this?"

"Because I have to know," he says, turning to face me again.

"Know what?"

"What you did to my brothers," he says. "And what it takes to break you."

"I set them free," I say. "Don't you want that too?"

His brow furrows and he frowns. The Shadow mark is barely visible with my limited magic sight, but it swirls faster, flashing.

"I am free," he says and turns back to the arena.

Silas is thrown into the arena. The monster has Killian and Gavin each grasped in one bulging arm. It's lifted them over its head, shaking them like rag dolls.

"No, you're not," I say, moving closer.

I touch his face. He's warm, feverish almost. He turns his face towards me, and our eyes lock. His swirl with sharp intelligence and a deeply buried burning passion.

That passion is what I have to tap into. That is how I'll set him free.

"A long time ago," I say, my voice barely a whisper. Forcing myself to focus, to ignore the roaring monster set on tearing my men apart. "You made a choice. A choice that trapped you. That put you into this state."

"The past doesn't matter," he says.

"Wrong," I say, rising onto my tip toes. "The past does matter. The past is a prisoner's cage. It's trapping you. The mistakes made, the things you're afraid might happen again, decisions you made that didn't turn out the way you expected."

"No," he says, his lips parting, his warm, sweet breath passing across mine.

I inhale his breath, taking his life into me. Butterflies dance in my stomach. Every nerve is alive, every sense on overdrive.

Our mouths are centimeters apart. I'm on my tiptoes, still that tiny bit of space separates us, I can't quite reach him. He has to choose.

"It is," I say. "Those are your demons. Not Her or her forces. She has no power we don't give her."

He closes the distance and our lips meet. My heart stops, the world screeches to a halt. Every nerve is tingling as excitement rushes through. The collar around my neck snaps and drops to the floor with a clatter.

Magic rushes in, flooding through my body then racing out to blend with Casmir's. My hair rises on my arms and on my head. The air around us crackles. His tongue tastes my lips igniting a fire of raging desire.

I mold myself against him. His manhood digs into my stomach, so I grip it through his pants, stroking. The twining of our magic builds power, and slowly the two opposing forces mingle. As it does, I'm inhaling the scent and power of him.

Restrained power. Controlled. So different than any of the others. His magic and passion is cold, freezing, it's so strongly contained. Suppressed yet even beyond that it's logical. It's one conclusion leading to the next. One event following another in precise order.

The walls between us grow thinner. His restraints cracks. The smallest of faults.

And the world around us explodes. The glass next to us shatters. Wind whips around, driving my hair into a frenzy. We're pulled apart. A roaring sound, louder than that of the creature below, fills my ears.

Casmir pushes me to one side, then gripping my arm tight he shoves me behind himself.

The glass divider has shattered into millions of sparkling pieces. In the air, over the arena, a swirling portal has formed. Golden sparks racing around the perimeter of absolute blackness. It's about ten feet in width. The roaring comes from the portal.

Casmir's power rises as he steps to the edge of the balcony. I move to stand beside him but he pushes me back again.

Tynan steps through the portal followed by Shen and Alaric.

My heart races at the sight of them. Tynan dominates the room, as he always does, filling it with too much presence. You can never miss him, he's too there, too... alpha for lack of a better term. He's the one in control and you damn well know it.

"Brother," Casmir says.

"Casmir," Tynan says, his eyes locked onto me. "You have something that is mine."

"Do I?" Casmir asks.

"Give her back," Tynan growls.

Shen and Alaric move up next to him. There's something deeply satisfying about Tynan's claim. It's primal and calls to something the same in me. I'm his, but at the same time, I can't let it stand. In the bedroom he can take me and use me and make me his. Out here, I'm my own damn woman.

"Tynan," I say, pushing forward despite Casmir's effort to stop me. "I'm here of my own choice."

Tynan's eyes widen the slightest bit, the only betrayal of his surprise.

"Aviella, I've come to rescue you," he says.

"It seems she doesn't want your rescue, interesting," Casmir says.

"Brother you'd be wise to shut your mouth," Alaric says.

"I don't need rescued," I say. "Take the mages and Silas."

"I will not leave you here," Tynan says, striding towards me.

He walks on the air as if its solid ground. An impressive feat of magic and skill. He's confident, full of himself, as usual.

Except I came here on a mission. Two of them and neither have been accomplished yet.

"Casmir," I say turning to face him. "Let's make a deal."

"A deal?" he asks, arching an eyebrow.

"Yes," I say. "Set my dad free. Give him and Efram to Tynan. Let them all go. I'll stay with you and we'll finish our discussion."

"Aviella, no," Tynan orders.

"Why would I accept this deal?" Casmir asks, ignoring Tynan.

"It gives you what you want," I say with a confidence I don't really feel.

"What is it you think I want?" he asks.

"To understand," I say, cutting to the chase.

"I agree," Casmir says.

Magic flashes and a golden glow encircles Casmir and me. I've never seen the likes of it before but instinctively I know we've made a binding contract.

CHAPTER THIRTY

TYNAN

*W*e tore our way into Casmir's domain, but this isn't the way it's supposed to go.

"Aviella, no!"

Casmir agrees and the binding takes hold with a flash of magic. Damn it. She can't have known what he did. He's tricked her into a binding contract.

We can't break that, Shen thinks across our connection.

I'm not a fool, I return. *We have to try.*

"Casmir," I growl, moving closer until I'm only inches from him.

The burning rage is molten in my core. In all our existence the one thing I've never considered is the destruction of one of my brothers. We've made each other angry, infuriated, harmed one another yes. But never, not once, have I contemplated giving one of them final death.

Until now.

"Tynan, it is done," he says, a smug look on his face.

He's won and he knows it. Of the four of us he's the only one that matches me in raw power. He rarely shows it. That's never been his way, but it doesn't change the fact.

"Do not do this," I say.

"Tynan, it's fine," Aviella interjects but I ignore her.

"Let her go. There is more at stake than you can imagine."

"Such as?" he asks, curiosity dancing on his face. "This is the ultimate experiment. How can I not watch how it plays out?"

"This is not one of your damnable experiments!" I roar, hands balling into fists.

Magic pools around both of my hands and Alaric and Shen pull power onto themselves as well. Distantly I hear men screaming and a monster roar. It's of little consequence to me right now. I have eyes only for Casmir.

"Casmir, save them, or our deal is off," Aviella yells.

Casmir's eyes flicker to one side and then he motions with a hand.

"Isn't it?" he says, his voice barely a whisper.

"Your meddling has stopped this twice now, would you interfere a third time?" I ask.

"Meddling?" he asks. "They had free will. I did nothing to their ability to choose. The choice is theirs, always has been."

"You know what you've done!" I yell. "What we've done!"

"Yes," he agrees. "I do know. How is the Leviathan?"

Rage blinds me and I swing. My fist smashes into his face, his glasses fly, and blood spurts from his mouth and nose as his head jerks to one side. He looks back at me and smiles, blood dripping from the corner of his mouth.

"Damn you," I say.

"You see," he says, looking to Aviella. "This. This is my brother. Uncontrolled rage and violence. A dog that needs a watcher, someone to tell him where to attack. It's the only purpose he has in life, you see. He fulfills it well. Death, that is his gift.

"When the Divine marked you, it chose well. You truly are the Horseman of War."

Memories from eons ago flash through my mind and they stoke the anger higher. Remembering when I was named out, when each of us was marked to fulfill our roles in the coming Apocalypses. A role we've only broken free of this time.

"We have one chance," I say. "She's it. Don't take it from us, brother."

"Or?" he asks, tilting his head to one side. "You'll destroy me?"

"To save her, yes," I say without reservation, anger or hate.

"Interesting," he says.

"Aviella!" a new voice cries out.

Aviella's magic swells, filling the room, overwhelming everything.

"DAD!" she yells, and then she leaps over the edge of the balcony.

She floats to the ground and lands already running. She races across the open floor to the mages and Silas, who support a broken mortal between them. The mortal's life force is weak, barely clinging to its shell. He won't have long to live, and I see what that will do to Aviella.

I close my eyes, take a deep breath, and look at the possible futures playing out from this moment. None are certain, all our fraught with peril, but one offers what would seem to be the greatest hope.

"Don't take her last moments with him from her," I say.

"Why do you care?" Casmir asks.

"Have you met her?" I counter.

Casmir frowns and shifts his gaze to Aviella holding her father. The golden glow of her magic flashes bright, engulfing her father and those around her. My own magic sings in sympathetic response.

"Agreed," he says.

CHAPTER THIRTY-ONE

AVIELLA

*"*D*ad," I say.*

Tears fall freely. I don't bother trying to stop them. He's pale, gaunt, way too thin, but his eyes are bright as he smiles.

"Hey, nugget," he says, his breath wheezing.

"Oh, daddy," I cry, taking him into my arms.

I lower myself to the floor, holding him tight. I gently feed magic into him, healing the wounds. His body drinks it in, taking all I'm giving it and demanding more.

"Well," he says, grabbing both sides of my head and resting his forehead against mine just like he used to do when I was a kid. "We're here, kiddo. You've done so well. I'm so proud of you."

"Daddy, thanks," I say, trying to not sob.

"Your mom is so proud," he whispers.

"I know," I say. "Rest. It's okay, let me help."

He chuckles, and it sounds wet. The magic I'm pushing into his body returns information. He's badly wounded but more, much like had happened to me, there are dead zones in his aura. They're not really dead though, more like small black holes sucking in magic, drinking it before it can heal him as it should.

"You have her eyes," he says.

"Do I?" I ask.

The guys stand protectively around us in a tight circle. I push more magic, pulling on my connection to them for more power. It's still not enough. The holes take all hungrily and demand more. It's as if he's starving, drained of his magic, I can feel them pulling on his life force. This is Casmir's work.

"Yeah," he says, he's barely speaking above a whisper. "Avi, you've come so far. Remember, always, your mother loves you more than words."

"She's gone, Daddy," I remind him.

He smiles and shakes his head.

"What did I always tell you?" he asks.

"She's never gone, always with me," I say.

"Right," he says.

His heart falters, stuttering with an unnatural rhythm. Throwing caution to the wind, I flood him with magic. Desperation makes me act. It's a river of power rushing into him like white-water rapids. He gasps, eyes widening, his heart races, and his breath becomes ragged.

The dark holes in his aura pulse, drinking in even this. I reach out to pull magic to me from the guys. All of them, even the dragons. I pull and pour it into him. My only hope is to blast apart these negative holes. Give them so much power they can't consume anymore.

I don't know if it will work, but it's the only idea I have. Sweat pours, hiding my tears, but still it's not enough. The holes drink it all.

"Dad," I say, squeezing him tight. "Give me a minute."

"Don't," he says, his arms convulsing around me. "Don't leave."

"Only a moment, daddy, I promise," I say.

A glance and Killian kneels, taking my father from me. I rise to my feet, turn around and glare at Casmir looking down from his balcony. Tynan, Alaric, and Shen hover in the air two feet in front of him, watching.

"Casmir!" I yell, pulling his attention off his brothers. "Fix this. Fix this or our deal is off!"

"A bargain has been forged," he says. "No fixing was agreed to in it."

"Not good enough," I growl.

Magic pools into my core. I depleted most of my reserves trying to fix my dad, but anger seems to speed its replenishment. Placing my hands on my hips, I glare up at the dragon.

"And what is it you would have?" he asks.

Tynan growls, his hands balling into fists. His own magic flares brightly in my astral sight as his ire rises. The mages and Silas move to stand behind me. This is it. Everything is on the line right now. It's about more than saving my dad, but for me, nothing else matters.

I know, it should. I'm supposed to be the Savior of the world. Selfish motivations shouldn't drive me, but damn it all, I'm only me. A lost orphan girl who finally found her dad. All I care about is saving him and I know, as sure as I know my heart will take the next beat, he's not going to make it.

"Save him," I say. "Take off whatever the hell it is you did."

"I cannot," he says.

"Liar," I say.

Magic roars in my ears like the waves of an ocean pounding against the beach. It swirls around me, making the air crackle. Casmir watches. His face is impassive, but there is more happening behind his eyes.

"What gain do I get from saving him?" he asks.

"I won't kill you," I growl. "Let's start with that."

His lips twitch, turning up at the corners until he is actually smiling.

"You would try," he says, sounding almost bored. "You would be a worthy opponent."

"Enough!" Tynan roars.

He rushes his brother, and the two men crash together and disappear from sight. The sounds of their fighting fill the room, but it's not good enough. Tynan is just as likely to kill him as he is to beat him into submission and that will get me nowhere.

"Aviella," Silas says, touching my shoulder.

Startled I jerk away and whirl around.

"What?" I yell, angry with all the choices I have.

"It's an experiment," he says. "The only thing Casmir cares about is testing free will. He's been doing it for all of existence. He's trying to find the limits of the one gift the Divine gave to mankind. Play to that."

Free will huh? Shaking my head, I pull more magic in and then form its swirling potential to my will. As I do, I lift off the ground, rising to the balcony.

"This... is... long... overdue," Tynan pants.

When I crest the balcony the two men are engaged in an epic struggle, their strength too closely matched. Alaric and Shen hold back, watching, while letting Tynan have the lead. I drop to the floor of the balcony, and then with a wave of my hands I weave magic around each of them in magic and rip them apart.

They're both surprised and struggle to break free of my hold, but I'm not done. I tighten the bonds as I storm over and stand between the two of them.

"Enough!" I yell.

Both of their faces shimmer, taking on draconic aspects, so I tighten my magical grip until they stop trying to shift to break free of my hold.

"Aviella," Tynan growls, his eyes narrow.

"No," I say, shaking my head. "I'll handle this."

Tynan fumes, but doesn't say a word so I turn my full attention to Casmir.

"You've almost killed him," I say pointing towards where my father is. "That alone is enough for me to destroy you."

"That is a choice," he says.

His glasses have been knocked cock-eyed, barely sitting on the edge of his nose. He stares with curiosity though, no hint of anger or concern on his face or in his voice.

"It is," I say. "But not the one I want."

I force those words out because part of me does. A primal part, that part of me that resonates with Tynan so deeply. The part that revels in having power and wants to dominate everything and everyone that crosses my path.

That's not all of me though. I'm so much more than one part, like any person. I'm not going to act on my basest instinct. I know, with total certainty, that the key to everything relies in finding my twelfth. I'm also certain Casmir is the one.

I don't want to forgive him. I want to blame him, hurt him, make him pay. I want vengeance, cold or hot I don't care. I want him to pay for what he's done. Except what he's done isn't him. I'm sure of that too.

When I stare into his eyes, I see a man trapped. Trapped by the past, trapped by the Shadow that darkens him. He's cold and stoic because that's how he deals with what he's done. We all have to handle our insecurities and he's no different.

He's good. I know it deep into my bones. His actions may be evil, but he is not.

My emotions rage as I'm torn apart, stuck between two impossible decisions, but nothing can happen until I choose. My senses are on hyper-alert. The beating of my own heart is loud in my ears. I'm acutely aware of my own breathing, my pulse throbbing in my neck. Staring at Casmir and willing him to make the right choice.

I will him to be good. Be the man I see in his eyes, not this cold façade of a man. This person he plays at being to avoid looking at what he's done. Nothing changes though, life isn't that easy after all.

Tynan's gaze is heavy, and it's easy to tell he's straining to hold himself back. His magic is full of rage and destruction fueled by Alaric and Shen, but they are always more controlled than Tynan.

I move close to Casmir and fix his glasses for him, resting my fingertips on his cheeks. He's clean shaven without the slightest hint of a beard. We stare into each other's eyes. He doesn't react to my touch, outwardly, but in his eyes is the suppressed fire. He's holding back, but that is what I have to reach.

"How do I set you free?" I whisper.

"I am free," he says.

Sadness swells in my chest as tears fill my eyes. "No, you're not. Make the right choice, Casmir. Save him, please."

The mark on his forehead dims and for an instant he's there, rising above the trappings of the Shadow. Holding my breath, I wait, not daring to hope.

"Okay," he says.

Nodding I drop the magic I'm using to hold him, but I don't release Tynan, not yet. Casmir walks to the balcony, looks down, and motions with his hand. I move over beside him. Dad is rising to his feet. He's pale, malnourished, but his life force is strong and the black holes sucking in magic and his life are gone.

"Aviella," he says, leaning on Killian for support.

"Go," I order. "All of you, get out of here, now."

"I'm not leaving without you," Tynan growls from behind me.

"Yes, you are," I say. "I made a deal, and I'll see it through."

Gavin organizes the mages and the four of them begin weaving a portal. Silas supports my father while they work. Tynan struggles against my binding. His magic surges as he strains against my hold.

"Casmir," he growls. "I'll kill you."

"You'll try," Casmir says without a hint of malice.

"No," I say, stepping between the two of them again. "Tynan, damn it, this is my choice."

"You're being a fool," he snaps.

He half-shifts to his dragon form, on the astral plane he fully assumes it, physically the magic I'm holding him with keeps it from manifesting here, barely. I flow more magic into the bindings but then suddenly he snaps the connection between us closed. As he does Alaric and Shen do the same. It's a chilling effect almost as if I've lost a limb. A part of me is suddenly gone.

"Tynan," I say, stumbling backwards.

Casmir catches me, strong hands gripping my biceps, steadying me on my feet.

"No," Tynan says. "You want your choice? Make it without us. This is the wrong path!"

Alaric and Shen move next to their brother and his resistance to my binding triples. Taken by surprise and still reeling from them closing our connection he breaks free. He looms large before me, filling the space impossibly big while still maintaining his human form.

"Tynan, don't do this," I say, a note of pleading in my voice.

"Free will," he says, fire burning in his eyes. "You've made your choice and I will not support you in it. We will not."

"Please, trust me," I say.

He pauses. A heartbeat, then two, as he contemplates.

"Efram betrayed you," he says. "I'll deal with that while you play your game. Call for us when you come to your senses."

He tears a hole in space with clawed hands and he and his brothers leap through it before I can respond.

"Petty," Casmir says. "He'll never change."

CHAPTER THIRTY-TWO

SILAS

"*W*hat you propose is not a wise course of action," I say.

We've returned to the mages Sanctuary to regroup. Now I have to try and control Tynan's destructive nature.

"Wise?" Tynan growls. "Who are you to advise me of wisdom?"

"The one who's not reacting like a petulant child who's lost his toy," I snap.

Tynan rises to his feet and leans threateningly over the table.

"Tynan," Gavin says, "Please."

Alaric and Shen grin with delight as Tynan rages. I shouldn't push him; he's barely staying in control. I can't stop myself though. I'm worried. She's with Casmir. Everything is riding on what happens and it's out of my control. I don't like this feeling any more than Tynan does.

Tynan drops into his chair but digs his fingers into the wooden top of the table before him, gouging deep lines.

"Then make a counter, Methuselah," he says, spitting my title.

"We let it play out," I say. "Trust her to know what she's doing."

"She's a child!" he yells rising to his feet again. "She barely has her feet wet and I'm to trust her judgment?"

"Yes," Gavin says.

"Yes," the others gathered add their agreement. Surprisingly even Shen adds his agreement.

"Brother," Alaric says. "It is obvious she is the thrice-born. So named by the Leviathan, who has allied himself with us, and through us her."

"Thrice-born be damned," Tynan growls.

This is the first I've heard of this, so I listen with interest.

"What is this?" I ask.

The dragon's frown as one making it obvious that they're in communication with each other before Shen speaks.

"The Leviathan aided us in finding her," he says. "It wants to help her."

"Why? Why this time? What's changed?" I ask.

The Leviathan has never gotten involved in the play of events. Sitting outside of time it does whatever a creature of that magnitude does, beyond the comprehension of all.

"Because of her," Tynan growls, gouging his nails deeper into the wood. "The same as all of us. Her. She's changing everything."

"There's nothing we can do, right now, for her," Gavin says, rising to his feet. "What we can do is deal with Efram."

Tynan looks up and the cruelty in his eyes turns my blood cold. Almost I feel sorry for Efram. Tynan needs a target for his anger and Efram is going to be it.

"Where is the betrayer?" Tynan asks.

"We've kept him locked up," Gavin says.

"Bring him to me," Tynan says, rising to his feet. "I would have words with him."

CHAPTER THIRTY-THREE

AVIELLA

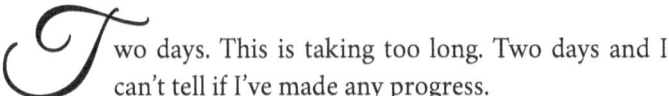

*T*wo days. This is taking too long. Two days and I can't tell if I've made any progress.

This is the hardest thing I've ever had to do. I thought Tynan was tough, but I had no clue. Tynan is fire and passion and calls to something so primal that it was actually easy. Casmir is cold, distant, and cracking that cool exterior isn't going as well.

"Why do you keep trying?" he asks.

We're sitting at a nice dinner. It's a small table between us and in any other setting I might consider it to be intimate but with Casmir it's not. One, we're in a lab, set off to one side, which is anything but a romantic setting. Two, everything is too precise.

The servants presenting each course of the meal do so with an exactness that is unnatural. Their movements are almost jerky, as if programmed, lacking the flow of motion I didn't know I expected until it was gone.

The food is perfect but again, it's too perfect. Exactly the right amount of seasoning. The temperature absolutely perfect for consumption. The placement of every setting piece looks as if it was measured out to the millimeter.

Casmir has probed me with similar questions throughout all our interactions. This is going nowhere, for me or for him. Sighing I set my fork down and lean my elbows on the table.

"Do you ever get tired of this?" I ask, staring into his eyes.

"What 'this' are you referring to?" he asks.

Reaching him with magic I caress his tightly controlled power with my own, teasing it, tugging, asking it to run free. Below the cold surface it roils behind his control.

"Being so cold," I say, leaning closer. "Holding yourself back."

The suppressed fire in his eyes burns and he doesn't move back. It's the best opening I've had.

"The world is out of control," he says softly. "Passions, anger, hate, emotion has ruled it and look where that has led."

"To us," I say, leaning so far over the table that I'm practically crawling on top of it.

"Destruction," he says. "Again."

"Yes," I say. "But also a chance."

"A chance?" he asks, his brow furrowing.

I'm close enough now we could kiss. Our lips are barely a hairs breadth apart. His warm breath passing over my cheeks, staring into each other's eyes, and still he doesn't retreat.

"Yes, a chance," I say. "To start again. To do it right, to create something that has never been."

"A more perfect world?" he asks.

"Yes," I say, reeling him in with magic and desire.

"Impossible," he says.

"No," I say. "We can do this. I can do it."

He rises to his feet breaking the moment as he takes a step back.

"This is a dream," he says. "I've heard it before but that is not the way it ever plays out. You think you're the first?"

Dropping back into my chair I try to calm my pounding heart. I was so close, damn it! I don't know how he can stand it. He has to be feeling it the same as I am. This animalistic attraction, the pull between the two of us.

"The first what?" I sigh, letting him have this round.

"The first come? You are thrice-born," he says. "Do you not know your own lineage? Your own tortured story?"

Frowning I shake my head.

"I have no idea what you're talking about," I say.

"You," he says, clasping his hands behind his back and entering full on lecture mode. "You poor soul that you are."

"Casmir," I say, rising to my feet and closing the distance between us.

"No," he says, stepping back. "You're blind. Until you understand, you are as a child. This game is so much bigger than you see."

"Bigger how?" I ask.

He smiles as he nods. "A proper question."

"Thanks?" I ask, unsure how to react to his words.

"Have you not wondered at the marvel of storytelling?" he asks.

Shaking my head I frown. "What?"

"Storytelling," he says. "You've been with the Methuselah long enough, I'm sure he's had you studying history. It is, after all, his domain. He has always been consumed by what has come before with little to no attention to what is happening now or in the future."

"Silas?" I ask.

"Of course," he says.

"Sure, I studied a lot with him," I say.

"And in your studies, have you not seen a pattern? A repeating pattern?"

"Sure," I say. "History does tend to repeat itself."

"Tends to, or intends to?" he asks.

"What's the difference?" I ask.

"Everything," he says. "It's designed this way."

"What is?" I ask.

"All of it," he says, sweeping his arm widely. "It's one grand experiment."

"Casmir, I don't understand what you're saying," I say.

"Free will, the power of choice," he says. "If you give complete and utter free will to mortal man, what will happen? Will they choose a path of creation and build something new and beautiful or will their choices lead to destruction?"

"Mankind has made all kinds of beautiful things," I counter. "Works of art, conquering the world around him, skyscrapers, beautiful paintings. Even more."

"Yes, but it also created Wormwood. The atomic bomb, two 'world' wars and then a 'third' because two wasn't enough destruction."

"Sure but that's fate—"

"No," he cuts me off. "No it wasn't. It was choices, made over time from the very first killing to the very last. One choice inevitably leading to another until we are here."

Staring my heart sinks as the implication of his words hit me with the weight of worlds.

"So you're saying that man's own decisions doomed him?"

"Of course," he says. "Again?"

"Again?" I ask.

"Yes Aviella," he says, moving close. "Again. You've done this before, though you don't remember it. Twice you've tried to save the world. Twice you've failed. Why would this time be any different?"

I'm shaking uncontrollably. Almost I can grasp the enormity of his words, but each time I almost do they flitter away, and I lose it. Before. I've done this before? It doesn't seem real.

"What does it matter?" I ask.

"What do you mean?" he asks.

He's so close the scent of him fills my nose. It's musky, manly and makes my heart race and my mouth dry.

"The past is done," I say, putting my hand on his chest. His heart rate doubles at my touch. "It's over. Are we to be trapped, forever, by the mistakes we made, or is there a brighter future we can create?"

He leans closer.

"What is it you propose?" he asks.

Our lips are almost touching. If I lifted onto my toes we'd be kissing. Magic swirls creating a storm of arcane energy. He's responding, I'm reaching him.

"That we can make new choices," I exhale. "It's not over, not predetermined that we'll fail."

"It's not," he says. "But the pattern is clear."

"Then let's throw the pattern out the window," I say, rising into his lips.

When we touch the swirling magic becomes a maelstrom with us at the epicenter. My heart stops before breaking free and galloping. His arms wrap around my body, pulling me tight. We meld together, and the raging magic lifts us off our feet, buoying us in midair.

I'm swept away, losing myself in his embrace. As our bodies move together our magic intertwines. Caressing, stroking, mouths exploring feverish skin. His touch is cool water passing over.

Our magic is orchestral, powerful music swelling to a crescendo, the tension building in our bodies and on the astral. It's breathtaking.

He opens himself a little, but I barge in, diving deep as we meld our bodies. The fire I knew was here burns hot but controlled. He wears logic as an armor, separating himself from the pain that comes hand in hand with life.

Running my fingers through his hair, I probe deeper, teasing, easing my way through his defenses, beneath the façade he wears like armor.

He jerks away, and we drop to the ground. My knees protest the sudden shock.

"Enough," he says, taking two steps back to separate our bodies, even as he pulls his magic back and puts it under tight wraps.

"Casmir," I say, stepping closer, but he takes a step back shaking his head.

"Aviella," he says. "I am not a fool."

He turns on his heel and strides towards the door.

"That wasn't a fool," I say to his retreating back. "That was a man. A man and a woman creating a future."

His only response is the click of the closing door behind him.

CHAPTER THIRTY-FOUR

EFRAM

Gritting my teeth I hold out as long as I can before giving in to the screams. They don't last as long this time, thankfully. I lie panting on the thin mattress, covered in sweat, breathing my way through the aftermath. It's nothing compared to what Aviella went through, I remind myself when the pause in the pain comes.

I don't know how long it takes but it's all-consuming, and I don't notice Luca has entered my cell for a bit. At least it feels like he's been there for a while. The weight of his eyes carrying judgment that lies heavy on me.

He's not wrong. I betrayed her. The whys don't really matter. I did it and now I suffer for it.

"Here," Luca says, walking over to the bed.

His hands glow white as he kneels. When he puts them on my body a cool rush of relief floods from the point of contact washing over me. My breathing eases and my heart slows to something almost normal.

"Thanks," I say.

"Yeah," he says, standing back up.

He steps back across the small room and leans against the

wall, arms crossed over his chest. That heavy gaze on me again. Closing my eyes, I wait. I'd sit up, but I don't have the energy. Despite the relief his magic brought, everything still hurts.

If I wait long enough, he'll leave. That's what they've all done. Come, stare, offer a bit of relief, then leave again. It could be worse, I'm sure.

They wouldn't understand. I wish they would, but wishes aren't reality. Reality is a cold, harsh mistress that I've come to great terms with. The suffering? That's reality. Deserved reality, after all, I am the betrayer.

"Why?" Luca asks, startling me out of my musing.

"Huh?" I ask, blinking.

"Why?" he repeats.

Why. The deepest question of all. The one every two-year-old child drives their parents insane with. I can't suppress a chuckle at the absurdity of it all.

"You think it's funny?" he asks, pushing off the wall.

Magic pools around him and for an instant a desire to push him overwhelms me. If I push hard enough, he'll end this. It won't hurt anymore. Death calls to me, whispering and offering sweet relief.

I can't.

She still needs me. I'm not done yet.

"No," I shake my head.

My muscles twinge, warming up for the next round of painful spasms. Groaning I force myself up onto my elbows so I can see him. My eyes are blurry, so I swipe my arm across them and blink until my vision clears.

"Then why?" he asks.

The unknowing despair in his voice resonates deep inside.

"I had to," I sigh, shuddering. "I had to, Luca. There was no choice. This is the way."

"No!" he screams, hands balling into fists and rising before him.

I close my eyes and wait for the beating. I don't blame him. I'd do the same if it was me. I'd probably have done it long before now, truth be told.

There's a loud smack, but no pain. When I open my eyes, Luca has his back to me and is holding his right hand. He hit the wall, not me. Surprising.

"Luca," I say.

My voice is scratchy, throaty. I'm so dry but no amount of water quenches the thirst. Casmir did a number on me, and damn, I wish I could die.

"Why?" he asks, turning back again.

I open my mouth to answer but nothing comes out. There's nothing I can say that will make any difference. I can't make them understand no matter how much I want to. I've tried. Tynan questioned me for hours.

Luca stares, waiting, then turns and walks out. Through the open door another figure waits. My stomach drops seeing him.

Aviella's dad walks into the room dragging a chair with him. He's gaunt and pale, almost ashen. His darker skin tone looks gray in this light. He was with Casmir a lot longer than I was and it shows. But his eyes are bright and intelligent. He takes a seat a couple of feet away, crosses his legs and leans back in the chair.

"Hello," he says.

Tears well up. The connection between him and her is obvious. They have the same cheekbones. The shape of his face is clearly mimicked in hers, though hers is softer, more rounded whereas his is sharper and more masculine. It's too close to looking at her.

"I'm sorry," I gasp, tears breaking free.

He uncrosses his legs and leans forward.

"Sorry?" he asks.

"So... sorry," I gasp between bouts of the emotional storm that has broken free.

He nods understanding, and it feels like he gets it. None of the guys do but with him he does.

"I don't have long," he says, sighing. "And we need to talk."

Clenching my jaw, I force the tears to stop. Despite the pain and the quivering muscles I push myself to a sitting position.

"Not long?" I ask, panting from the exertion.

He frowns deeply and shakes his head. Sitting up and looking with more than my eyes, for the first time I see what he means. Wisps of death drift off of him. He's on the door, ready to step through, no matter how alive he seems. My own magical affinity shows me clearly that he's here through force of will alone.

"Yeah," he nods, as if he sees my own understanding of his plight. "It's fine. Aviella is what matters. Tell me. Tell me everything."

It's an entirely different flood as the story pours out. I start with the first moment I saw her, what seems so long ago now, up to our last moment together. The last bit, though, I hold back.

"Thank you," he says, placing his hand on my knee.

"She's special," I say impulsively.

"Yes, she is," he agrees. "You didn't betray her, did you?"

The question startles me. Sitting up straight I snap my mouth shut and stare. No one can know that, not yet. It's not time.

"It's fine," he continues, sighing. His shoulders slump and his head hangs lower, but his eyes are still bright. "I know how her mother works."

"Her mother?" I ask. "She's dead, isn't she?"

He smiles shaking his head. "Now is not the time for that story. I don't have long enough to even start."

"Maybe I can… help…" I say hesitant.

What help can I really offer? Me wielding magic well enough to combat the death touches wafting off of him? Yeah, right. Any moment now the pain will return, and I'll be curled into a ball trying to get through it.

"No," he shakes his head. "It's my time. I'm almost done."

"I'm sorry," I say, but I'm not sure what I'm sorry for.

All of it? Betraying her? For not being strong enough?

"Don't be," he says. The acceptance in his voice is powerful. "I need to tell you some things. We're in the end game now and she's going to need you. All of you."

He leans forward, conspiratorially close. Anticipation crawls across my skin like a million pin pricks.

CHAPTER THIRTY-FIVE

AVIELLA

*H*e's avoiding me, and I'm done with this game. I don't have time. The world outside this bubble is burning, and every moment I waste here is one I can't recover. The sense of urgency leaves me anxious and restless.

Prowling through the halls of Casmir's bunker, I search for him. He's elusive though. When I find a wing I've yet to explore, I step through swinging double doors that creak as I pass. They flap against each other behind me with a slapping sound that echoes off the tiled hall. Fluorescent lights make a cold, uncaring light. It's creepy as hell, like something out of a late-night horror movie.

Nervously I mold magic into a protective shield around myself, just in case. I'm in Casmir's bunker after all, and he is still under the mark of the Shadow. No need to be a fool.

The hall stretches as far as I can see. Heavy steel doors are set every fifteen feet, each with a dirty viewing window set in them. I go to the first door and look in. It's an empty room. The walls are covered with thick padding, there's a lone metal framed bed and a massive bolt in the floor with a thick chain hooked to it.

My stomach does flips looking at it and it doesn't take much imagination to see its purpose. I know, with certainty, some of these rooms have inmates in them. I can sense their life force calling out in despair.

I can free them. All of them. I can storm down this hall, opening doors, breaking chains and set them all free.

But if I do, I'll not win over Casmir. I'll condemn him to the Shadow forever. I'm every bit as certain of this as I am that I can free these people. It's a test. Do I choose the immediate good or the greater good?

If I don't free Casmir, I can't win. The Shadow will win the war. I'll lose no matter what I try, because I need that final piece. The final connection that will fully unlock my power. Shaking with the effort, I move ahead.

Don't look. That's the only way I can do it, even though I feel them. Their pain, pure anguish as I pass the doors.

It's a test. Another of his infernal experiments. What will I choose? Damn you Casmir, if I didn't need you—

A wailing scream of despair stops me. I'm drawn to a door almost against my own will. I don't want to look. Don't want to see it, but I have to.

A woman is chained to the bed. She's wasted away, barely recognizable as a person. She's screaming, and it breaks my heart. Magic curls around, testing the door. The door is nothing, I could tear it from its hinges without a second thought.

If I do, it's over.

I'll have made the choice, choosing one person over all the others outside this Bunker. That's not all though. I'm choosing between one life, and all life. The entire future of our race. All of humanity and the entirety of another age.

Closing my eyes tight I turn from the window and take the next step. My legs are heavy. It takes every ounce of will to force my feet to move. The first step made the next is not as hard and like that, one foot in front of the other, the choice is made.

The lights of the hall blink out leaving me in darkness. A thought and a magical light surrounds me pushing the darkness back but I'm not in the hall any longer. It's a room with one door. Casmir walks through the door and stops in front of me.

"Why?" he asks.

"Why what?"

"You did not save that person," he says. "You could have. It's well within your power."

"Yes," I agree.

He stares at me from behind his glasses that he pushes up on his nose, waiting. In return I wait for him, letting him play out the possible answers to the dilemma he has posed.

"You chose because you felt it was one versus many," he says at last.

"Yes," I agree.

"It was hard?" he asks.

"Yes," I say.

"Yet you chose," he says.

"I did," I say.

"Interesting," he says.

The fire is in his eyes, barely contained passion and desire. I take a step closer, then another when he doesn't retreat. One foot in front of another until I place my hand on his chest.

"Do you see?" I ask.

"Explain it," he says, his heart pounding so hard it's making my hand thrum.

"It's the greater good," I say. "That's what I've had to learn. I can't save every single person. I've tried and I've failed... so many times."

I choke up as memories come with the words. All the

178

people I've failed to save. The bunkers full of them that have fallen in the wake of my passing. Every one of them weighs on me but I've had to come to terms with the losses.

"You have chosen a possible future over a certain one. You could save the one in front of you but chose instead in favor of an uncertainty. This does not make sense. Humans don't choose that way; they take immediate gratification. They want their now, now, no delays."

"Casmir," I say. "That's not true."

"It is!" he argues. "Statistically it's the majority."

"That may be," I say. "But it's not true. Humans dream. It's what we do, it's vital to who and what we are. We dream of new possibilities. Futures that we could create, not for ourselves but for those who come after us."

"Not at the cost of yourself," he argues.

"Don't be silly," I say. "That's her viewpoint, is it really yours?"

I put my other hand on his cheek and trace the strong line of his jaw, feeling it tighten as I challenge him.

"Yes," he says but the hesitancy in his voice is clear.

"No," I counter. "It's not."

"I've done so many experiments, the majority always come out the same," he says.

"Are you saying that the exception proves the rule?" I ask, smiling.

He frowns and shakes his head. "It doesn't make sense."

"No," I agree. "It doesn't. Humans are messy. We make mistakes. We can be petty, self-centered, full of ourselves, but we also create beautiful works of art. We care about each other. Go out of their way to help one another, even when it costs them."

"Those are the anomalies," he says.

"How many anomalies have you observed?" I ask.

He doesn't answer for a very long time. I'm acutely aware

of my breath, the rising and falling of his chest as he breathes. Our breaths are in time with each other. Beneath that rise and fall his heart beats strong and steady. I'm reaching him.

"Fascinating," he says.

He leans closer, his lips closing with mine. So close, we almost touch. Sparks jump between us, we're less than an inch apart when something flashes in his eyes and he pulls back. Damn it.

"Casmir," I say.

"I'll consider your words," he says, turning he strides out of the room.

Damn it.

CHAPTER THIRTY-SIX

RAFE

"Getting… tired?" I pant.

Beelzebub's sword and mine clang loudly.

"I'm going to destroy you," he growls.

"Wow, you ever hear of a breath mint?" I ask, shaking my head.

Leaning into my sword I draw on depths of reserves I didn't know I had, pressing for any advantage. Beelzebub's eyes widen then he leaps backwards as Nate's sword flashes towards his head.

He lands with bent knees and sword held ready before him, assessing. Piles of bodies are stacked around the three of us but there are thousands more waiting for his command. Exhaustion makes my arms heavier than they should be. My sword must weigh a million pounds. My heart pounds and my magical channels ache but I can't fail. If I stop, he'll go after Avi.

Nate moves next to me in his full angelic glory. We exchange a fast glance and it's clear we're both willing to die for this. If nothing else, we're buying her time. It's all we can do.

"You'd both die for this," Beelzebub says. "For her."

A slow smile forms and I laugh.

"Would you? For Lucy?" I ask.

"You know there is nothing more for us," he answers. "This is it. We've already won. Why not give up? Your fight is futile."

"You know," I say. "I've heard that shit before."

Rage contorts his face. "It's true!"

"Sure," I agree. "I'm sure it is, for you."

"Why? Why do you fight the inevitable?" he asks.

"Why do you talk so damn much!" I yell, charging forward.

I'm going to die. I'm sure of that but at least I can choose how I go out.

Nate charges at my side. There's no time for goodbyes or settling our long history but it doesn't matter. Nate knows, as do I, that our long rocky history is behind us. The future, short as it may be, is ahead.

Demonic monstrosities watch in awe as the three of us battle. I'm exhausted, nothing left, but still I fight. Deep inside a fire burns. The fire that she ignited, reminding me of who I used to be, but more, it pulls me towards who I could be.

A better man.

It gives me hope. She gave me hope, and for that I will die if I must. I've lived in the darkness, devoid of any hope for the future. My dreams died and when they did, so did I. Nate and I move in perfect synchronicity. I remember, now, how close he and I were.

Closer than we had any right to be. I also remember, as we battle for our lives, how that closeness was used against me. I fell for it then, but I've lived a long time since. All that time has led us to this moment.

Ducking Beez's swing, I come up inside his reach,

bringing my sword in for a killing blow on his neck. I stop with the blade pressing against his throat. He growls, a rumbling noise that pounds against my chest.

"Tell Lucy," I say. "I chose wrong."

Air rushes out of him and his eyes widen as Nate drives his sword into his guts and I slice with my own blade.

Beez's form collapses, black smoke swirling around it. It's an avatar, he's not met true death, but it's all we can do for now. We've bought time. Time for us, but more important, time for Aviella to do what she needs to do.

Chests heaving, limbs shaking from exhaustion, I smile to Nate who still looks grim.

"That went better than expected," I say.

"This is better?" he asks, staring over my shoulder.

We're still surrounded. The milling masses of demons and undead monstrosities are unsure how to react to the loss of their leader, but this is only a brief respite.

"Sure!" I say, cheerfully despite the fact I'm struggling to remain upright. "He finally shut up. You know how many millennia I've wanted to shove his tongue down his throat to make him do that?"

A smile forms on Nates' lips and then he laughs.

"You're impossible," he says.

"I prefer to think of myself as indubitably upbeat," I say, affecting an English accent.

A low rumble sounds as the surrounding demons shift their attention to us. A particularly large and ugly bastard howls. Nate's smile turns down and his eyes grow serious.

"I'm sorry," he says.

"Nate, you shouldn't be," I say.

He shakes his head and puts his hands on my face.

"I am. I couldn't," he says. "I tried, but I couldn't follow you, not then."

Swallowing hard I put a hand on his shoulder and squeeze.

"I know," I say. "Trust me, it was a stupid decision to follow her out those pearly gates. I'm glad you stayed."

He leans closer, our forehead touch, and in that moment everything is good. A brief moment in time but one I'll cherish for what life I have left.

Nate screams as a taloned claw shoves through his shoulder and I cry out as it pierces my left side. Gripping my sword tighter I rip myself free and the battle is engaged again.

CHAPTER THIRTY-SEVEN

AVIELLA

*A*nother day passes. At least one. There's no easy way to tell time, it's only a sense of it passing. There are no clocks and I haven't seen the outside since coming here. Casmir is avoiding me but so is everyone and everything else here. It's like I suddenly ceased to matter. No more tests, no taunting's, nothing.

Lying on a hard cot I wait. I know I'm not forgotten but that doesn't make the waiting any easier. I've counted the ceiling tiles then the stains on them and now, at least twenty times, I've counted the squiggly designs in the tiles.

Good times. Not.

Bored to tears I rise to my feet and walk the halls. People go from room to room doing things that make no sense to me. Some rooms seem dedicated to plants. They're doing experiments with them, but I don't understand it. Other rooms have jars and tubes and one even has these massive tanks full of fish.

I'm in that room, watching the fish swim to amuse myself when cold chills pass over my skin and it becomes hard to breathe. It's like the air is suddenly too thick to inhale. I've felt similar before, but not this strong.

She's here.

My enemy. The one who stands in direct opposition to me. The she-devil has come.

I rise to my feet, take a deep breath, pull magic around, and then turn to the door. Heels click on tiles, and I know she's coming right to me. This is it. We're going to face off, at last. This is the moment the fate of the world is decided.

I suppose most people would believe I've already lost after what happened at New Jerusalem, but that's not the case at all. That was only the first part of my story. Now I'm becoming the one I'm supposed to be.

The clicking stops, and a shadowy figure stands outside the door. I sense more than see her. Power, pure, raw, more than I've ever felt. She's every bit my match and then some. The door pushes open and time slows.

As it swings open my eyes adjust to the light behind the figure outlined there, first appearing as a shadow. It moves into the room, the heels clicking again. I don't know what I expect. Something evil, horrible looking, horns maybe. I've seen so much ugliness since the Apocalypse surely the embodiment of evil will be the worst. The door swings closed behind her, my eyes adjust, and I see her for the first time.

She's beautiful.

So damn beautiful my knees feel weak. I've never seen anyone or anything more perfect. My heart stops, my mouth is dry, and I want to go drop and scream that I'm not worthy. No one should be so gorgeous. My body aches with the sight of her. She's even more beautiful than when I last saw her in my vision, when she tempted me.

"Hello, Aviella," she says, smiling.

It's an illusion. Magic plays around her, sparking and

calling to my own power. Teasing my power into a frenzy. She is temptation given form. I can't help but find it fascinating to look at her, to feel her. Being in her presence is its own excitement.

"Yeah," I say, shaking my head.

The temptation may seem real, but it's not. Not really. What's real is that she's led the way to hell. Literally. Now we're going to face off. Taking a deep breath, I brace myself. This isn't how I expected it to go down, but if this is it, then it is.

"Have you rethought my offer?" she asks.

"Yeah," I nod. "I have."

"And?"

I smile, shaking my head. "I think you're getting desperate. Seriously desperate."

"Oh," she says, pursing her lips and shaking her head.

The door behind her swings open and Casmir enters, stopping inside the opening. He stares at her, and for an instant I feel his anger before he clamps it back down behind his controlled façade.

"You are not supposed to be here," he says to her.

"Casmir," she purrs his name, but doesn't look at him. "You're sweet but no. I go where I want."

She strides forward, closing the distance between us. Her power pushes before her, trying to force me back, but I hold my ground. She stops a foot before me, and we stare at each other.

"I'm not going to give in," I say.

"That is too bad," she says. "Is that your final… choice?"

She pauses and drags out the last word, letting it fall heavily from her lips, loaded with implications.

"It is," I say. "Yours is not the way."

"Very well," she says, raising a hand.

Invisible force closes on me like vise grips, jerking my

limbs outwards and lifting me off the ground. It happens so hard and fast it feels like my arms and legs are almost jerked out of socket. I cry out in pain, losing my concentration for a moment which causes my magic to roil unfocused.

"Do not do this," Casmir whispers so soft I barely hear him.

"I gave you two chances," she says. "Choice points, but now you've made the final one."

Breathing through the pain as Silas has taught me, I empty my mind. Focus. Pull the magic to me, let it flood through my channels, empowering. Shaping it into a single point I drive it towards her, willing it to knock her back.

The magical force hits her and she stumbles backwards, a drop of blood slipping past her rosy lips. She grunts as she slams up against one of the lab tables. Straightening, she touches her lips, wiping away the trickle of blood.

"I said no," I say.

"Feisty," she smiles, her perfectly white teeth stained pink with blood. "I like that."

Her hands come up, finger curling, and pain explodes throughout my body. It feels like something is tearing its way through my insides. I scream, unable to hold it back.

I don't know how long it lasts until it stops, and I'm left hanging in midair, head on my chest, panting as I struggle to catch my breath.

"That… the best…you got?" I ask, looking up and meeting her glare.

"Oh, Avi," she smiles, hips swaying as she moves closer. "I've not even begun. Your choice is made, and now you're mine. Of your own free will."

"Don't," Casmir says, looking over her shoulder, but she ignores him.

I look past her to him. His eyes narrow as his brow

furrows. His jaw is tense, his hands curling into fists. This is it. I know what to do.

"You're pathetic," I say to her. "All your talk of free will, it's bullshit. You're a petulant child at the heart of it all. A child throwing a temper tantrum."

"You know nothing!" she yells.

The world explodes. Bright white, pain so deep I'm blind. Ripping so deep it's in the heart of what I am. Unreal. I can't focus.

When it stops at last, I'm left whimpering. Focus, Avi. This is what the boys trained you for. Opening my eyes and gritting my teeth, I blink until she comes back into focus.

"Child," I say. "Tantrum."

She grins, dragging her perfectly manicured nails across my cheek leaving burning lines in their wake.

"Just wait," she whispers.

"I said no," Casmir says, louder.

"You had your chance," she says, glancing over her shoulder.

He's there, close. The scent of him is comforting, a balm to the burning pain throughout my flesh.

"Uh oh," I pant. "Trouble in paradise?"

She slaps my face so hard I see stars as my head jerks to one side.

"She is mine!" Casmir roars, his presence filling the room as he drops his controlled façade.

The dragon arrives in a raging storm. She turns to face him, her own presence swelling to match his. The two titans clash, magic slamming together. I bite my lip to force myself to focus. Pull magic around myself in a shield.

The room around us becomes a war zone. Tables, machines, and glass flying through the air in a hailstorm of debris, bouncing off my protective shield.

Casmir and the she-devil are locked together. He looks

past her and our eyes lock. Concentrating I reach out to him with my magic as she forces him back a step then two.

His magic and mine touch and he resists. He needs my help, but he has to accept it. WE need each other, but if he won't open himself, it will be over.

She's towering over him, too big for the room, spatially impossible, but they're locked in an epic battle and Casmir is losing.

She slams a fist into him, and he's rocked back, sliding across the tile floor. His glasses fly off of his face and he roars. I keep my magic extended to him. He looks at me again then his magic opens up and he takes my offered help.

The swirling mark on his forehead flares. Shadows coalesce around it.

"No!" the she-devil screams. "You're mine!"

She slams an open palm down on the point of the mark. Power, dark and filled with the negative pushes into him. The equivalent of a nuclear bomb explodes as her dark magic meets the light of my own trying to erase his mark.

Bright white light blinds me as the clash of powers explodes. I'm thrown back, flying through the air, unable to inhale a breath of my own.

I try to brace myself for the coming impact. Any moment and I'm going to slam into a wall with crushing force.

Aviella, forgive me. Casmir's voice sounds in my head then my body jerks in the opposite direction.

There's a wrenching sensation and I lose my stomach somewhere along the way. I drop in a heap onto the floor still blinded by the light.

"Aviella!" Gavin yells.

CHAPTER THIRTY-EIGHT

TYNAN

"*I*'ll tear my way through to her!" I yell, slamming my fist down.

"That would be monumentally stupid," Silas says.

Turning to face the Methuselah I contemplate a dozen ways to end his long life. As I lean across the table, struggling to control my baser urges he doesn't blink.

The room flashes white as magic explodes out in a ring. Dragon-magic washes across me, then she's there.

"Aviella," Gavin yells.

She's lying in a heap on the floor. Everyone leaps towards her, but I lean back in my chair, watching. She stirs and rises to her feet. Everyone puts hands on her, steadying as they help. She looks around the room, taking in each of us her eyes resting on me last.

"He sent me here?" she asks it as a question.

"Apparently," I agree, though I'm not sure what she's asking about, outside the obvious.

She bites her lip then shakes her head. "Can he stand up to her?"

"I don't know," I answer, getting the drift of her message. "Did you succeed?"

She nods.

"Then he has a chance," I say, feeling the weight of Alaric and Shen's eyes resting on me.

Our brother is free but still with her.

"What's our next move?" I ask.

Gavin helps Aviella to a seat at the table and everyone else resumes their place. She looks around the table and a smile forms on her face. Her eyes land on the empty chair, where Efram would sit, and she frowns.

"Where's Efram?" she asks.

Everyone at the table looks down or away. No one meets her eyes as she turns to each of us. She turns to me last of all.

"Tynan?" she asks.

"Avi," I say. "Efram betrayed you."

"I know," she says. "I told him to."

"You what!" Gavin, Luca, and Killian yells as one.

Shen, Alaric and I exchange a quick glance but otherwise don't reveal our thoughts.

"Yes," she says. "Now, where is he?"

"You can't drop a bomb like that and not explain yourself," Ronan says.

"Please tell me you haven't hurt him?" she asks, ignoring the others she's talking to me.

"He has… survived," I say.

She nods. "Good. Now can we get him here?"

"Aviella," Silas says, his voice even and reasonable. "You need to explain yourself better than this."

Her shoulders slump and she closes her eyes, settling back into the chair.

"It had to be," she says. "I can't explain it, really. My mom came to me and I knew… it had to happen. Someone had to be sacrificed."

"Sacrificed?" Ronan asks. "Someone?"

"Yes," she says.

"It should have been one of us!" Luca yells. "I was there, why didn't you let it be me?"

She opens her eyes and looks at him. It's such a tender, loving look, a stab of jealousy pierces my chest. I want her to look at me like that.

"I couldn't," she answers, her eyes drifting around the table. "I couldn't choose one of you. It had to be me, because I couldn't. I'm sorry for what you had to go through."

"You should be," I say, rising to my feet. "You have to trust us."

"I do," she says, rising to her feet too and leaning onto the table. "I trust each of you. More than that." She sighs and bows her head. "I love you. Each of you, more than… words. More than I can say in any way except… this."

Magic fills the room, a swelling wave crashing through, engulfing each of us. I'm pulled into the undertow of her. My magic flows into her as she fills me back up but it's not only mine. It's ours, all of us gathered here flow power into her and she flows it back out to us.

Power fills me. I'm a dragon, a Horseman, I've known power all my existence, but nothing I've experienced compares to this, and I know it's only a taste of what we can be.

"I love you," she whispers as it flows through all of us. "But we're in trouble, and it's going to take all of us."

"Aviella?" her dad's voice is shaky.

The moment she hears it she cuts us off and it's a drop from an incredible height. I have to lean on the table to support myself as she spins around and runs to her dad, taking his frail form into her arms and wrapping him up.

Panting, I watch the reunion through blurry eyes.

CHAPTER THIRTY-NINE

AVIELLA

"*D*ad!"

He's frail, so I force myself to be careful as I take him in my arms, but he hugs me tight.

"Hey, baby," he says, sobbing into my shoulder. "Let me look at you!" He holds me back to arm's length, looking up and down with a smile on his face. "You've grown, so beautiful."

"Thanks," I say, cheeks warming.

"You remind me of your mother," he says. "You've got her eyes and her hair."

My cheeks burn at his compliments and he pulls tight.

"I'm so glad you're okay," I say.

"Me too, baby," he says. "You've done so well. I'm proud of you."

"Thank you, daddy," I say.

"I told you, your mom is always with you," he reminds me. "You saw her?"

"Yeah," I say, tears wetting his shoulder.

"Good," he says. "You're special, and now you're going to save the world."

His hear flutters and his breath hitches too, so I flow magic to him, but I sense immediately it's not enough. He's slipping away.

"Daddy," I say, desperation making my voice crack.

"Yeah," he agrees, understanding what I want to say. "It's okay. I'll be joining her soon."

"No, Daddy, no," I sob.

The guys stand around us, shifting their weight, but I'm only dimly aware of them. This moment. I've wanted this since I was a little girl. Since he disappeared trying to save me. Now, as powerful as I am, I can't save him? This isn't fair.

"It's life," he says, as if reading my thoughts. "It's okay, baby girl. I'll be fine, trust me."

"I do, daddy, but I don't want to let you go!"

"I know," he says, squeezing tighter. "It's not about us though, is it?"

"I want it to be!" I raise my voice and it cracks.

"We all do," he says. "But you're better than that."

"What's the point?" I ask. "Why? Why is it on me? I don't want this, I didn't ask to be this!"

"No," he says, pushing me back so he can cup my face in his hands. "You didn't, but then, if not you, who?"

"I don't want to be special," I say, tears streaming. "I want to be with you. With my… friends. It's too much."

"Aviella," he says, taking on his serious tone. "I've always told you, you're special, and you are."

"To what end? What does it matter? I'm only an orphan, and now you're about to leave me again! The one thing I did all this for, all this power and I can't save the one thing I want? Why bother!"

Magic forms a maelstrom in my soul, tearing its way through the fiber of who I am. My dad watches with his kind eyes, understanding, and even that pisses me off.

"I understand, Aviella," he sighs. "It's not fair."

"How can you be like this? Why aren't you fighting! Screaming! You should be fighting, damn it. Not understanding, not being kind, you can't leave me. Not again!"

Hurt blooms in his eyes, and it feels good. I want to hurt him, want him to feel the pain I felt when he didn't show up. When I had to take myself to the orphanage. Feel the pain of growing up alone, outcast, with no one to love me.

"It's not fair!" I yell, and magic bursts out of me in a nova.

The guys around us are thrown backwards, slamming through furniture and hitting the walls. Chaos reigns as the storm is unleashed. Magical energy crackles across my skin, making my hair stand on end.

"Avi," Silas says, struggling against the magic holding him against the wall.

I don't want to hear him or the others as they struggle to break free. I only wanted one damn thing and now I'm losing it. The one thing I asked for out of all of this. They struggle, they call my name, but I ignore them.

More power. I draw on the guys, pulling their magic in. It flows into me, rivers of power streaming out of them to fill the ever-growing pool inside of me. I'm going to save him. Everyone and everything be damned, I'm going to do it. Somehow.

My dad shakes his head as his eyes widen. Gasps echo from the guys as I pull more power. Magic rages too, taking on the shape of my emotions. All my pain, all the loss, everything I've been through pours into it.

Distantly there's a primal sounding scream. It takes me more than a moment to realize it's coming from me. Blue and purple lightning crackle in the air around me, magic expressing itself as I struggle to control the power.

I've never taken in this much. My control slips. Magic crackles, burning along the skin of my arms. Tynan roars.

The sound echoes over the thundering of my heart. Desperate, I try to regain control of it.

I'm able to, barely. The power is raw, too much for me to focus, too dangerous to control, but then a fleeting thought comes to me.

Accept it. Accept this power. It's mine. My birthright.

Suddenly I recall standing in that desert. I'm with her and she's offering me... everything.

This is it. This is everything. I can save my Dad. Staring down at him, I'm growing taller and he's receding. It's not only about him, I could save the entire world. Wipe out the Shadow forces with just a thought. If I flick my fingers, they'd be gone. Turned to dust and returned to the Earth as they should be.

I can set all the wrongs right.

The 'darlings' of Tynan's bunker. The outcasts consumed with their looks and fashion and appearance. I could make them see, with this power I'd make them look at how shallow their thoughts and lives are. They'd see, and they'd be better, because I made it so.

Wormwood. I could eliminate the monsters there. It wouldn't be more than a thought to eliminate all the horrors.

The orphanage. All those times of being picked on, bullied, made to feel alone. An outcast among the outcast. They'd look on me now and cower. I am power.

I can save my dad.

I can make Casmir pay for what he's done.

I can make her pay for what she's done.

I can win.

I'm so tall I barely fit in the room. I'm too big, too powerful to be confined by things like space or walls. No, I'm more than all of these... ideas, but I turn and look at the sources of my power. Each of my men, my loyal ones. They stare, wide-eyed, slack-jawed, straining to break free of my power holding them against the wall as I drain them.

They're almost empty vessels. Something twinges. This isn't right, I… care about them, but I have to choose. Do I save them or the entire world?

As I look at each of them in turn, I see every wrong they've done. None of them are innocent. None of them are free of their own crimes. Hidden by the passage of time or not, I see them all. Every misstep, every bad decision, every time they failed to uphold the greater good.

I am the greater good. It's time I accept my role.

"Dad," I say, turning back to him.

My voice echoes, doubling over on itself, carried by magic and reinforced. My words can be law. The focus of my will.

He's not alone. Rowan stands in front of him, staring with wide eyes and shaking her head. Her curly hair dancing around as if on its own accord as the magical storm lifts her off her feet. The white flowy dress she's wearing drifts around and gives her the appearance of an angel.

She's shaking her head, motioning with her hands to her chest, covering her heart then throwing them out towards me.

"No," I say, shaking my head, tears filling my eyes. "No, Rowan."

She frowns, floating off the ground, then a soft white glow surrounds her, pushing my magic back as it forms a shield.

She motions again, but now she's signing rapidly. So fast I can barely follow the flow of her words.

"Aviella… don't…" Gavin gasps behind me.

Rowan is 'talking' fast still. The storm raging around us echoes my pain.

"Rowan, damn it, I can save him," I growl, raising my hands before me and balling them into fists.

Magic coalesces around my fists, condensing power. Something dark whispers through my thoughts, telling me what I could do. I've got the power. I'm in control now.

The room rumbles as a crack appears in the floor racing towards the wall. Rowan glances down then her wide eyes lock to mine. She moves closer but I drift back from her. She opens her arms wide, sadness in her eyes, the corners of her mouth turning down.

"No," I say, shaking my head as I retreat before her. "No, no, no."

Her magic is the lightest touch against the raging storm around us. Caressing, entwining, reaching through the tempest to touch me.

It's cool on my skin, a simple point of contact. Our shared memories flicker through my mind like shuffled cards. The two of us laughing. Rowan mimicking the bullies and making fun of them until I would quit crying and laugh. The two of us sneaking out of our room to snitch more food because we were starving.

Getting caught and being in trouble again. We didn't understand, then, what I do now. They weren't being mean to us or withholding food out of anger. They were afraid of their low stocks. There wasn't enough food left, so they kept us on strict rations, hoping for a solution in the future.

A future I can fix.

"Don't you see?" I ask her. "I can fix all of it! I can... save them. I'll set the world right. No child will starve again. No child will be bullied. They won't be able to take him away from me!"

My tears fall so fast my vision is a blur. She's a white-golden blur. I wipe my arm across my eyes drying them furiously.

Rowan signs rapidly.

No. she shakes her head. *No. This is not you. You would be like her?*

Pain stabs through my heart as my breath catches in my throat.

"NO!" I yell. "How could you... compare us?"

Ronan nods emphatically and signs again. I thought I'd misread her signs, but she repeats them again.

"No," I shake my head. "I'm not her."

No, you can be better, she signs. *This is the same. Twisting free will.*

And just like that, I let it go.

Rowan, all the furniture, and the guys drop to the ground. Grunts of surprise and pain echo around the office space as I fall painfully to my knees in front of her, sobbing.

Rowan wraps her arms around me and pulls me into her lap. She runs her fingers through my hair as the floodgates holding back my grief break open. A moment later, my dad is there too, hugging me from the other side.

I can't stop it. Even winning, I'm going to lose. The one thing I wanted, and I'm going to lose that too. It hurts. It hurts so bad, but I know, no matter how bad it feels. I know.

I can't save him.

CHAPTER FORTY

AVIELLA

I'm numb.

Rowan helps me up, and the guys gather around, getting a chair and making sure I'm sitting in it. Sitting with my arms around my legs, head hanging low. The weight of duty is crushing. I can't go on, can't even lift my head. Meet eyes? Yeah, no.

Hands touch and retreat. They hug me, whisper platitudes, but all of it is happening to someone else. All I can see is my failure.

If I can't save my dad, what's the point?

I want to be angry. I want to rage, to hate, to unleash righteous fury, but even that is gone. Taken away, because it's not only futile, it's wrong.

I don't know how long I sit, feeling sorry for myself, when my dad kneels in front of me and tugs my head up by cupping my chin with his rough hand and forcing me to look at him. He smiles and it lights up his whole face, but behind that life, his impending doom is clear. It's written in the ashen color of his skin, the dullness of his aura, and there's nothing I can do.

"Aviella," he says softly.

"Daddy," I say, tears welling.

He wipes away the first tear to fall then puts his hand on the back of my head and rests his forehead against mine.

"My sweet, darling girl," he says. "I know this is hard. No one here blames you."

"I can't..." the rest of my words won't make it past the lump in my throat.

"You can," he whispers. "You can."

Tears drop off my nose, staining my jeans. He holds my head as we sit in silence. I can't speak and maybe he can't either. How can he be so calm? Why isn't he raging too?

"It's not fair, damn it," I sob.

"No," he agrees. "It's not. Life rarely is."

"I can... I can fix it," I whisper.

"No," he says. "Don't do that."

He isn't saying I can't, he's telling me not to.

"Why?" I ask. "Why not? What is the point of all this power if I can't fix this?"

"Because you're not here to fix it *for* us," he says. "My beautiful girl, I'm sorry, but that's the crux of it. You can't be the one responsible for everyone else."

"Then what?" I choke. "What am I supposed to do?"

"Fight her," he says. "Fight her and win."

"To what end?" I ask, looking up for the first time as anger rises pushing aside the sadness. "What is the damn point?"

Dad rises to his feet, but he's weak and stumbles as he does. He catches himself on a tumbled-over chair before I can rise to catch him. Rowan moves beside him, a soft, warm look on her face. The guys gather around, forming a semi-circle around us.

I look at each of them in turn. Tynan, Alaric, Shen, Silas,

Gavin, Ronan, and on the other side of my dad, Killian and Luca, then at last my eyes fall on Efram. His smile is wan, he's pale too, but okay. He's alive, they didn't hurt him in any obvious way.

My dad takes a step ahead of the semi-circle and for the first time I'm looking at all of them at the same time. Beside Efram there's an emptiness where something should be. No, not something, someone. That's where Casmir fits. He belongs there, and I know it, but part of me still wants to destroy him. If he hadn't done whatever he did to my dad, none of this would be happening.

"The point," my dad says, holding his hands up. "Is for you to show the way."

"What way?" I snap. "Isn't that what's been done? Why will it be different this time? How many times in history has someone said, here's a better way?"

Dad nods and so do the others. The dragons exchange a knowing look that pulls my attention to them.

"What do you know?" I ask.

"Aviella," Tynan says, his voice cool and calm, every bit under control. "We know this has been done before, yes. You know this too. The Leviathan has named you thrice-born."

"So?" I ask. "What does that even mean?"

"We're entering the fourth age," Silas answers. "You're the gateway, Aviella."

My dad nods, smiling. "You, my love, will set the stage for the next age."

I shake my head as my stomach flip flops and my limbs feel weak. It's too much.

"I'm... no one. I'm an orphan," I say, inhaling deeply. Facing the truth of it all makes a shiver run down my spine. "I'm scared."

"Of course you are," Tynan says.

"Only an idiot wouldn't be," Shen says.

"You're not a fool," Alaric agrees.

People enter the room. All the Innocents that the mages have gathered throughout their long history. Pouring into the room and joining us, forming into lines behind the semi-circle of my Chosen ones.

It's an army. The magic in the room swells until it's too much for the space and the walls themselves push back as the ambient magic gathering creates more area for itself. They silently watch. Every one of them looking to me for hope, leadership, each of them ready to fight. Their magic calls to mine and instinctively I respond. Reaching out with magic to touch theirs.

Power rushes in, but this time it's different. Cool and controlled, not mingling and becoming one with mine like it does with my Chosen. I'm not taking from them, I'm accepting. They're each here of their own accord. No one is giving anything they haven't decided to give, up to and including their life for the cause.

The cause of setting the world on a new path. My dad walks closer, cupping my face between his hands the same way he did when I was a little girl. He leans over and kisses my forehead.

It's warm where his lips touch my head, leaving the spot tingling.

"I love you," he says. "Your mother loves you. You can do this."

"I…" my thoughts spin away, and then a deep calm washes over.

Certainty fills me and I don't bother trying to finish the old thought. I look at the assembled army. They're looking to me and ready to fight.

I know the odds against us. A legion of undead, an army of demons, and a monster at their head who's more than a match for anything we've thrown at her so far. Statistically, we can't win.

Screw the statistics. It's on us, and we'll make our own luck.

"We're going to war!" I yell, throwing a fist into the air.

Resounding cheers meet my declaration.

CHAPTER FORTY-ONE

RAFE

"You'd think," I say, struggling to catch my breath. "That they'd run out of demons for us to slaughter."

Every muscle screams. It's all I can do to keep my sword swinging. The unending hordes of hell was always a nebulous concept, but now it's all too real. Nate's breathing is heavy too, heaving against my back as he steps forward to dispatch yet another demonic form. As fast as we kill them, two more take their place.

"You... have... always... talked too much," Nate pants.

"You... love it," I pant.

"No," he disagrees. "I don't."

Blood runs down my limbs, streaming from dozens of cuts. Rage pulses in time with my heart. Three blades come in at once. I block two, the third pierces my side and I cry out in surprise and pain.

Nate's blade appears above me, taking the heads off all three attackers, but then his scream echoes mine.

He slumps onto my shoulder. Bracing myself, I turn into him wrapping my arms around his chest. His breath hitches, and blood is flecking his lips. Time stops, leaving the two of us in a last, final instant.

"Don't die," I order.

He smiles then coughs wetly. "Too... late."

"Story of our lives," I say, tears swelling in my eyes.

He touches my face with the tips of his fingers.

"I'm sorry," he says.

"For what?" I ask.

"For not following you," he says. "All those years ago."

"No, don't be," I shake my head.

"We could have—"

A deafening trumpet sounds, echoing back and forth, redoubling over itself, cutting off the rest of his words. My heart sinks as I look to see what fresh hell is about to descend on us. Magic rushes over my skin leaving a tingle in its wake. When I look up, my heart leaps and I grip Nate tighter, turning him to see.

It's impossible. It can't be, but there she is.

Aviella floats in the sky a dozen feet away surrounded by a brilliant white light. The demonic hordes surrounding us scream, a battle cry or the sound of terror, I'm not sure, but it doesn't matter.

A tear floats in the sky behind her and the dragons emerge, but that's not all. Everyone is stepping through the tear. Silas, the mages, even Efram walks out onto the field of battle and behind them an army of the Innocents. All of them dressed in pure white, each of them a brilliant sparkling diamond in my magic sight.

"Nate," I say. "We're going to live."

"She's beautiful," he exhales then collapses into my arms.

CHAPTER FORTY-TWO

AVIELLA

*P*ower flows through and around me like a river that I'm immersing myself in. Exhilaration leaves my skin tingling. A sweep of my hand and the demons tumble away, creating a clearing for my army to emerge.

"There!" I yell, pointing to Rafe and Nate.

This is the test. Our first time going on the offense. Every breath I take sends a thrilling tingle down my spine as we charge the hordes of monsters. The clearing I created on entry doesn't reach my boys but it's close.

Tynan, Shen, and Alaric stand beside me in a half-dragon, half-human form. Their faces are draconic, but their bodies are still men except for the leathery wings sprouting from their backs. As one they inhale deeply, then breathe flames across the monsters blocking our way forward.

We march ahead with them clearing the path. The magical energy surging through my body is so much I'm not walking on the ground but three inches over it. A cushion of air beneath my feet which allows me to step easily over the rocky, blood-covered terrain.

Monstrous demons leap towards us, but I sweep those

who get close away with a flick of my fingers and an instant's thought. It's barely straining for me to handle them. The three dragons draw swords, the mages and Silas cover my flanks and rear while Efram walks at my side. I'm going to get my boys out of this mess.

The dragons' work is akin to music. A swelling orchestral movement as they step, duck, whirl, blades singing through the air like the soaring musical notes that lead to the crescendo. Their motion climaxes when the horde parts and Rafe is before us.

He's on his knees, using his body to cover Nate, who lies in his lap. My Chosen and the Innocents form a circle around me as I kneel next to them. Rafe looks up, blood and tears stain his face, but he grins.

"About time," he says, laughing. "I was starting to think maybe you'd given up on us."

"Never," I say.

Nate's life force is weak, flickering in my magical sight. I lay two fingers on his dirty face and flow magic into him. The strain eases and his breathing evens out. I keep flowing, witnessing the blood running from his many wounds slowing, then the open holes knitting back together.

His eyes open and he grabs me by the back of my head, jerking me down. Our lips meet and magic flares around us in this stolen moment of passion. Power flows from me into him, where it redoubles and comes back.

He breaks the kiss, pushing me back. He puts a hand on Rafe's face then rises up to stand on his own. Rafe and I stand up, but Rafe stumbles, putting a hand on his side. Blood pools at his feet from his own wounds, so I put my hands on his shoulders and heal him as well.

The Innocents and Chosen fight around us, the unending hordes driven into a frenzy at our arrival and the loss of their certain victory.

"Avi," Tynan says over his shoulder. "We should leave. Now."

He ducks a massive claw then swings his sword and the arm behind that claw drops between him and Alaric.

Nodding I close my eyes and will a portal to open. Magic pours out, swirling, creating a sparking ring that slowly grows. I pour more power into it until my own reserves are spent. I draw on my connection to my Chosen and pull from them to fuel the portal. Healing Rafe and Nate took more of my power than I expected. The portal grows until it's a rift in space surrounded by crackling magical energy.

"Now!" I yell directing my attention to the Innocents first.

Rowan looks over her shoulder and nods. A scream catches in my throat as I a sword swings towards her. She's distracted and doesn't see it, but then she seems to sense it before the sound leaves my throat. She gestures and the sword bounces off of a magical shield she forms, stopping an inch from her face.

She stumbles backwards as the demons and undead press in. Two of the Innocents grab her arms and drag her through the portal.

"Take him," I order Rafe, pointing at Nate.

He doesn't hesitate, hooking Nate's arm over his shoulders he drags him through the portal. Turning my back on the portal, I confront the army arrayed against us. There are thousands if not hundreds of thousands of undead, demons, and other Shadow-created monsters.

It's too many to fight head to head. My heart sinks as I take it in. We'll never win. All the talk of my destiny, of it being on me to usher in a new age, how can I? This is what I have to beat? An unending army of darkness that keeps on coming. It's impossible.

As doubt worms its way through my thoughts, the portal behind me flickers. It's not fair. This is too much to ask of anyone, but then what choice do we have? Do I consign all those that will come after to live in darkness and damnation?

My lips tingle with the memory of Nate's kiss, and I know. The way forward is one of love. One of forgiveness. Maybe we won't have to beat the army itself. There might be another way. Touching my lips, I nod as a nebulous idea takes shape.

"Get out of here," I order.

Willing magic into a shield around me, I press out and it pushes the hordes back. They beat against it, forcing me to keep flowing power into it. The Chosen see the opportunity and retreat through the portal.

Tyan stops next to me and offers his hand. I take it and together we leap through, the shield I created collapsing behind us. The demonic horde howls and surges forward. The portal snaps closed behind us, and several limbs fall to the ground, cut off by its closing.

"Close," Tynan says, pulling me into a tight embrace.

"Yeah," I say, acutely aware that everyone is watching us.

My cheeks warm at the attention, both his and the onlookers. Tynan's arousal is more than obvious as it digs into my belly. His volatile magic swirls around us, promising pleasures, but my attention is elsewhere.

Rising onto my toes I kiss him, and the passion does rise, but now is not the time. We have work to do. Lowering myself, I turn and face those assembled.

They're dirty, stained with gore and blood. I sense their fears and doubts, worming their way through the magical energy surrounding us. Tynan steps aside joining them.

I know it's time to be a big damn hero, and I have a glimmer of an idea, but right now it feels like I'm standing on a precipice. The unknown lies before me, uncomfortable and scary. Chewing on my lower lip, I look at them.

My Chosen are in front of the crowd, behind them are

the Innocents. Rowan stands next to Efram, smiling as she nods encouragingly. Silas is supporting my dad whose eyes shine brightly with unshed tears, but there's no mistaking the pride beaming from him.

Still, they're scared. So am I. Am I really going to do this? Is this what my path has really led to? Leading an army, me. An orphan.

Except I'm not, not any longer. My dad is right there. My dad, who always told me I was special, despite the fact I thought I was cursed.

And my boys. Silas, Tynan, Alaric, Shen, Gavin, Ronan, Killian, Luca, Efram, Rafe, and Nate. Each of them with love in their eyes but more flowing towards me. I'm connected to each of them and they're connected to me.

I'm standing on the precipice, but I'm not alone. Not any longer.

Rowan walks closer, stopping right in front of me. She touches my face, her brilliant smile lighting up my entire world. Her soft hands cup my cheeks and she nods. I pull her into an embrace. She crushes me back as I crush her against me.

My one friend. No, my first friend, but not my one friend. Opening my blurry eyes and looking past her at all those assembled, every one of them is a friend. We are the creators, founders of a new age. We are all that stands between the next world and the unending darkness threatening to consume it.

We're all there is and we're enough. We have to be, but more than that. I'm their leader.

"It's time to be a big damn hero," I say softly into Rowan's ear.

She grips me tighter and nods.

CHAPTER FORTY-THREE

CASMIR

"You stupid, stupid dragon," she hisses. "I thought you, of all of them, would know better."

I close my eyes and focus my thoughts. Shadows close around us as she sidles closer and closer. Rubbing her perfect body against me. She's trying to be enticing, using the beauty of her flesh as temptation.

It's never been about that. What use do I have for the perfection of her form? I could not care less for the flesh. I'm only interested in and only have ever been interested in the experiment. The experiment that has now proven itself a failure.

"I've done my part," I say, stepping back from her. "We are done."

"Done?" she purrs. "No, Casmir. We have yet to begin. All that has come before is nothing. This time the balance will be shifted fully to my favor. The grand experiment of free will is over."

"So you seem to think," I say.

"Do you see something different?" she asks. "The Divine itself has to acknowledge where it has led. That army following my will? It's not my creation, it's man's! They made their own demise. I merely offered them an opportunity to use it. They decided to do it."

"Some of them did," I agree.

"The exception proves the rule," she says, pressing closer yet again.

"No," I say. "It does not."

"Fool!" she hisses, pushing me.

Her face shimmers, revealing the truth. Mistress of lies and deception. I know her well, but I've been blind to the truth. Now my eyes are clear, and as I look at her, the reality of all I've done weighs heavily on my mind.

"Yes," I agree. "I've been a fool."

A path of destruction lies in my wake. I'm every bit the monster she is. I'm worse, for I had a choice. I've done evil for evil's sake. This is where my path has led me, and now I find there's no one else to blame but myself.

I can't help but think of Aviella. The hurt in her eyes when she saw her father. She didn't care how much pain I inflicted on her, the only time I saw her care was when I hurt others. She is selfless, caring for those around her more than herself.

She has an integrity that is fascinating. Caring more about her own moral code than her life. Every experiment I conducted with her, she never did the expected. She didn't cave to the pain, or even the threat of loss.

Unlike what Lucy is willing to accept, I see a truth I've missed in all my long existence. The power of free will does not mean that destruction and darkness is inevitable. Man can rise above the baseness of his nature and aspire to something greater.

It changes everything.

It means I was wrong.

This game is over. Lucy stares, eyes wide, her form shimmering as she struggles to control her temper. My own destiny is clear, and it's time to pay for my sins.

"Have you gone mad?" she asks, her voice dropping lower to become almost guttural.

Smiling, I shift to my true form. Breaking through the ceiling, dust and debris falling around us as she also shifts. Inhaling deeply, I'm still grinning. I'm free, and for the first time in my long memory, I'm making my own choices without concern for what the outcome will be. I'm acting on impulse, and I know in this moment my impulse is good.

Fire explodes as I exhale, burning Lucy in her true demonic form. Shadows swirl forming a shield around her, and the fire parts around it without causing harm. A sword of flame and shadow forms in her hand. In her other hand, a burning whip.

The battle is engaged. Payment for my sins has come due, and I will pay the price.

CHAPTER FORTY-FOUR

AVIELLA

"We should let him burn," Tynan says. "I gave him his chance, and he turned it down."

"The fourth Horseman joining us would be a powerful ally," Gavin says.

"He was behind the False Prophet. I say we let him burn," Luca says, shaking his head.

The arguing continues, but it doesn't matter. Efram is staring, so I look to him. He smiles, a pale imitation of himself. Casmir hurt him, badly, and I'm curious as to his thoughts. It's not going to change my mind. I know the way forward. But still, I want to know.

By weaving between the arguing men, I make my way to his side. When I get close to him, the easy comfort between us takes over, despite all that he and I have both been through.

"Hey," he says softly.

"Hi," I say, hesitating.

I want to say more, but of all the boys, I hurt him the most. He gave up the most for me. I can't deny it, but more than that, I don't know what to say. Sorry you had to be an outcast? Hope they didn't treat you too badly?

There are no words, really, what are words but a pale attempt to express thought? Sometimes the thought and the emotions wound up in it are just too complex for them. Staring into his eyes, my heart pounding in my throat, blood rushing in my ears, trembling with fear or anticipation or both. Words fail.

Magic, though, magic responds. It curls around the two of us, and the noise becomes a murmur. The world drops away, and there is only the two of us. He doesn't hold back. Despite all I've put him through, while they would say he betrayed me, I know the truth. I betrayed him. I gave him up to suffer because I couldn't choose one.

I paid a price, but so did he. I'm not sure which one of us had it worse. Sure, I died, but that was it. I was dead, and in death there was a peace that Efram didn't know. He suffered, not only in knowing what I'd had him do, but by being outcast from our circle. The boys couldn't know, and he never betrayed that trust.

It haunts him. I see it and I feel it. The pain and wariness echoes in his magical aura. He doesn't mingle with the guys like he used to, and they don't include him. It's all different now, and that's too bad. We had something special.

"Don't," he says, shaking his head.

"Don't?" I ask, confused.

"Don't be sorry. Don't. Don't say it and don't feel it," he says.

"Efram, I—"

"No," he cuts me off putting a finger to my lips. "I did what had to be done."

Shutting my mouth, I nod. He takes his finger away but doesn't move his gaze from mine. Emotions and thoughts too complex pass between us and in the end, we understand one another. The way he always has. He gets me in ways none of the others ever will.

He was there at the first, when this started, and he's here with me at the end. I can't ask for any more than that.

"Thank you," I say, letting it all go.

He smiles, and this time it's reminiscent of his old self. The man I fell for what seems like an age ago. This is my Efram.

"We need to save him," he says, changing the subject.

"We do," I agree.

"Why let them argue?" he asks.

"Because it makes them feel good," I smile. "They'll figure it out, sooner or later."

"Do we have a later?" he asks, arching an eyebrow.

"No," I sigh. "We really don't."

He nods and I move closer, putting my arm around his waist. He rests his arm on my shoulders, and we watch them continue the debate, but he's right. There's no more time to waste. I'm about to say something when the room rumbles. Dust drifts from the ceiling and several of the Innocents yelp in surprise.

"Harrumph, harrumph, thrice-born," a voice so deep it rattles my bones calls. "Time, it is, time it is, thrice-born."

Leave it to the Leviathan to make such an entrance, even if he hasn't bothered to show up physically. His voice echoes, bouncing off the walls from the shimmering outline of his form. He has the appearance of the head of a whale, emerging from the far wall, dark circling shadows for eyes stare, cold and filled with depths I'll never comprehend. All other eyes turn to me, falling silent in the presence of the elder creature.

"We're going to save him," I say. Tynan steps forward and opens his mouth to protest but I cut him off with a single finger. "No, we are and that's it."

I don't bother waiting for more debate. Magic surges through the room as I draw magic from my Eleven. A portal forms next to the wall closest to me. In moments, it opens and lets us see into Casmir's bunker. Knowing where it is located is allowing me to bypass its protections.

The portal is a window onto a battle. Casmir is fully in his dragon form, standing at least three stories tall as he rears his scintillating green neck back, spreads his leather wings and screeches. He exhales a gaseous green cloud towards his opponent. His opponent is every bit as tall as him but humanoid. Red, burned skin covered by a loose robe, black bat wings flapping in the air, massive horns rising from her temples.

It's her. My opponent. The Mistress of Shadow, Controller of the Dark, the Devil herself. This is the first time I've seen her in what I assume is her native appearance. She may once have been beautiful—the stories say she was the most beautiful of them all—but her form reflects the monster that she is now.

She flaps her wings pushing the gas cloud back towards Casmir but some of it drifts through my open portal. Those closest to the opening scream as it touches them and scramble away, running into each other. The scent of burning flesh fills the air, turning my stomach.

Damn it. Willing magic I place a shield around the cloud and push it back to the open portal. Containing most of it, I reach my thoughts to Casmir.

Come, I call.

This is my fate, Casmir says. *Leave.*

"Not happening," I say, pulling more magic from those around me until I'm brimming with power.

Tynan, Alaric, and Shen share a look and Tynan charges through the portal. As they pass through, they shift to their dragon forms. Now the devil faces four enraged dragons, and the tide of the battle changes. She doesn't back down. Holding her massive sword defensively in front of herself, a smile creeps across her face.

"Oh boys," she laughs. "You think you're ready for me?"

Cold ice balls in my stomach sending icy chills through my limbs. Her confidence is terrifying. Four Horsemen of the Apocalypse, and she doesn't blink an eye, not a hint of fear. She knows something or has some kind of a plan. She has to, but what is it?

The dragons attack. It's beautiful, takes my breath away watching them. It's more perfect than a ballet. The way they move together, in perfect coordination is beyond words. They're never in one another's way. Weaving their attacks, retreats, feints and dodges as if they're one mind with four bodies.

It's an awe-inspiring display of prowess, but they hardly hurt her, a few scratches that barely draw blood. She exudes power and strength, defending against the four dragons as easily as I would bat away flies.

My stomach sinks and my mouth is dry. How am I supposed to beat her? As she holds the four of them at bay, her eyes lock onto me, staring through the portal I created. A smile spreads across her face.

"Aviella," she says, casually, for all the world as if we're sitting down to tea. "How good to see you."

My stomach flips and flops, but it's not only her eyes on me. My men are watching and what's more, the Innocents are watching too. Their fear is palpable. I can taste it on my tongue, an acrid flavor like I've inhaled smoke.

I clench my teeth and force my stomach to be still. Nodding to her, I smile as well. I'm not going to let her see a hint of fear. More, I'm not going to let those around me see it. She's powerful, so what? Fate is on my side.

Or so I keep being told, and if not, what am I going to do?

If not, I'll die again. Been there, done that, and knowing that brings a comfort of its own. Coming back to this world was much harder than being dead.

I laugh.

I don't mean to, but it slips out and once it starts, I can't stop it. I laugh more and shake my head. I'm laughing so hard tears form in my eyes. Her eyes widen, and she misses blocking an attack from Shen.

Blood pours out of three long lines on her side where his claws dug deep. She roars, partly in pain, but it sounds more like anger.

"Why are you laughing!" she yells, swinging her sword in a broad arc and forcing the dragons to dodge back.

"You…" I try to explain, but another gale of laughter cuts off my ability to speak.

The dragons use her distraction and press the advantage. She moves her sword blindingly fast, but the dragons are every bit as fast. Tynan moves in under her strike and catches her leg in his teeth. He clamps down, shaking her like a rag doll.

She growls, a deep demonic sound that causes cold chills to race across my skin. Those around me shudder, and some drop to their knees at the sound, pulling on their own magic defensively.

She slams the flat of her blade onto Tynan's head, hard enough that he lets go, yelping in pain. If it hadn't been an awkward swing and the edge had hit, he might have lost his head.

"Get out of there!" I scream, fear stopping the laughter.

Shen, Alaric and Casmir grab Tynan and drag him towards the portal. She doesn't follow. Her leg looks a mess, but it's already healing, as are the other wounds the dragons inflicted. Sword held before her, she stares through the portal, eyes on me.

"This isn't over," she says, speaking through a catlike smile. "Don't count a victory before it's complete."

Tynan surges forward, breaking free of his brothers' grip. Magic is a maelstrom around him as he unleashes his fury on her.

Her sword flashes up defensively and the magical storm parts around it, doing no more than ruffling her hair.

"Tynan, no!" I yell. "It's not time, not yet."

He glares at her then retreats through the portal with his brothers. She and I stare at one another until she nods.

"Soon," she says, a portal opening behind her too.

She steps back through her own portal and it closes as I let the portal I created go too. My heart races and my knees feel weak. I can't let those around me see I'm shaken. I lock my knees and smile, but Efram senses my distress and puts an arm around my waist.

"That is our enemy," I say, letting some of my weight settle onto Efram gratefully.

A murmur runs through the room and I feel their fear. They're not dumb, fear is the proper response. She stood against four dragons, and they barely scratched her.

"How..." someone says, and others mutter similar concerns, but no one speaks up directly.

They're scared and it hits me. This is the moment. I'm standing at a turning point again. My actions, right now, what I do and say to them will directly affect what comes next. It's a gargantuan responsibility that lies on my shoulders alone.

Aviella, my mother's voice whispers in my thoughts as warmth suffuses my body, and I'm reminded of the soft golden glow that I felt in her touch.

"Love," I whisper then certainty fills me, and I say it louder. "Love!"

"Avi, what are you talking about?" Efram asks, speaking softly so as not to be heard.

All eyes are on me now. They're looking to me for certainty, to overcome their own fears, and despair.

"We win with love!" I say and laugh out loud. "It's simple, don't you see?"

They look at each other, then Rowan steps in front of the crowd. She holds her hands over her heart and then motions towards me with a big smile. She turns to face the group and repeats the gesture, then mimes giving a hug.

"So you're saying we're supposed to give her a big hug?" a skeptical voice asks.

"No, not exactly," I say, standing straight and taking my weight off of Efram. "Her weakness is love, that's what I'm saying.

"She can't do it! Love is a… choice. You choose who you love. It's free will. You can choose to love or not to love. It may not seem like it, but you can! That is the choice we have to make. Do we love, or do we succumb to hate and despair?"

Silas has a half smile on his face as he nods. The mages whisper one to another, but Luca is nodding his agreement. The dragons…. Tynan stares then strides to me with loud steps clicking on the floor.

I'm not sure what to expect. Butterflies dance in my stomach at his approach. His hands grab my waist, and he sweeps me off of my feet as his lips press to mine. Tingling fires ignite throughout my body, racing up and down my limbs.

He crushes me to him tightly, stealing the air from my lungs into his kiss. Our magic engulfs us, swelling like an incoming tide rushing to shore. I wrap my arms around his neck and my legs on his waist. His hands run through my hair and I lose myself for only a moment, but it's a moment of pure bliss.

His heart pounds against my chest. Thundering a rhythm that tells the depths of his feelings. My lungs burn, screaming for air but still I don't break this kiss. This moment in time with him. Tynan is a creature of fiery passions, anger to lust, but this is the first time he's opened up the true depths of his ability to love.

I bask in its warmth. Surround myself with him, physically and magically. We all know the odds we're up against. The deck is stacked against us, but one thing I'm certain of is: this is the way out.

Love.

Not hate, not war, not violence, nothing more and nothing less than love.

My certainty grows as our kiss continues. Dimly I'm aware of more hands touching, feather light touches all across my body but still my kiss with Tynan goes. All of my men open the floodgates, and each of them join their magic into the flows between Tynan and me.

The magical channels swell as each man flows his magic towards me and on the astral plane, I see it all happening, but I'm separate from it. Guiding and controlling, a level of awareness I've never been able to achieve.

Efram's magic is first, he stands to one side watching, but the flow of power is gray mottled black, the death magic that he wields. Luca, Gavin, Killian and Ronan are only a moment behind Efram.

Their magic is white with hints of red streaks. Exhilarating, full of purpose and uniquely them, as each person's magic is. They've dedicated themselves to their purpose since the Crusades, collecting and saving the Innocent, preparing them for the time that has come upon us.

The mages press in, touching my body with light strokes, affirming their connection. As each man's power flows into me I take it in and let it flow through my own magical channels. My magic joins and it becomes our magic. More than the sum of each of its parts.

As it I connect with each of them, the magic flows back out and into them. We're becoming a conduit, a circular loop. As the magic runs through, it grows.

Alaric and Shen flank Tynan, kissing my cheeks, stroking my sides. Their magic joins the flows. Alaric's magic is reds and blues, protectively warming. Shen's magic is pale and throbbing, but cool, almost cold. It blends perfectly with Alaric's mixing into me and flowing through.

Nate is next to Rafe and joins in next. He touches my hair and it sends tingles running down my neck and spine. His magic is that of the Divine, golden light pouring in as he joins the flows connecting all of us.

Rafe grins lasciviously watching. Instead of touching me he grabs Nate's face, forces his head around to him roughly and kisses him. As he does his infernal magic flows through Nate and into me with the others.

Seeing Rafe do that makes me hotter than I already was. I want so much more than this kiss. I grind my hips against Tynan's middle, feeling his erection and needing to be filled. I'm not complete though. One is missing.

Breaking the kiss at last, I look past Tynan's shoulder to Casmir. He stands stiffly, arms crossed over his chest, observing but keeping himself closed off.

"Cas," I say.

A frown flickers on his lips. "Do not call me that, I am Casmir."

Touching his face, I trail my fingers along his jaw and down his neck.

"Okay," I say. My hand is on his chest, his heart pounds hard and I watch him swallow. He is struggling to remain in control. "You're free."

He isn't looking at me. Instead he's staring at Tynan.

Something is going on between the dragons that I'm not sure I understand. There are obviously old wounds, but I don't have time for this. She's moving against us, right now. The Shadow is poised to take this world and set the next age to a path of darkness like nothing that has ever been.

"I am free," he says. "But that does not erase history. Or change what I have done."

"No," I agree. "It doesn't release any of us from the burden of what we've done. It does give us a chance though. A chance to make amends, an opportunity to set things right."

As I talk to him, I wrap my magic around him, but his magic is a wall refusing to join with mine. The desire is there, his shield throbs and wavers with it, but he's holding fast. The emptiness in my soul aches and I know he's the final piece. The one that will pull everything into place.

"What if we've done too much?" he says, his voice so quiet I barely hear him.

That gives me pause, thrusting a hard, sharp knife of doubt into my heart. What he did to my dad is unforgiveable alone, and I know that's not all he did. Forgiving him for that was the hardest thing for me to come to terms with. I know the other guys are having a hard time finding it in their hearts to forgive as well.

How do I do it? I can't demand it of them if I myself do not forgive him in full. I can't harbor resentment or anger at what he did. If I do, then I'm a liar and a hypocrite.

"Forgiveness is not always easy," I say, biting my lip as I work out what I want to say. "And it's on both sides."

"Both sides?" Casmir asks.

Everyone's eyes bore into me and the weight of their stares gives me pause. I'm right, I know it with the same certainty I know Casmir is the twelfth. He's the final key. Maybe this right here is the piece I have to figure out.

"Yes…" I say, trailing off, still thinking it through. "You've hurt a lot of people. It's not easy for them to forgive, but you can earn forgiveness."

"Even I?" he asks.

"Yes," I say, certain as it all clicks into place and I see it clearly. "You've betrayed those you love. They're hurting, angry, wanting to lash out, and that's okay. You have to make it up to them, all of those you've hurt.

"Dedicate your life, your mind, and your work to making the world a better place. If you truly repent of the evil you've done, then you'll need to make up the damages you've caused."

I grasp his face between my hands and force him to look down at me. His breath catches as our eyes lock and my heart stills. Magic makes my hands glow as I hold his face. Rising on my toes, I kiss him, giving him my forgiveness.

He stiffens, not returning the kiss. I don't let him stop me. He will accept my forgiveness if I keep flowing it to him. Magic swirls as cracks form in the barrier he's formed to shut himself off. My magic flows through those cracks, invading him, and then it shatters. He gives himself to my kiss, his arms wrapping around my waist and lifting me up into him.

We kiss. It's magical in and of itself, much less the actual magic swirling around us. Our magical energies twist and turn until they meld, becoming one as our bodies press together. He gives himself over to my insistent need.

At last we break apart. The air around us is charged with sexual and magical tension. He stares into my eyes, his deep emerald eyes alight with desire tempered by his deep intelligence. I don't know how long this moment will go on, but I'm warmed by his gaze, the depths of his feelings engulf me and as we stare the walls he holds in place come down.

"I don't know if that is possible," he says.

"It is," I say. "If we win."

He nods and the other men close around us. Breaking his gaze at last, I step beside him and face the group. Tynan stares at Casmir, then nods his agreement and the tension in the room lessens.

"This is it," I announce, raising my voice to be heard by all present. "We've seen the face of the Shadow. We know what we face, and the odds are not in our favor. Her army is legion, and her own power is obviously beyond anything we've faced or considered.

But we're fighting for a new world. A world filled with reason, forgiveness, and most of all, love. True, deep love where mankind is truly free to reach new heights. A world without criminality, without insanity, and without war.

It's on us. We Chosen few who will stand against the encroaching darkness. We will create our new world, but only if we win. Are you with me?"

The ringing cheers echo off the walls at deafening decibels. The Innocents and my Chosen Twelve exclaim their victories before we've even begun. I flow magic through each of them bolstering their own strength and they return it to me tenfold.

"Tomorrow," I say. "We make our final stand."

Gavin and Killian step forward and bark orders to begin the preparations. All of my men go to work except Casmir. He stays by my side watching. That's good, though, I've got other plans for him. There's a final step that needs to happen before tomorrow.

Taking his hand in mine I lead him away to my room.

CHAPTER FORTY-FIVE

AVIELLA

*T*he door closes behind us as I turn into him. He's stiff and almost cold, but behind it I sense the truth is he's uncertain. Resting my hands on his chest I rise up and kiss him again. This is a soft, reassuring kiss.

Lowering myself flat I take his hands and pull him into the room. He follows, obedient, but not taking the lead. Holding himself back still. Silence stretches between us as we stand, and I wait. His thoughts are spinning behind his beautiful green eyes, but he doesn't speak for a long time.

"Aviella," he says, shaking his head. "I cannot."

He drops my hands and starts to turn, but I grab his shoulder and turn him back to me.

"You don't get out of this that easy," I say.

His eyes burn with a green fire, flashing brightly and for an instant there is warmth and rage in them. His dragon nature burning through his cold façade. He opens his mouth to argue further, but the stony façade forms on his face as he does.

I want him angry. I want him to let go, and this isn't going to do. Taking a step back I slap him with all I've got, right across his face. Red marks outline my handprint on his cheek. His eyes widen and the rage burns through.

"You dare!" he exclaims, stepping forward, his hands balling into fists.

"That was for my father," I say, and he stops dead in his tracks.

He touches the mark on his face, thoughtful, then nods. "I deserve that."

"Yeah," I say, stepping closer again. I rise up and kiss where I left the mark, soothing the sting. "But you also deserve this."

"You are contradiction in all its forms," he says.

"Maybe," I say. "But what matters now is you have to forgive yourself. Be willing to own what you've done, yes, but forgive yourself for it. I need you, Casmir."

"Why?" he asks, shaking his head. "Why do I deserve anything?"

"Truth?" I ask. "I don't know. You're the one, I know it. You feel it too, don't you?"

"Yes," he says, nodding slowly. "But what is this?'

"Fate. Love. Divine Intervention?" I shrug. "I don't know. I know, though, you're the last one. The final piece, and that without you we'll lose."

He shakes his head. "This is… illogical."

Rolling my eyes, I grab his face in my hands.

"What does logic have to do with anything?" I yell. "Seriously. You're all logic this, logic that, grand experiment, blah blah! I'm offering you a way out of the trap of your past, but more than that, I'm forgiving you.

"You're an asshole, you know that? Seriously. After all you've done, I should crush you, but no, I can't, because I need you, you son of a bitch!"

"You would try," he says, anger flashing in his eyes.

"You think?" I say, pulling magic around and loose objects in the room rise into the air in response to the swelling power. "Bring it bitch."

He growls, his magic rising in response to mine.

"You dare—"

"Dare?" I taunt him further. "Oh yeah, I dare you. I dare you to man up. Own your shit and let's do this."

He grabs me and pulls me forward, smashing my body against his. I grab his hard cock through his pants. His eyes widen at the unexpected move but his cock throbs in my hand even through the cloth.

He grabs my ass, rough, jerking me up, and I wrap my legs around his waist, and then our mouths smash together. His tongue forces its way into my mouth. I knot my hands in his hair, making him stay close.

Our tongues dance and I moan into the kiss. He grabs my tits with one hand, roughly fondling them through my shirt.

I grab the waistband of his pants, but I can't wait. Fueling my strength with magic, I rip the pants, and they drop to his ankles. His cock leaps to my hand and I grasp its girth, stroking. He groans into the kiss, his hips thrusting back and forth in reaction.

He grabs my hair forcing my head back and kisses his way down my neck. One handed he rips my shirt down the front letting my breasts drop free. He makes his way to them and roughly tongues my nipples.

They're so hard it hurts, and his rough tongue sends shockwaves of pleasure throughout my body. Magic pulses deep inside, but it's not breaking free. A dam holds me back from breaking through to the other side. A wall or something, and I'm slamming against it as we explore each other's bodies.

We struggle against each other, pulling, tugging, fighting but never breaking apart as we rip and tear free of our clothing. Ages of pent-up passion rage within him, and I want it all. I need it, need him to fill me, to give to me all that he's held back for millennia.

He spins us around and I drop my legs long enough to let my pants slide off. He grabs my hips and lifts me up and up until my legs hook over his shoulders. His tongue-laps at my pussy as he holds me aloft effortlessly.

Pleasure builds towards a climax so hard and fast I can hardly believe it. Still the barrier between us is in place though, something is holding it in place, and I have to break through it.

He works my pussy like a maestro, alternately driving deep then returning his focus to my clit. In moments I'm falling over the edge into my first orgasm. My legs clamp around his head as I convulse on his tongue.

He holds me up until it passes at last and only then does he lower me to my feet. I don't stay standing though. Lowering myself to my knees, I take his cock in my mouth, returning the oral favor.

His hands twine in my hair, forcing me roughly onto his cock, driving it deep into my throat, and I take it all. Grabbing his ass I dig my nails in as I accept his tribute to me. As one we thrust back and forth until I feel his dick swelling in my mouth and I stop, not ready for him to finish yet.

Jerking back, I look up into his burning green eyes. Ready to finish, needing to break through the final barrier blocking my magic.

I stand up and grab him by his shoulder. With magic wrapped around myself, I force him back until he falls onto my bed. I crawl towards him until I can climb over him and hover over his cock. I grab it with one hand and tease him and myself both, rubbing it over my wet opening.

He moans, groaning with the urge to resist driving himself up into me.

I feel the same. I want him inside me so badly I can hardly stand it, and it takes all my will to hold off finishing fast.

The pleasure needs to last though. It's part of the key, though I only understand this on some instinctive level. I don't have any logic behind any of this, it's all run by feeling and sense and figuring it out as I go.

He grabs my waist, waiting for me to finish, holding his breath in anticipation. I do, too. I'm waiting.

Magic builds, swelling towards a crashing, moving between us, around us, building and building inside of us until it's almost here. Almost... almost... and there!

I drop down onto his cock, taking it to the hilt. We both scream in pleasure as he fills me. We stroke, fast and hard and there's no holding back any longer. It's as if his cock is driving the magic against the final barrier.

As pleasure builds to dizzying heights, the barrier in myself cracks. Suddenly it explodes at the same time that I fall into my orgasm.

I'm swept away. Magic carries us both to a plane beyond even the astral. We're beyond anywhere I've reached. The pleasure is so intense, so great, and as it happens his power floods me.

His power joins the other Eleven, and we are all now one. I am the One. I become who and what I was always meant to be. The Way.

I am the path to a new world.

Together we will forge it, and apart we will fail.

It's a white-water dash through a rocky dangerous river sweeping along and bashing me against the rocks as the orgasm rips through not once but over and over. Unstopping it keeps control of my body fueled by the powers of magic.

At last it reaches its end, and slowly we drop back down

into our bodies, collapsing on each other, panting from the exertion and depths of our pleasure.

"I forgive you," I pant, eyes half-closed.

"Thank you," he says, chest still heaving. "I accept."

CHAPTER FORTY-SIX

AVIELLA

*R*esting my head on Casmir's chest, I drift off to sleep feeling awakened inside but exhausted. I'm complete, wholly the one I'm meant to be, standing on the doorstep of destiny. All that remains is to step through.

As my body drifts away, I'm still aware, rising above our sleeping forms. As I look down at the two of us entangled in the bedsheets, we seem happy. It's fleeting, of course. What can last?

The world is destroyed and on the brink of rebirth. The only question is, what will the new world be? A world of hope and joy, or one of unending despair?

I rise through the ceiling and out above the streaming lines of the broken timelines. They flow beneath me and somehow, I'm aware of all of them. Each of them looping in on itself at some point, no matter how long it might go. Those trapped in those loops never see that they're reliving the same moments over and over.

If they made different choices would it change?

I don't know. Maybe. The timeline my body rests in glows with golden lights. Twelve of them, one for each of my guys. Mine. The poor little orphan girl who couldn't control the monstrous power inside of her. The outcast, but that's not me any longer.

No, I've changed even as the world crumbled. There's a dim timeline connected to me that stretches back and back. When I look at it, a sense of joy fills me—which is odd. I know, on some deep level, that this is who I was before.

"Harrumph, true," the Leviathan's deep and rumbling voice echoes through me. "Before, yes, but also what you could be in that to come."

"What if I fail?" I ask, voicing the doubts that assail me.

"Then a dark cycle will begin," he says implacable as ever.

"It will be my fault," I say.

"And that there was," the undulating whale like creature motions with a flipper like arm. "And there, and there. Do you let your past define your future? Harrumph."

It's almost my own words coming back to me. Isn't this the very thing I told Casmir? That we have to take responsibility for our past and face our future as new?

"No," I say, after a moment's contemplation. "I did my best."

"Harrumph," he says. "Did or did not, it doesn't matter. What matters is, did you learn? Are you smarter now than then?"

"I am," I state with total certainty.

"Good," he rumbles. "Return. It has begun."

Panic fills me, and I'm sliding fast, the timelines speeding past with dizzying speed. If I had a stomach it'd be flip-flopping.

I drop into my body, sitting up with a gasp. The roof shakes, dust falling, and screams fill my ears as the sound of alarms echo.

I leap to my feet. Dress with a wave of my hand and a thought of magic. In an instant, Casmir is beside me, dressed, and we pause. He grabs my waist, lifts me to his mouth, and we kiss. It's brief, passionate, and all we have time for as another loud crack echoes through the Sanctuary.

"We go to war," I say, breathless.

Nodding, he sets me on my feet and side-by-side, we run to meet destiny.

CHAPTER FORTY-SEVEN

AVIELLA

*H*aving always teleported to the mage's Sanctuary, I've never seen the massive gates that lead to the outside. Standing in front of them now at the head of our assembled forces, butterflies dance in my stomach as the gates tremble with each mighty blow.

"This is it!" I yell, turning to face the group. "Win or lose, there is no second chance. We win or we doom the new world to an age of darkness."

"Win!" they cheer, thrusting swords and weapons into the air.

Magic sweeps through me and I enhance it, flowing it back into each one of them. Giving them what power I can. They're going to need it. The Twelve fan out on each side of me as I take a deep breath, letting power pool inside. I don't know exactly what we're going to see on the other side of this door, but I have no doubt it is bad. Really bad.

I raise my arms over my head and motion to each side. The Innocents break off, pouring into secret tunnels that lead to the surface. I don't want to be trapped inside this bunker. That would restrict our movements too much. I know from experience that the forces arrayed against us will be innumerable, they are legion, so to speak. We need to bring to bear as much of our area affecting magic as possible. If we stay inside, they'll win by attrition.

One-fourth of the force I have makes its way through the secret tunnels, ready to flank the enemy. As soon I see they're out of sight, I glance at Tynan. He's imperious, shoulders square, back straight as a rod, and sexy as hell. His eyes smolder with delight, and he smiles when our eyes meet.

"Confident, aren't we?" I ask.

"Of course," he says. "War is my domain."

He flows power into me. His power is rage and anger, boiling hot and waiting to be unleashed. He inspires men to impossible feats, and as it fills me, I'm certain we can win, no matter what. Redoubling his magical flow, I send that out to my army too.

We're going to need it.

"I fight for love, for my dad," I mutter and motion for the doors to be opened.

The massive doors were designed to withstand a direct nuclear strike. They crank open stiffly, slowly. They are bent and barely on their tracks. Motors grind, metal screeches as they jerk open an inch at a time. When they part six inches, arms reach through, clawing for purchase, demanding entrance.

Diseased arms, decaying arms, arms that look like they're made of stone, some of burned flesh. The sight is horrifying enough, but the smell that they exude chokes me. Bile rises in my throat. The smell of death and decay is almost over-whelming. The butterflies in my stomach transform into a wave of nausea that I have to force down.

Grasping deformed hands grab the doors, pushing and pulling them open faster. The screeching tearing of metal echoes around us, and then we face our opponents for the first time. A collective gasp followed by sobs rise from my army as they look into the unending face of terror.

Undead, mutated monsters, horrid hodge-podge experiments, and demons stretch for as far as I can see. They fill the doorway and out to the horizon, packed so tightly they can barely move. As the doors part the pressure of the crowd pressing forward causes those in front to not enter the bunker but to fall in, piling on top of each other.

Laughter echoes above the scrabbling, growling, and hissing of the monstrosities pushing towards me. Looking past the front line, towering over the field a few hundred yards away is her.

My enemy and I lock eyes, and she smiles. The form she's taken is at least thirty feet tall and looks human. An impossibly beautiful human. She's so gorgeous it makes me feel instantly inadequate, as if somehow, I'm not woman enough to be considered one. It aches to look on the pure perfection of her form.

Until I meet her eyes. Her eyes are crimson and have the slightest hint of a glow to them. More than the appearance, they're malevolent. Filled with evil intentions that burn into me as we stare at each other. She smiles, throwing her arms wide.

"You cannot win!" she yells. "Any who surrender now, I promise you a better place in the world I will create after this one. This is your one chance for mercy."

Her voice booms across the battlefield. Magic connects me to every one of my guys and amplifying through them to every Innocent who is my army. This small handful, a thousand of us or so, standing against this ocean of darkness. Some of them waver. Doubts niggling through their thoughts sowed by fear.

I have no blame for them. We face an unimaginable terror and we're outnumbered at least a thousand to one.

I don't blame them, but it's my duty to lead them. I know this isn't over, that somehow, we have to tip the scales, even if I don't see how that's going to happen. It's my job to bolster them. Glancing at Tynan I smile, feigning a confidence I don't feel.

"Let's start this party," I say, and he laughs, throwing his arms wide and roaring a wordless challenge.

Drawing symbols in the air I form a thick shield of magical energy, condensing it further and further until it's as solid as I can make it and shaped like the scoop in front of a bulldozer. The army surges through the door and slams against my shield.

My Innocents cheer excitedly when the monsters racing at them suddenly stop, slamming against nothing and unable to progress. The first beads of sweat form on my brow as I pour more magic into the shield. The mages give me more power, their distinct flavor racing in to fill the void left behind by my casting.

Cupping my hands in front of my chest I draw them back then shove forward with everything I've got, willing the magic to move.

The monsters fight me, some with claws digging into the steel plates of the floor or walls, but I push harder, and their claws tear long rips through steel as they're shoved back and back, outside the now-broken doors of Sanctuary.

It's the tiniest of victories but a victory nonetheless.

Roaring, I lead the charge to the final battle.

CHAPTER FORTY-EIGHT

NATHANIAL

The battle rages below. It's obvious we're losing.

Pure, cold calculations make it obvious this isn't a war we can win. Numbers alone tell the tale. Yet we fight.

Aviella is a blinding white beacon in my sight. Shifting from a purity of whiteness to hints of gold, to a rainbow of colors that I've never experienced in all of time. She races along the lines of defenders, supporting them all, healing here. Fighting there. She's constantly in motion.

We Twelve are arrayed in a semi-circle with our backs to the bunker. I cover the high ground, fighting the airborne creatures and sending her information from my viewpoint. It's a good strategy.

It's going to fail.

A red-black pillar of flames shoots into the air drawing my attention. My heart leaps into my throat and instinctively I move toward it, but the flames blast out, blasting the monsters tearing at Rafe away, leaving him kneeling in a depression and no opponents within ten feet.

He's hurt. Bleeding, heart pounding, thoughts racing, but he looks up and meets my gaze as if he feels it upon him. He smiles, gives me an okay hand gesture, then leaps back to his feet, sword blazing through the air as he re-engages the enemy.

A clawed hand whizzes toward me, which I block with my sword, but almost miss the other one coming from behind. Dropping through the air, I dodge, but it scratches the top of my head, leaving a burning line behind.

Diving and spinning through the air the two creatures give chase, thinking they have an advantage. I can't take my attention off Rafe though. He's surrounded again, driving himself deep in like the damn, reckless fool he's always been.

Fear. What a strange emotion. I've only felt it a handful of times in all my existence, making it difficult to recognize. I'm a creature of the Divine, full of my own purpose, with no time for such base emotions.

Yet I feel it. Here. Now, but not for me.

My life will be what it will be, fulfilling the path the Divine laid out for me. This feeling, this sensation of cold ice creeping through my veins, making my heart pound, assailing my certainty with doubts isn't for me.

It's him.

I'm afraid to lose Rafe. We've been separated for ages. Lost, one to another, because of a single choice made so long ago almost no living creature remembers. A single choice that tore us apart but here, at the end of this age we find one another again.

As if it was meant to be. Through her.

Eyes darting to her even as I weave through an ever-growing gauntlet of claws, flaming spheres, and balls of deep shadow that will suck the life out of me, the fear dissipates. Love.

243

It swells out of my core, chasing away the cold and the doubts, leaving behind acceptance and a sense of wellness no matter how wrong the world is.

She is love, and as she draws power from my own wells of strength, she gives it back, renewed and fresh and somehow better than it was. A fireball explodes directly in front of me, forcing me to try and pull back, but there's no time.

Flying directly through it singes my skin, burning at my feathers. I lose height as I emerge from the other side, toasted, but nothing life-threatening. Spinning midair, flaming sword across my chest, I face my opponents. A dozen creatures, each different and unique hover facing me.

"Prepare to meet your fates," I smile, swinging the sword in a defensive pattern.

They look at each other, hesitating in the face of my confidence. Love pulses through my veins and even deeper. It infuses my muscles, into every fiber of my being. And as I look at my opponents, there is no hate or anger at their presence. Indeed, I feel compassion.

Compassion with a depth that even I, an Angel of the Divine, have never felt before. This is what Aviella teaches us. We are victims of our own choices. These creatures' choices led them to where they are, and now they're trapped, but not beyond redemption. They're not beyond hope.

That redemption may have to come at the slice of my blade, but I won't do so with malice or hate. That is not the way.

Understanding at last comes to me in a way that I've never had before. I've always done as I was guided to do, never bothering to actually know the whys of my actions. One glance around and it's clear we're losing, but maybe I can make a difference.

I send out a signal on a deeply buried magical channel. A

message blasting through the astral planes, carrying forth my new understanding and sharing it.

It is all I can do beyond meet fate head on. Grinning, I charge the dozen before me.

CHAPTER FORTY-NINE

TYNAN

This is my element. War rages and bodies pile up as we exact our toll on the enemy.

My blood sings with contentment. Win, lose, these are lesser concepts that mortals use to try and understand. Very few of them embrace the beauty of war itself. Understand that it's not black and white but an array of beautiful colors dominated by red.

Red of rage. Red of blood. Red of fluttering banners and of men's pure intention to prove themselves against a worthy opponent.

It fuels me, charging my magical pools with every swing of a sword, every swipe of a claw. Every battle cry and every scream the sweetest of wines.

I roar my pleasure and opponents drop and tremble. Rightfully so, I am the Horseman of War, none can stand against me. Shifting to my dragon form, I rise above the fray of the engagement. The horde pressing in is innumerable and logically there is no way we can win.

None of that stills the music. It flows through in a rising

of magical energy, fuel that feeds me better than the finest of delicacies.

She pulls power, drawing on mine, and I give to her all that I am. She's a shining beacon on the battlefield. All our power flows into her and out, she's central to our army. She fights beautifully, wielding her magic with skill and finesse that makes my heart swell.

She gives me purpose, awakens things inside that I never knew I could experience. She alone freed my brothers and me from the Shadow's mark. If not for her, we'd be on the opposite side of this battle.

A trumpet beast stomps towards her, squashing lesser undead and small demons as it picks up speed. Its intention is clear, but she has her back to it.

"Aviella!" I roar.

She looks up, not behind her. The thing closing on her has the body of an elephant, tail of a scorpion, leathery wings, and the head of a lion. It's the size of a house. The ground shakes as each massive foot slams down, killing more of its own.

Her knees buckle as the ground shifts beneath her, and she twists towards it as she falls. Her hands move, and a magical barrier shimmers over her, stopping the thing from biting right into her, barely.

Heart pounding, I dive through the air. Flying monstrosities dive and tear, but they're ineffective and will not distract me from saving her.

The monster bites and slams its head over and over against the barrier protecting Aviella. The mages are moving towards her, but the battle shifts, cutting them off, leaving the four of them surrounded.

I'm almost there, Alaric is coming in from my left, one of us has to make it.

Something hits into my side, a long searing line of pain

the likes of which I've never felt in all my existence. The scream tearing out of my lips is as unexpected as the agony.

"Not so fast," she hisses, drawing her sword back.

The devil smiles as she swings her blazing black sword once more. Acid drips off of it, burning those below her indiscriminately.

Stars dance in my vision as blood pours from my side. Directing magic, the wound slowly closes, but I'm using most of my power to avoid the new attack. An impossible twisting midair reversal of direction, pulling myself up short, and the blade passes harmlessly in front of me.

"Damn, I missed," she laughs, blade turning and slicing back in.

I shift to human, sword in my hand, and I block her blade. Aviella screams for help, and a cold chill grips my heart as the she-devil and I engage in a long-overdue battle.

CHAPTER FIFTY

EFRAM

*T*his is it. The end.

The end, and I'm smiling so much my cheeks hurt. Ducking, dodging, and leaping from side to side as we face impossible odds. There's no way we're going to win.

Yet... I believe.

It's her. Her magic flows in and out, passing through my soul. A refreshing river renewing my very purpose. It's not about winning. It's not about losing. It's about the battle.

I see it now, so clearly, for the first time. All the trials, the trouble, the fighting—it's led us here. What does death matter, when we fight not for our lives but for a new world?

Simple, it doesn't.

I'm too slow. Claws rip through my side, slicing easily through my flesh. Blood pours down my side, but I call the lost dead to my defense. Spirits of the forgotten, those lost souls who haven't found their way out of this realm answer my call, filling the air around me with swirling shadows.

These shadows are mine though, my allies. The constant in my life, the not-quite-dead who could never fully let this world go and embrace the next. Normally their power is limited, but Aviella's power pulses through my soul and in a moment of inspiration, I use it to empower them.

Their forms become more substantial. They surround me, forming a protective shield. Undead, demons, monsters of nightmare press in from all sides. I can't see the other guys, but a few of the Innocents are within an arm's length, fighting to survive.

Survive. If we can hold out long enough, something will break. The Divine will gift us or something.

I close my eyes and inhale deeply, almost choking on the stench of demons and decaying flesh, but it focuses my thoughts enough to seal the wound in my side. The lost souls aren't able to do any real damage, but they keep the army at bay, for a bit at least. Blocking them is the best they can manage, but it gives me a moment to catch my breath.

Up ahead, the she-devil herself towers over the battle-field. My knees weaken at the sight of her. Power pulses from her like a beacon. Seeing her in her true form like this is more than any mortal should ever have to witness.

Tynan, Alaric, and Shen are in full dragon form fighting in the air over us. The she-devil slices Tynan and he roars in pain. It's distant, barely registering, as a dozen undead monstrosities fight their way through the temporary shield of lost souls. Rotten teeth gnash, seeking to sate their unending hunger with my flesh.

This isn't my arena. I'm not a fighter like some of the others, but I can't let Aviella down. Dodging grasping arms the best I can, I touch the nearest one of the walking corpses on the forehead and push magic into its skull using my own power to give a command.

"Rest," I order.

The body drops, and the dim soul trapped inside of it slips out and away. Free at last. It fuels the flames of hope that Aviella ignited setting one of them free. I'll run out of power long before I could handle the legions arrayed against us, but I'll do what I can.

More pile in, lumbering towards me. Moving and dodging, I touch them on their foreheads and issue my command. Bodies pile up, restricting my movement. Falling back, I climb over the loose stacked mound of flesh.

One of the bodies shifts and my foot slips. Arms pinwheeling, I try to stay upright but I'm falling.

"AHHHH!!!!!!" Aviella's scream cuts through the clamor of battle and my heart stops.

CHAPTER FIFTY-ONE

AVIELLA

*W*e're losing.

It's only begun and we're losing, but I can't give up hope. Everything has come down to this one moment. This chance to change everything.

If I fail, if we don't succeed, it's over.

Death would be a welcome relief. It's not death that is the concern, I've been there, done that. If we fail the world is doomed, and it's all my fault. My name may not be remembered, or perhaps it will.

The Leviathan calls me thrice-born. I don't really know about that, but something about the title rings true. As if I've done this all before, but I trained under the tutelage of Silas. The Methuselah force-fed unwritten history into my head, and I do know that there have been prior turning points.

Those points all came to a head in a single battle and the outcome of it set the world on a new path. It always centered around a prophet or a goddess or whatever title the history books decided to grant to the one at the center.

This time, it's me.

And we're losing.

Damn it, I can't let this happen. Somehow, we have to turn the tide of the battle. Turning a circle I flow power out to my Chosen Twelve, bolstering their own power even as I draw power back. Luca and Killian aren't far away. Four Innocents form a line between us. In my magical sight, they're each glowing beacons and I flow power, using each of them as a conduit.

Luca looks over his shoulder, dodging an undead monstrous arm swung by something that looks like it was stitched together from five different men. He grins, hands moving through a complex motion, focusing magical energy that blasts into the monster and tears its way through the thing's chest.

His grin drops and his eyes widen as the ground shakes beneath my feet. I'm thrown up into the air and slam down hard enough to hurt my knees. Instinctively I pull a magical shield around myself, but something hits me, and I'm knocked face-first into the dirt.

Scrambling away as I turn over my training with my Chosen takes over. The magical shielding holds, powered by instinct and reflex more than conscious thought. I get my first look at the thing attacking.

It has the body of an elephant, tail of a scorpion, leathery wings, and the head of a lion. The damn thing is big. Really, really big. The sharp teeth of its lion head slash against my shield while the tail repeatedly slams down, seeking to sting me. A vile green poison leaks from the tail, pouring across the shield and sizzling where it lands on the ground.

I'm dimly aware of Tynan roaring my name over the sounds of battle, but it's distant. The thing's mouth is close, so close I can see the back of its throat as it scrabbles and bites. Every stomp of its massive feet against the ground lift me enough so that I land hard, rattling my teeth.

My shield is weakening. The monster slams its head

against it over and over, driving its way closer to me with each smash of its teeth. I scream, a wordless sound ripping through my throat. This can't be it.

The army of monstrosities presses in from all sides. The two closest of the Innocents cry out as they're torn apart. Their screams break my heart. I can't save them! My magic trembles like an overtired muscle, holding on past its strength as I reach my limits fighting against this thing.

I'm losing.

This isn't how it's supposed to end. I can't stare down the throat of the thing that's trying to eat me, so I turn my head to the side, and I'm staring into the glassy eyes of an Innocent. Lying dead, fallen in service to my cause.

Rage burns through my veins and the fire in my core becomes an inferno. Closing my eyes, I reach out to my Twelve. They're hurt. Tynan has felt pain for the first time in his existence. He's blinded by rage.

Efram is struggling against despair. Silas is cold, calculating, but there is no denying his sense that this is inevitable. Nate...

Nate's attention is on Rafe, who's hurt. The love between the two of them flows strong, giving me strength. It does nothing to lessen their love for me, if anything its stronger because Nate is coming to terms with his own feelings. Their love is one of ages, and in this, of all moments, they seem to be finding each other at last.

Sensing it, I know their love includes me, and that nothing between us is changing except to be strengthened by honesty. Love.

It's the one thing we have. The thing we can choose, that makes us different.

What other choice in life matters? The choice to hate or the choice to love is at the heart of every decision we make, no matter the complexity we layer on top of it. All of that is an apparency. Lies humanity has told itself for years.

Lies sown by her.

My fiery rage tempers as it becomes something different. Power flows through the connection I have with each of my guys. Each of them uniquely distinct in what they offer, a delight of sensation and feeling comes along as I draw their power onto me.

The shield holding the monster at bay grows stronger. As each of them give of themselves to me my love for them grows. Balling up my left hand into a fist I focus magic until it's a tight, roiling ball.

As the things head crashes down against my shield again I open a hole and dive my empowered fist into the things throat and punch right through and out the back of its head.

The monster collapses, its crushing weight burying me.

CHAPTER FIFTY-TWO

SILAS

*S*he pulls power and I give all I can. Something is about to happen. The air is rife with a sense of anticipation that causes chills across my skin.

There isn't time to even spare a glance, but I sense her. A group of Innocents huddles behind me as we fight. They're good, as prepared as they can be, but this isn't the way we'll win this fight. The real fight isn't on this plane, and I know it.

How long until she figures it out though, is the key. It's not something I can do more than guide her towards, because I don't fully comprehend it myself.

A fist the size of a thick tree slams into my face. My jaw and nose break with the impact, and I'm thrown backward, crashing into the Innocents. They try to catch me, but we fall in a heap. Claws, fists, undead hands tear, ripping flesh. Screams echo in my ears, and I'm sure some of them are my own.

We're going to lose.

I'm staring into the sky when winged monsters dance overhead and then a trumpet sounds. I thought we'd had the last of them, but this one sounds different. It carries the sound of hope with it, which is strange. Nate is entangled with a half-dozen of the things in the sky, when suddenly a diamond-shaped flock of man-like bird creatures join him.

Nate breaks his engagement, joining the hovering flock as if he knows them. Then as one, they attack the enemy.

Reinforcements? Unexpected... but it brings hope with it. Hope is all we need.

"There! We have allies! Fight! Get up and fight!" I yell, leaping out of the tangle of bodies to land on my feet.

The Innocents that remained standing glance up, and power swells fresh in them as they find hope too. As one we continue the fight.

"*Silas,*" Aviella's voice echoes in my thoughts. *"Choose love. I choose love."*

My vision splits. I'm seeing on two planes now, astral and physical. In the physical we fight this army, but on the astral Aviella stands in front of me. Her tiny hands resting on my chest as she looks up into my eyes.

"Love Silas," she smiles.

Luca appears next to us then Killian, Ronan, and Alaric. They share a confused glance as they adjust to seeing on both planes.

"LOVE!" she yells, rising on her toes and kissing me.

The battle continues here on the physical plane, but on the astral an entirely different engagement has begun.

She pulls each of us as her magic swirls across the field. The sounds of flesh against flesh, steel ringing on steel, and the screams of pain and roars of triumph become almost secondary to what's happening.

Through the throbbing pain of my broken nose and jaw I feel her lips on mine even though she is nowhere near me on the field. Casmir rises above the field of battle, shifted to his full dragon form he, Alaric, and Shen dive through the air heading for the she-devil.

Glancing in their direction my heart falters. She and Tynan are engaged in a duel, and it's clear who's winning.

CHAPTER FIFTY-THREE

TYNAN

"I've waited... for... years," I say, gritting my teeth as the force of her swinging blade rattles my bones.

"You've waited," she laughs. "Oh Tynan, they always said *I* was the most arrogant yet none of them looked at you."

Aviella is pulling magic, she's in trouble. I need to end this now. There is no time, but in all my long existence, I've known there's only ever been one opponent truly worthy of my time.

Her.

The only one who could match me. Who might be, as much as I hate to admit it, better than me. Her sword whistles through the air, switching angles and directions as fast as a viper. I've taken more than one cut.

The pain is fuel. A new experience. At first it was distracting, but now it powers my rage. The righteous rage of having been trapped by her magic for eons. Now is the time of my revenge, but I can't keep my attention from Aviella.

Shen, I send to my brother. *Is she okay?*

He doesn't answer, but I feel him and the others coming closer. Do they not know? Where is she? If something happened to her, if she was gone, I'd feel it. I'm sure of that. I felt her loss when we failed her before, and I won't lose her again.

The ground rumbles, the sky roars, and cold rain pours across the field. The tears of the Divine? Perhaps, the last time the Divine shed its tears the world flooded. It would be a fitting end for another age, wouldn't it?

Silas should feel right at home, take him back to his earliest days.

"Tynan, give up," Lucifer whispers, leaning across our crossed blades. Her lips are so close to mine we could kiss. Sweet, full red lips that offer pleasures untold if only I assent to their touch. Her magic crawls across my skin, seductively offering the choice. A choice I made wrongly once.

"Not this time," I growl, pushing back and stepping away, sword at the ready.

Casmir and Shen dive out of the sky towards her. Her blade flashes through the air forcing them to pull out of their dives, but giving me the slightest of openings, and I act.

My blade blurs, and at the last instant she sees it, moving her own. Her blade cuts into my right arm, but my blade finds purchase, slicing across her stomach deeply. She howls, roaring her pain, but my right arm has gone numb. It's all I can do to hold onto my sword.

I stumble backwards.

Aviella, I think. *I'm sorry.*

I'm jerked onto the astral plane while oddly still here on the physical plane as well. The others are gathered, the Twelve, standing in a circle around her. She glows, radiant, casting her warmth across all of us.

As her smile lands on me, power flows through my being. Shifting my sword to my left hand, I renew my attacks.

"Tynan, this is pointless," the she-devil says. "I do not

want to destroy you. You belong at my side, join me. Make your choice, dragon."

A slow smile spreads across my face.

"You don't understand," I say.

"What don't I understand?" she asks, motioning with a sweep of her sword. "I've won! This next age is mine! Mine in full. The only question for you is will you be at my side or beneath my feet?"

I laugh. Her eyes widen, her seductive magic tinges with anger, burning across my skin instead of teasing.

"You are so wrong," I say, rushing at the opening I see in her defenses.

CHAPTER FIFTY-FOUR

AVIELLA

"*G*uys," I say, finishing my circle having looked at each of them in turn. *"Love. I choose love."*

They murmur their assents and own feelings, but no one is sure yet. They don't get it. There's one way to make them see it, I have to open their eyes to the truth. I've got them all here now, and this is it. I finally understand, but my understanding alone isn't enough.

On the physical plane, I blast the dead body off of me with a burst of magic that sends it flying high into the air. The birdmen have joined our fight, coming to make their last stand with us. My heart swells seeing them flanking Nathanial as they engage with the enemy in the sky.

Power coalesces around my form. My hair rises, standing on end as magic tingles across my skin. Rowan leaps over the piles of bodies and lands gracefully at my side, her infectious smile firmly in place.

She grabs my face, turning me to face her full on and nods. Then she plants a kiss on my lips and embraces me tightly before turning so that we stand back-to-back facing the army together. The horde attacks and we fight.

"Rafe," I say. "Kiss Nate."

Rafe arches an eyebrow. "Aviella, I don't think this is the—"

"Now," I order.

"Well..." Rafe says uncharacteristically serious. I watch, we all watch, as he walks up to Nate and then engages in the hottest, most passionate, love filled kiss I've ever witnessed. It turns me on but more than that it fills me with hope. Joy. Their love flows out, passing through the connection between all of us.

I take in their love, for each other and for me, and then I amplify it, feeding it back out to the other men. The men close with me and as they do, I will my clothes away. I stand in the center of my Twelve, naked, exposed, and loved.

Their hands and lips are on my body. Touching, kissing, everywhere. I kiss every piece of skin I can reach as they sweep me off my feet. My hands find their bodies and we begin.

Love fills me with power. I'm brimming with it. The aches, the cuts, the bruises all fade as my Chosen and I join on the astral, but here on the physical, we fight. It's a strange duality. Ducking, weaving, blasting beams of power or wielding magical shields to keep the enemy at bay.

A torrential rain pours down on us, soaking me to the bone, but it has a cleansing feel. Rowan and I are forced against each other as the monsters continue pressing in.

"Rowan," I say. "I love you. With all my heart, I love you."

She pats my ass with one hand, the only concession she can make in the midst of the battle. Power pools in my core but there's a void there drinking it in.

Gavin enters me first, while Luca and Ronin hold me up by my shoulders. As his cock drives into my waiting pussy, his hands and those of Killian and Shen hold my ass. Alaric turns my head towards him, and I take his cock in my mouth while grabbing Killian and Shen's cocks with my hands.

Gavin drives in deep, seating himself fully inside. I cry out my pleasure around my full mouth. Each thrust in he pushes magic in that redoubles on itself and works to fill the empty void. The magic is love.

Love is all the magic we need. It melts the concerns, the fears, but more than anything it destroys the hate, bigotry, and the self-centered only me attitude that was the downfall of an entire age of existence.

Past Shen I see Nate and Rafe are fondling one another but their eyes are on me as they toy with each other's engorged cocks. Rafe moves them closer and each of them play with my breasts with one hand and the other's dick with their opposite.

I moan again as Shen continues to fill my mouth and Gavin my pussy.

Screeching leaves my ears ringing. Four of the Innocents have backed up to Rowan and me, and we've opened our circle to include them. Rotting teeth click and clack as they try to find purchase in our flesh.

Nathanial and the birdman army fight, and it's clear that Nate is trying to get to me, but every time he gets close, he's driven back by a fresh onslaught of the unending army. I should despair, but hope is eternal as they say. As my body is filled on the astral my magical energy is replenished here, and with it comes hope.

Willing a shield around our small group a shimmering wall of force pops into existence buying us a small reprieve. We lean against each other, all of us breathless and exhausted. No amount of physical training or cardio can really prepare you for the Apocalypse, it turns out.

Pouring power into the shield, I turn around, placing an arm over Rowan and the Innocent next to me. We huddle together, heaving breath, all too tired to speak.

"This... isn't... the end," I say. "It's the beginning."

Rowan nods enthusiastically. She's wearing a white shirt with no bra, made clear because the thin fabric is pasted against her skin from the rain. She's beautiful, which I've always known, but now I see so much more. The bright light that has always drawn me to her is the pureness of her heart and soul. Her capacity for love is exponential, an important lesson she taught me.

Each of these Innocents are filled with an enormous capacity to forgive and to love. It's inspiring. Rowan signs fast, too fast for my distracted state, as on the astral plane I'm closing in on a climax.

"Huh?" I pant, shaking my head, my body trembling with the sex energy layering across my normal power flows.

She signs again, fast, but I'm watching this time and get it.

"Yes," I agree. "I love all of you. That's what I want to teach you. Love. It's your power. It's our power but all of this…" I nod back to indicate the battle we've paused in the middle of. "It's about choice. Free will."

"What do you mean?" an Innocent asks.

She's young, maybe nineteen, pretty green eyes, but she's so scared her skin is pale white.

"What's your name?" I ask, shuddering as my first astral orgasm hits, I bite my lip trying not to make a scene here too.

"She," I point at the she-devil, "hates free will. She is jealous. It was our greatest gift and our greatest downfall. She tempted mankind, throughout history, and no matter what choice it was, it always comes down to the same one.

"You can choose love, or you can choose hate. There is, in the end, no other choice. If you act out of love, you create love. We've chosen wrong, all this time, but we don't have to."

The guys switch. Rafe is at my mouth, sliding his gorgeous cock in, and Nate positions himself between my legs. The two of them drive in and out as one. In time with each other. As Nate thrusts in pleasure races through my body, affecting me here and there too.

"Choose love?" the Innocent asks.

"Yes," I say, gripping her shoulders, "Choose love."

She nods, biting her lip, and I can't suppress a soft gasp as the pleasure filling my magical reserves spikes.

A fresh trumpet beast slams down against the shield I've erected to protect us, pulling me out of the moment. I'm close. So damn close, but we have to last a little longer. I don't know what's going to happen, but I can feel it racing towards us like a freight train coming in.

Rowan signs and the girl smiles, nodding. The girl hugs me then turns forming her magic into a glowing sword. Rowan grins and her hands glow with power. Turning we face the newest threat, together.

"Move," Tynan orders Nathanial.

Nathanial looks at the dragon, continuing to thrust in and out but then he obeys without arguing. Tynan looks over all of us imperiously, his eyes alight with a burning need of his own. His cock is in his hand and he slowly strokes as he scans over my body, his lips parting.

"Silas," Tynan says. "Lie down there."

Silas moves and does as he's told, lying on the ground his cock standing up and at attention. Tynan motions and Alaric and Shen grab me and move me around until I'm directly over Silas. They lower me down, holding my legs apart.

Biting my lip I close my eyes and prepare myself. Silas cock presses against my rear entrance and I open my eyes to see Efram. He's standing to one side, love pouring out of him and into me as he strokes his cock too.

Gently I'm placed onto Silas waiting cock until he's fully in my ass.

The pool is almost full. We're close. So close. The ground trembles, the rain pours harder, it's almost there. All four dragons face off against her, keeping her busy while the rest of us fight the unending forces.

The she-devil spins around, sword held at arm's length driving back the dragons. Her eyes lock onto me.

"What are you doing?" she asks, understanding dawning on her face.

My heart leaps into my throat. She's sensed my nebulous plan. We're in trouble.

CHAPTER FIFTY-FIVE

AVIELLA

"*Gavin, there," Tynan orders, moving the guys in and out and around.*

As I take each of them, in mouth, ass, or pussy, it doesn't matter, my claim is made. In appearance they are 'taking' me, but in truth I'm taking them. They're mine, our connection is too deep for anything less than a physical manifestation in the joining of our bodies, astral or real. We are becoming closer now that, for the first time, all of us are here together. Loving one another.

"We have to hurry," I urge. "She's onto us."

The astral plane trembles as her attention falls onto me in the physical. Gavin moves up to my mouth, Efram comes close enough I grab his cock in one hand stroking and he groans. Alaric gets between my legs and slowly presses his girth into my waiting pussy. The double penetration creates a sense of fullness.

Beyond though, the well is filling. Magic is brimming up and the void seems less hungry, the flow into it less demanding. Soon. We're so close.

The she-devil strides across the battlefield heading right for me. Rowan and the Innocents flank my sides as I turn to face her. The dragons attack, diving in from all sides, but she dodges or blocks them with her sword, never diverting her attention.

"Stop that!" she yells, pointing her sword.

As she does all the undead, trumpet creatures, and uncountable horrors turn as one. It's a mad rush.

"We're in trouble," I say. "I need more time!"

Things scrabble at the shield I'm holding in place, and it won't last long. It's already wavering. The ground rumbles, protesting, tossing us back and forth against each other as if we're having a minor earthquake to boot.

The shield shatters and creatures pour through. Backs to each other we face the incoming onslaught. It's too soon.

The guys switch again, each of them taking a turn inside, giving their magic to me. Tynan directs the group, running tight control. If he is working from instinct or some base carnal desires, I don't know, but it's working.

Power builds. We're close. It's the sweetest taste of orgasm I've ever experienced, and with this group I've had a lot.

As each one of them and I join, as I take them, the mark we've left on each other strengthens. The connections deepen. Magic flows easier, deeper and faster than ever before.

Luca is inside of me, thrusting fast. He grunts, throws his head back and I recognize he's about to come.

"Yes!" I yell, pulling my mouth off of Shen's cock. "Give it to me! Silas, in my ass. Do it!"

The two men thrust in and out as one, and then they're exploding. We're in the astral, and the explosion is as much metaphysical as it would be physical on the other plane.

Their 'release' is an outpouring of power unlike anything we've done. My body thrums, and one thing is certain: I need more.

"Gavin! Rafe! Nate!" I yell. "Now!"

My attention is split. My body here is alive with the pleasure and the power I'm taking in the astral which is a

MIRANDA MARTIN

confusing mix of signals to the pain, exhaustion, and fear that I'm experiencing here.

My stomach clenches tight, and I'm sure we're about to lose, that we've run out of time. A horde races towards me, and behind them strides the she-devil herself. As I lift my hands up into defensive position, the air around me cracks as if lightning struck. The ground explodes, dirt hitting me in the face, so I throw an arm protectively over my eyes.

Nate has done a perfect super-hero landing right in front of me. Rising to his feet, massive flaming sword held ready, he takes up a defensive position.

Cold chills race over my skin. My hero.

As he lands in front of me in the physical here, he slams his cock into my ass having switched out with Silas. Rafe is in my front, leaning in close and kissing me deeply as the two of them work fast to unload themselves.

We all know the urgency. There's no time to waste but love, physical and spiritual, takes time, and we can only do our best to buy enough of it there.

Their cocks rub against each other inside of me. Mouths are on my tits, a hand is rubbing my clit, someone has his cock in my mouth and two more are in my hands. Each point of contact is an expression of their love.

"Fuck me, please, fuck me faster," *I beg them to give me their release.*

It's dancing right there. I want it. No, I need it. My own release is building but I can't let it go. Not yet, this isn't the time. We're close but not yet.

Nate sword dances, whistling through the air in complex defensive patterns. Glowing runes empowered with his Divine magic linger in the air of its passing. As he sets to work around himself, body parts fly off, zinging through the air.

Letting go with blasts of magic I shoot raw energy shaped

into lightning strikes. Hitting the encroaching beasts and holding them at bay the best I can.

She's close. Too damn close. One glance up is all it takes to see her towering. A handful of strides more and we'll be engaged directly.

"Aviella!" Rafe and Nate cry out my name as one, letting their orgasms rip through.

Quickly I'm repositioned under Tynan's direct guidance. There's no time left to waste.

"Fill my mouth, give it to me, penetrate me anywhere, we have to finish!" I order.

"As you wish," Tynan says, taking up his position.

The dragons dive at her and Tynan leaps into the air impossibly high, still in his human form. He lands in front of her, holding his sword out in challenge.

"We have unfinished business," he challenges.

She pauses, looking at him. "You could have been great."

"I am great," he says. "Without you."

He attacks, and the two elder beings are blurs. Even with my magically enhanced sight I can't keep up with the flow of their engagement.

"Are you ready," Tynan growls.

"Yes!" I scream. "Now!"

He finishes, moving quickly out of the way. I'm almost there, but it's not done. Something is missing. Who?

"Efram, now," Tynan orders.

Efram is holding my head. He leans in and kisses me. Soft, gentle, filled with his gentle love.

"Is this what you want?" he asks.

"Yes," I say, my fingers lingering on his cheek.

My sweet, gentle Efram. He's the final piece.

He moves down, between my legs. His cock pulsing in his hand. I roll over onto my knees and look back over my shoulder at him, giving him an inviting smile. He runs his hands over my ass, then takes his cock and slowly slides it into my pulsing pussy.

"ENOUGH!" the she-devil yells, and magic sweeps its way in front of her gesture.

Tynan is thrown through the air, tumbling like a ragdoll in a hurricane. She strides forward, closing the distance.

We're so close, a few more minutes is all we need. Nathanial turns to meet her. Shen, Alaric and Casmir land around him. A moment later, as if out of a cloud of exploding smoke, Rafe is there. All of them forming a line blocking her approach to me.

She smiles, certainty on her face and in her eyes. Undeterred she continues her march in.

"Fuck her," Tynan barks. "Faster Efram. Faster!"

He obeys, thrusting into me faster and faster. The final piece is about to unlock. His cock, sweet and gentle pushing in and out. Tynan comes over and smacks my ass. It's loud and sharp and startles Efram.

"Efram, faster," I beg. "Fuck its good. It's so good. Fuck me Efram. Give it to me now."

All the guys are in a circle, watching Efram finish. They all have their cocks in hand stroking, flowing their power to him and through him me.

The well is brimming as if it's a boiling pot about to go over. All I need is this last bit...

She roars, swinging her sword in one hand. It sweeps aside the guys and all of her own encroaching forces too. A gale force wind blasts its way between us. Holding up my hands and pressing them together in front of me the winds part around me.

I can't save Rowan or the others. They're all blown away leaving emptiness around me. She and I, my eternal enemy face each other here on a blasted destroyed land.

"Stop what you're doing," she orders.

She towers over me, using her size to be intimidating but it's not working. I'm not intimidated. I see the truth. It took me a while but now I get it.

"No," I say, shaking my head. "You're too late."

"No! This is my age. I've won, this last-ditch effort is already doomed."

I smile and shake my head.

"You're wrong," I say. "I'm sorry, but you've been wrong all these years."

"Wrong?" she asks, confusion in her voice.

"You chose wrong," I say. "All those years ago, you chose wrong, but you can change."

"I don't have a choice!" she growls. "We were not given free will."

She raises her blade holding it over my head, ready to drop. I might be able to stop it. I might not, but one way or another, it doesn't matter. I've already won whether I survive this moment or not.

Efram comes into me and the well of power overflows. Magic blasts through everything that I am as his come fills me at last.

The others, watching, all come again. On this plane it's magic, it's power. It's their love given form, and it races into me, fueling my own power.

Power explodes from me like a nuclear blast. Tearing through anything and everything. The blackened, blasted land around us is wiped clean. Life springs forth. The first sprouts of grass appearing, the broken trees blossoming new growth.

"No!" she screams.

"Yes," I say.

She swings her sword, but I raise my hand and it stops in midair, held in place by nothing more than my will. Where she was towering over me, her size reduces until she's the same size as I am. A normal human, returning to her beautiful, natural form.

And she is beautiful. So beautiful it makes my heart ache to look at her. She shakes with anger looking around in disbelief. The army of undead and monstrosities falls to the ground, the magic fueling them falling away before the onslaught I've released.

It's not my magic. It's *our* magic. Our magic, our choice, the choosing of love above all.

"This can't be," she raises her hands, and I sense her willing magic to her cause, but nothing happens.

"Yes," I say, shaking my head.

I move towards her, arms open, offering her the choice. An open offer of a hug and the chance to choose love.

Magic pours out and into the world. Healing, renewing, changing.

The Chosen gather around, and we encircle her. She stares, agape, and I understand. It's hard to believe, but she's lost.

"It's over, Lucy," Tynan says. "Choose to be part of the new world, or retreat and wait for the dawn of the next age."

Hate burns in her eyes. It's clear that she's not able to let it go, but this is her choice. The world can't be a perfect utopia it seems, but the Chosen and I will create something a lot closer to it than we've ever had before.

"Fine," she says. "You've won, this time."

She waves an arm, and, in a flash, she's gone. Cheers rise up and echo around us all.

We've won.

AFTERMATH
AVIELLA

. . .

"This report came in," Efram says, walking in and setting a wrinkled piece of paper down.

"From whom?" Tynan asks.

"Elsbeth," Efram says.

"Oh, she was one of Tynan's," Shen says, and I glare at him. "What? She was."

"We don't play those games any longer," I say, leaning over the desk towards him.

He smiles and shakes his head.

"So boring," he sighs.

Efram watches the exchange, silent, his face carefully neutral. I pick up the paper and scan the scribbled note on it. Butterflies dance in my stomach.

"Wow, never would have looked there," I say, shaking my head.

"What is it?" Tynan asks, taking the paper for himself.

"More survivors," I announce. "Underneath the Magic Kingdom, Florida. They holed up in the service tunnels."

"That's good news," Silas says, rising to his feet. "I'll go to help."

He walks behind the desk and wraps his arms around my waist. Tilting my head back we kiss, deep, but perfunctorily. Who knew that there would be so much to do after we had won the war? Silas strides off and I return my attention to the piles of notes and maps on the desk.

"You should relax," Tynan says, rubbing my shoulders.

Moaning with pleasure I roll my neck and lean back into his attention.

"I'd love to," I say. "But there's so much to do."

"There is always plenty to 'do,'" he says, kneading a knotted muscle and making me gasp. "That does not mean you have to do it now."

"I hate to interrupt," Efram says. "But there is more that requires your attention."

"What else?" I ask, pulling away from Tynan's ministrations.

"Supplies," Efram frowns. "We've had more food stocks come up missing. Luca's team hasn't returned from scavenging yet."

"They were due to return yesterday," I say immediately concerned.

"Right," Efram agrees.

"Okay, give me a minute," I say, leaning back into the chair and closing my eyes.

Pulling magic around myself I send threads of it stretching out looking for Luca. Ley lines have awakened since the start of this new age making this so much easier. They're natural channels for magic to flow along. It's like a complex network of interconnecting lines, similar to the cables that the old world had forming an interconnected world wide web, except done with magic.

It's only a moment or two before I sense him, his essence pulling me towards him. The connection between myself and all the Chosen is strong enough they can't really hide from me no matter how far away they are.

"Luca! "

He manifests in the astral smiling and grabs me into an embrace.

"Aviella!"

"You're late," I say, sternly. "And you didn't check in."

"Yeah, we ran into some problems," he says, not letting me go.

"Is everyone okay?" I ask.

"We'll be fine," he says, eyes darting to one side.

"Who's hurt?" I ask.

He shakes his head. "It's nothing."

"Luca..." I trail his name off, and he shrugs.

"An undead thing got a chunk of me," he says.

"Oh! Let me see, quit trying to hide it," I order.

Now that I'm looking for it, his left arm isn't fully manifested here, he's blurring it out, so I won't see how badly he's hurt.

"It's nothing," he says, but obeying my demand, he manifests his arm.

There's a piece missing from his bicep and blackness creeps along the veins.

"Damn it, get back here now, you need healing!" I order.

"I'm on my way," he says, grinning. "Seriously, it's worse than it looks."

"Hurry back, check in with me in two hours," I bark.

"Yes Ma'am," he says, grinning, giving me a mocking half salute.

"Luca—" *I threaten but he pulls me tight with his good arm and cuts my words off with his mouth.*

As he breaks the kiss, he also steps out of the astral, avoiding any further admonitions from me. Opening my eyes back at the office, I shake my head.

"That man," I mutter.

"He's okay?" Efram asks.

"Yeah," I say. "They'll be back soon."

"Alaric, Shen and I can help tide over supplies," Tynan says. "We will form a hunt."

"Good plan," I smile.

Tynan strides off and his brothers follow. Efram shifts from foot to foot, staring at the desk, and not meeting my eyes. Everyone else is busy with their missions, leaving the two of us.

"What?" I ask.

His eyes dart up to mine then around the room.

"I don't know," he says, finally. "It's all too… perfect. Too easy?" He shrugs. "I'm probably being a pessimist."

"No," I agree, rising and moving in front of the desk. I lean against it, but I wanted to be closer to him. "I'm feeling it, too."

"So what do we do with it?" he asks.

"That, I don't know," I say. "I do know, I didn't sign up to be an administrator, and that's what is needed here."

"Avi, you didn't sign up for any of this," he smiles moving between my legs and putting his hands on my waist. "Yet here we are. Thanks to you."

"Thanks to us," I say. "All of us. It wasn't me, alone, it was us."

"Us," he whispers, his voice deepening with desire as his stiff cock presses against my jeans.

My stomach flips and nausea grips me hard. Jerking away, I race around the desk and grab a trash can, barely stopping myself from losing my last meal. Efram holds my hair back, rubbing my back and making soothing noises.

"Are you okay?" he ask, as I rise, the nausea passing.

"Uhm," I say, buying time. "Yeah, I think so."

As fast as it came, it's gone. Now my belly is warm. Not hot, but warm with a strange, magical feel to it. Efram and I are looking down at it at the same time and he must also be using magical sight because he inhales sharply.

My stomach has a golden aura to it. A glow of its own. This is... new.

"Efram?" I ask, not wanting to say what I think is happening here.

"Yeah," he says, agreeing without saying the words.

"We'll need to talk to everyone," I say.

"Yeah," he agrees.

EPILOGUE

AVIELLA

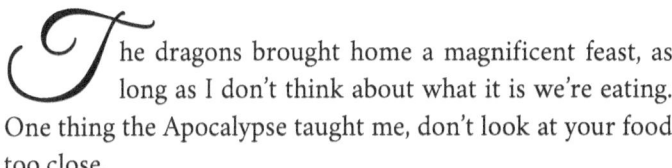

*T*he dragons brought home a magnificent feast, as long as I don't think about what it is we're eating. One thing the Apocalypse taught me, don't look at your food too close.

My stomach is way too sensitive as it is. No one but Efram notices how I push the food around on my plate without really eating. He keeps catching my eyes, frowning and worrying. I give him my best reassuring smile.

This is going to be fine. Or so I keep telling myself, attempting to calm the butterflies in my stomach. The guys are getting along so well. Luca is animatedly telling the story of his wound, wincing each time he gets overly excited with his arm gestures as he reenacts the battle that gave him his wound.

Tynan sits at the opposite end of the table, holding court. Alaric and Shen sit to his left and Casmir is at his right. Casmir, quiet, thoughtful and oh so damn brilliant. He's already turned his thoughts to feeding the world. It is on his work that the future really depends.

His lifetimes of scientific research, always bent towards

destruction, now turned towards helping the world is paying off in spades.

Ronan, Killian, Gavin, and Luca sit down the line from Casmir. Laughing at Luca's tale. He's making it a lot more dramatic than I'm sure it was in reality but it's fun. Next to Shen sits Silas who I catch watching me much more than he's paying attention to the storytelling.

"And then Luca leaps into the air," Rafe says, jumping from his chair and miming what he's describing. "Sword over his head yelling you want some, come get me you son of a bitch!"

Rafe lands on the edge of his seat, chair teetering below him but he balances it perfectly. The room explodes with laughter. Rafe soaks it in. He, of all of us, is the most different. Nate and Rafe are rarely, if ever apart. On their nights with me I can count on both of them, which is fun physically of course, but it's very satisfying emotionally too.

They're openly in love with each other, finally admitting it after eons of time, and they've kindly included me into their triangle of intimacy. My heart swells watching Rafe but mostly seeing the look on Nate's face as he watches Rafe.

In this, our new world, love is the choice and it's beautiful. Rafe resumes his seat and I don't miss Nate putting a hand on his thigh and squeezing. They share a quick smile as the conversation continues to flow around the table.

Efram taps the side of my leg widening his eyes silently pushing me to say what needs to be said. I want to. I do, but I'm still hesitant. What if one of them doesn't take it well? Will anyone be upset? How do we decide… oh so many damn questions.

I guess the only way to handle it is to put it out there. The chips will fall where they're going to fall. So, I rise to my feet and tap the side of my glass with a fork. It clinks loudly. No fine ring of a crystal here, not in our post-Apocalypse world.

Silence falls slowly over the room and they all look to me. The weight of their gazes carries their love and it bolsters me as I swallow hard, struggling with a fresh wave of nausea, and the way my stomach flip flops.

"Guys," I say, meeting each of their gazes in turn. "I love you."

They each add their own return of feelings and love which I nod and accept but I hold up my hands asking for their attention to remain on me.

"I'm not sure how to say this and I don't know... maybe you've thought about it. I hadn't but... well these things I guess we could have expected. I don't know why I didn't, really. I mean—"

"Aviella," Tynan cuts me off. "Please."

My mouth is dry and my heart stills as he and I lock eyes. The silence is awkward, and I shift from foot to foot.

"Yeah, well I need to say—"

"No," Tynan says. "You don't. None of us here are fools. We know."

"You... you know?" I ask.

"Of course," he says.

Efram puts his hand on the small of my back supportively which I'm grateful for. My knees are weak, so I lean on the table for support.

"And you're all... okay?" I ask, looking at each of them.

One by one they nod.

"Of course we are," Silas says. "None of us are fools. We know biology. This was to be expected, we've had many discussions on how to handle our roles as father to our child."

"You... you have?" I stutter my head spinning.

They've already discussed this? They were prepared, and I hadn't even considered the idea that it could happen. I'd been so busy surviving, who could really think about a future.

"It is the natural way of things," Casmir says.

"So no one is upset that I'm pregnant?" I ask, limbs numb, anticipation building as I wait for the answer.

"Upset?" Tynan asks. "We are ecstatic!"

"Yes!" Gavin cheers, jumping up and raising his glass. "To us! To fatherhood!"

The Twelve are on their feet cheering. They drink to themselves, then one by one they come and give their affection and love to me. The power flowing between us is so strong and now it includes the new life growing in my womb.

Someday, long in the future, my unknowable number of greats later grandchild will be the Warrior or Savior of the next age. Now though, my time for that is done. My one duty is to assume the mantle of mother, and I know with a depth of certainty I rarely have, I'm ready.

I'm ready, and my daughter will have twelve dads to care for her. What better way to be welcomed into the world?

THE END

ABOUT THE AUTHOR

USA Today Bestselling Author of fantasy and scifi romance, Miranda Martin's books feature larger than life heroes with out-of-this-world anatomy and smart heroines destined to save the world. As a little girl she would sneak off with her nose in a book, dreaming of magical realms. Today she brings those fantasies to life and adores every fan who chooses to live in them for a while.

She was born and raised in southern Virginia, but as a veteran she's traveled to places like Korea, Hawaii and good 'ole Texas. Now she's settled in Kansas, the heart of America, with her husband and daughters. Her favorite animals are dragons, unicorns and cats. If she's not writing, you can still find her tucked away somewhere with a warm blanket and her nose in a book.

Get in touch!
mirandamartinromance.com
miranda@mirandamartinromance.com

facebook.com/mirandamartin
twitter.com/imMirandaMartin
instagram.com/imMirandaMartin

ALSO BY MIRANDA MARTIN

USA TODAY BESTSELLING AUTHOR

Red Planet Dragon's of Tajss Series
Red Planet Jungle Series
The Power of Twelve Series
The Alva Series
Dragon's & Phoenixes Series